Death on Demand

Also by Carolyn G. Hart

CAROLYN G. HART

Death
on Demand

A PERFECT CRIME BOOK
DOUBLEDAY
New York
London
Toronto
Sydney
Auckland

A Perfect Crime Book
PUBLISHED BY DOUBLEDAY
a division of Bantam Doubleday Dell
Publishing Group, Inc.

DOUBLEDAY is a trademark of Doubleday,
a division of Bantam Doubleday Dell
Publishing Group, Inc.

Library of Congress Cataloging-in-Publication Data

Hart, Carolyn G.
Death on demand/by Carolyn G. Hart.
    p. cm.
"A Perfect Crime book."
I. Title.
PS3558.A676D45   1993
813'.54—dc20   92-27739
CIP

ISBN 0-385-42597-X
Copyright © 1987 by Carolyn G. Hart
All Rights Reserved
Printed in the United States of America
January 1993

10 9 8 7 6 5 4 3 2 1

To Kate Miciak, an imaginative, creative, exciting editor

Death on Demand

One

ALONE, EACH ITEM was insignificant. Some were easily found. A few were stolen from friends or acquaintances, but their value was so slight that the losses occasioned mild puzzlement and nothing more.

A pair of doctor's rubber gloves.

A spool of black extra-strong button-and-carpet thread.

A handful of assorted keys.

Clear fingernail polish.

Polish remover.

One dart.

There was just one more item, the most important one of all.

Two

THE BIG COLLIE barked first, then the cockers chimed in shrilly, shifting nervously in their pens. The deep-throated *woof* of the German shepherd boomed against the plastered walls.

In the hallway, the figure bending near the keyhole of the third door stiffened.

Goddam those goddam dogs.

Sweat slid between skin and the tight sheath of the rubber gloves, making it hard to work the keys.

All the dogs barked now, even the sleepy, ancient dachshund.

The fourth key worked. The lock clicked and the door swung open. Once inside, the figure shut the door, then switched on the flashlight. The bright beam danced over the immaculate linoleum floor, bounced up to the worktable, then to the rows of wooden cabinets. These, too, were locked.

It took patience. The dogs continued to bark, and the frantic yelps rebounded from the walls and tore at the senses. When the fifth cabinet door was open, a gloved hand reached up to pull out the third drawer. There were two small plastic vials in that drawer. The labels read *Succostrin.*

Jill Kearney always drove too fast, with the windows down. She loved the feel of the cool October night air against her face. She'd always liked nighttime. Nothing looked quite the same after dark, not even this road, a road she knew so well she could drive it automatically. She hummed softly. What a wonderful job she had, even if everyone thought she was crazy to love it. Usually, she didn't have to go back to the hospital after her ten o'clock check, but that big Doberman had to be turned every three hours after his surgery to prevent pneumonia.

The road dipped just before her turnoff. The lights from the Honda skimmed across an automobile parked deep in the shadow of a live oak. Odd place to park. Must have had car trouble. The Honda picked up speed, and she leaned into the curve. Because the road curved so sharply, the Honda's lights flashed up into the sky, and the moving beam of light in the third window on the east side of the clinic was sharply distinct.

As the Honda squealed to a stop, Jill flicked off the motor and the headlights, staring at the now dark row of windows.

Something had disturbed the dogs. Even out here in the parking lot, the sound of their frantic barking rose and fell.

A light had moved behind one of the windows. She was sure of it.

She looked around the graveled parking lot. It was empty, of course. No one had any business at the Island Hills Veterinary Clinic at one o'clock in the morning. No one but she.

Perhaps she had imagined the light, but she wasn't imagining the barking. She'd better check the rooms on the east side. Just to be sure. She picked up her ring of keys and slipped out of the car.

Opening the back door, she flipped on the hall lights. Except for the almost deafening rumble of barks, accented by the high-pitched yapping of the cockers, everything seemed just as usual: the hall floors glistened from their final swab of the day, the air smelled of disinfectant and dogs.

Jill hesitated, then pivoted and walked up the hallway, unlocking doors as she went.

She unlocked the third door, the door that led into the dispensary, pushed it open, and reached out to turn on the light.

Her hand never touched the switch. The side of her head exploded in an agony of pain.

Three

ANNIE LAURANCE stared first at the telephone, then at the list she held in her hand.

Should she call all of them? Tell them it was canceled?

What could she say? That she had smallpox?

She took a deep breath and glared at the telephone. It was *her* shop, *her* Sunday evenings. If she wanted to call it off she . . .

Beneath her hand the phone rang. Annie and her black cat, Agatha, both jumped.

"Agatha, love, it's all right," she called, but Agatha was already streaking toward her usual hiding place.

The phone shrilled again.

Annie yanked it up, remembering at the last moment to insert a modicum of cheer in her voice.

"Death On Demand."

There was an instant's pause, then a familiar voice, an upsettingly familiar voice, inquired mildly, "Do you provide a choice? Defenestration, evisceration, assassination?"

"Max!"

She winced at the enthusiasm of her greeting. Determined to put that right, she repeated crisply, "Max," the inflection pleasingly even.

"I liked the first Max better," he said in that lazy, good-humored, oh-so-Max-satisfied voice.

"Where are you?"

"Dear Annie. Always straight to the point."

"Look, Max, I'm busy, and I've—"

"No time for old friends? Dear friends?"

She could picture him, leaning casually against something, a newel post perhaps, as if it were a play. Or he might have a cellular phone in his Porsche. Max always liked to have the latest in everything. His blond hair would be rumpled, his mouth quirked in an expressive grin, and his blue eyes, those damnably vivid blue eyes, alight with laughter.

"I've had the devil's own time finding you, love. You could at least ask me how I did it."

She waited. Max never needed encouragement to display his cleverness.

"They were very friendly to me at your old alma mater, via long distance, of course. I spent enough to keep Sprint solvent for another quarter."

"You called SMU?" She heard the bleat in her voice and winced again.

"Did you think I didn't listen to your tales of college days?"

"You have a brain like a sponge."

"I will take that as a compliment. When I explained to the drama secretary that I was casting director of a new off-Broadway play, and that we'd lost your number . . . Well, it worked like magic."

Annie objected, "They don't know where I am."

"But they knew the name of your best chum, one Miss Margaret Melinda Howard, who now lives in Lubbock, which sounds like a cross between a hillock and a sick sailor. I chatted long enough with Ms. Howard to finance a major promotional campaign by Sprint. She was thrilled to tell me that you, her most favorite orphan friend, had inherited the not-quite-beneficent estate of your crusty uncle Ambrose and were now living on an island off the coast of South Carolina, which I brilliantly located on a large-scale map."

Annie almost corrected him. She wasn't really an orphan. Her parents had divorced when she was three, so she didn't remember her father, and the fact that he was apparently alive and well in

California wasn't important. Margaret knew of her mother's death, of course. Annie realized she was twiddling her mind with every extraneous detail possible to avoid responding to Max's magnetism. It was to no avail. She felt the same old weak-kneed dizziness that swept over her every time he used to come around her tiny Greenwich Village apartment. But she had settled with that, done with it once and for all, and she wasn't going to stand here and let it all start up again. Besides—she glanced at the antique clock above the mantel—she was running out of time.

"Look, Max, it's great to hear from you. But I've got to make some phone calls, something I have to attend to."

Unintentionally, the worry throbbing deep inside spilled over into her voice. She knew he heard it just as clearly as she did.

"What's wrong, Annie?" The light tone was gone.

"Nothing big," she said lightly. "Just some stuff with the shop."

"You're upset."

She took a deep breath. Upset was putting it mildly, and if she didn't get busy on the phone right this minute . . .

"Max, it isn't your problem."

"Come on, my love. What's upset you?"

She forced a laugh. "Nothing. I just need to cancel a party for tonight."

"Where's the party?"

She was so obsessed with her problem that she'd forgotten everybody didn't know. "It's here at the bookstore."

"Bookstore? Oh, hey, I like that—Death On Demand."

She glanced at the clock. "Look, Max, it's swell to talk to you." It wasn't swell. She steadied her voice—good, straight, crisp inflection. Good girl, Annie. Always knew there was a superb actress in you. "But I've got to get off the phone and cancel that party."

"Don't cancel it, Annie. You know I love a good party."

She stiffened. "Look, Max, you *are* in New York, aren't you?"

He chuckled. "Not by a long damn shot. See you at the party."

The line went dead. Annie glared at the humming receiver.

He couldn't be in South Carolina.

Max here. She looked out the front windows of the shop at the green water surging against the rock wall of the harbor. He couldn't actually be here.

Before she could assimilate the thought and order her emotions, her heart—that untrustworthy, undisciplined, irritating member—gave a happy leap.

Annie banged down the receiver. All right. Let him come. If he'd ferreted out her new home, followed her down here, just let him come. She'd never change her mind, no matter how much he piled on his careless charm.

They were poles apart, and apart they should stay.

She was poor.

Max was rich.

She'd grown up in a shabby frame house in a Texas prairie town.

Max had lived in lots of houses: a white stone mansion high above a Connecticut river, a rambling, weathered summer home with its own tennis court on Long Island, a penthouse high above Fifth Avenue, a medieval castle near a Scottish loch.

She'd scrimped through school on a drama scholarship.

Max lounged languidly through Princeton.

She liked life to be foursquare, aboveboard, and predictable.

He delighted in ambiguities, disdained certainties, and loved above anything to puncture pretensions.

But oh how happiness bubbled inside her. Max in South Carolina.

Footsteps sounded on the wooden porch. The shop was closed on Sundays, so it couldn't be a customer.

But it was. Annie felt a spurt of irritation and wished she had a flag just like Dell Shannon's, complete with a striking snake and the legend DONT TREAD ON ME, to hoist outside the main door when she wished to be undisturbed. Of course, Shannon raised her flag when she was hard at work on a new Luis Mendoza. And Annie doubted whether any flag would ward off Mrs. Brawley, who now stood with her fox-sharp nose squashed against the north window. Her snapping black eyes quite clearly saw Annie standing beside the cash desk next to the phone. Trust Mrs. Brawley. She must have followed Annie here from the early service at St. Mary's-By-The-Sea.

Mrs. Brawley tapped on the window.

Mrs. Brawley bought books by the *carload.*

Resignedly, Annie moved through the foyer. She opened the door and stepped out onto the slatted wooden planks of the verandah which fronted all the shops. The smile she managed wasn't exactly hospitable, but it would do for a Sunday morning.

"I'm sorry, Mrs. Brawley, Death On Demand isn't open now. I'm just here to catch up on—"

Mrs. Brawley had learned early on in life that persistence might outrage, but it was effective. She ignored Annie's opening salvo.

"Miss Laurance, you *promised* you would get the latest Mrs. Pollifax for me. I came by the store Friday, and here it is Sunday, and I thought it might have come in on the late ferry yesterday. Couldn't you just check your shipments and see?"

But Annie, standing with the shop door open, wasn't listening. Her eyes were on the tall figure striding negligently across the plaza, obviously en route to Death On Demand. A wolfish smile exposed strong white teeth as Elliot Morgan looked up and saw her discomfiture.

Elliot Morgan. The last person in the world she wanted to see right now.

Four

MAX PRESSED THE SWITCH on the dash and a softly humming electric motor opened the Porsche's sunroof. The marsh-scented air swirled gently around him. Damn, he liked this country! Enormous pines hugged the narrow blacktop. The dense woodland was broken by watery stretches where golden-stalked grasses rimmed dark green pools. He began to whistle, a slightly off-key but cheerful rendering of an almost forgotten tune about a happy wanderer. And that's what he was, a happy wanderer. His goal was almost at hand.

Annie.

He frowned slightly. Annie with her sunny smile and serious gray eyes. Flyaway hair that couldn't quite decide between spun gold and chipmunk brown. His happy . . . Max's frown deepened. Not so happy at the moment, from the sound of her voice when they talked that morning. Well, whatever it was, he would soon put it right.

Coolness suddenly tingled beneath the warm sweep of air as a cloud briefly obscured the sun. He looked up, then squinted against the brightness as the cloud sped on. A road sign flashed by. Broward's Rock Ferry, 5 Miles. He grinned and again sounded the song's refrain. Nice place, all right. But he would be happy slogging up a rutted trail in the Mojave Desert if Annie waited at journey's end. Still, South Carolina charmed him, although this narrow road left a little to be desired. Finally the Texaco truck straddling the center line pulled off into a two-pump country station. For the moment, the road lay straight and empty before him.

Leaning forward, he pressed the accelerator. The Porsche leaped ahead, and the handful of varicolored speeding tickets jammed behind the visor fluttered hard.

Intent on her mission, Mrs. Brawley ignored Elliot Morgan. "I don't want to be a bother," she prodded, clearly not meaning a word of it, "but if you will just *check* your storeroom." Her ingratiating smile had all the charm of the shark in *Jaws.*

"Mrs. Brawley, I phoned the publisher on Friday to place a special order, but even special orders take a few days."

The sharp eyes flickered past Annie to the open bookstore door. "I talked to Mr. Parotti and asked him if you received any packages this weekend. He said you did."

Annie accepted defeat.

Both Mrs. Brawley and Elliot followed her down the central aisle, and they all turned left to troop into the storeroom at the back, where Annie slit open the shipping carton and displayed forty copies of the latest Dick Francis—and nothing else, despite Mrs. Brawley's energetically skeptical probes into the packing material.

"Well," she sighed. "I do so *want* that latest Mrs. Pollifax."

Annie took her firmly by the elbow, without a great deal of subtlety, and tugged her away from the storeroom.

When they were even with the watercolors displayed along the back wall, Mrs. Brawley jerked to a stop.

"Miss Laurance, I've just got one question about that second one—"

"No hints," Annie replied firmly, and gave a little shove toward the central corridor.

Deigning to move, Mrs. Brawley twisted her head to stare back at the paintings.

"These are just *too* hard," she complained peevishly. She hugged a worn brown purse to her skinny chest and wriggled her bony shoulders in irritation. Then her face brightened. "I'm ahead of everyone else. This time I'm going to win. Just you wait and see." She shook free of Annie's restraining fingers. "If I figure out that one, then I'm going to be the winner this month—and I'll get my Mrs. Pollifax *free.*" She peered anxiously at Annie. "Have you heard anything about it? Is it supposed to be as good as the others?"

"I'm sure it will be wonderful, and I'll call you as soon as it arrives." One last push, and Mrs. Brawley was out the door and onto the porch.

Annie closed the door, took a deep breath, and turned to face Elliot Morgan.

"One of the joys of running a bookstore—dealing with book-lovers," he observed.

"Don't enjoy it so much," she said sourly. "I was just going to phone you."

He grinned. Again she was reminded of a wolf, dark eyes deep set, pugnacious jaw. He stood at ease beside the enormous stuffed raven which perched on a pedestal just inside the door. The raven's feathers shone a glossy black, uncannily like Elliot's hair.

"Two minds that work as one?" he inquired lightly. "I dropped by to see if you wanted to lunch at Smuggler's Inn."

Annie was nonplussed, then infuriated. How could he possibly think she would lunch with him—ever—after his performance last week at the meeting of the Sunday Night Regulars? She stared at him, feeling wordless rage begin to boil.

He looked down at her, his darkly handsome face tilted. When she'd first met him, she'd been mildly impressed. Physically, Elliot was an imposing man—tall, lean, and well-built, with a bold, uncompromising Roman face. She realized now that he always turned a little to the left to present his best profile. He had the same pose on his most recent book jacket. That book sat right now in a ten-deep pile on a table behind her that held local authors' latest efforts.

Annie had never before felt the urge to engage in book burning.

Still, maybe it wasn't too late. Maybe she could keep disaster from happening.

She made a muscle-hard effort to sound pleasant. "I need to talk to you."

"Oh?" Another wolfish smile. "Now what could you want to talk to me about?"

A dull flush spread over her face. *Oh, Lord, don't let me lose my temper.* He was obviously going to be difficult.

Quirking an inquiring eyebrow, he lit one of his ever-present, abominable Turkish cigarettes.

"Those are going to make you very sick someday," Annie commented through clenched teeth. A wisp of acrid smoke spiraled past the No Smoking sign prominently posted over the raven's head.

He shrugged. "If I need a nursemaid, I'll pick a nubile Swedish import. Besides, living too long is folly."

"If you keep on the way you're going, you may not live past tonight."

That amused him.

"Are some of the pigs squealing?"

"Elliot, these are your friends. Why are you doing this?"

"So who needs friends?"

"Who do you think you are, Sam Spade?"

"I was a private investigator once and a damn good one. Everybody will see that tonight." He blew several perfect smoke rings, enjoying himself enormously.

How could she ever have thought him attractive?

He picked up on that, too.

Elliot reached out and his fingers brushed her cheek. "Now, Annie, don't be so damn soft-hearted. It will stir them up. They'll probably all write best-sellers in revenge."

She jerked away from his hand. "It isn't funny," she snapped. "You know, Elliot, you're a louse."

"Really?"

"For the last time, will you change your topic tonight?"

He drew deeply on the cigarette and pondered the smoke. "No."

Her hands clenched. His face was very unpleasant now, the heavy bones bunched up in a tight, hard frown.

"Then the party's off."

Lazily, he shook his head.

Annie exploded. "Look, this is my bookstore—I set up these sessions—I can cancel them."

"Sure. But you won't."

She dug her nails into her palms. "You didn't listen. *The party is off.*"

Taking one last puff on his cigarette, he moved casually around her to snuff it out in a small skull-and-crossbones tray on the cash desk, scattering paper clips. "I guess I never told you that I invested my money from *Blood Tales* in island real estate."

Annie looked at him blankly. *Blood Tales,* his most successful book, was a current Edgar nominee.

He tossed his head toward the dim interior of the shop. "Check your lease, Ms. Laurance. This belongs to Pleasanton Realty, lock, stock, and John D. MacDonalds." He paused, then said coolly, "And yours truly is Pleasanton Realty."

Elliot shook loose another cigarette. "Screw with me, baby, and you'd better be ready for a little increase in rent. Like another thou a month."

Annie took two quick steps and yanked open the door. "Get out of here, Elliot."

He didn't hurry. He sauntered out onto the wooden porch, then looked back over his shoulder at Annie, a small, furious figure in the doorway.

"I thought we might go eat clams, but something tells me you aren't hungry. Oh well, I'll live. See you tonight, Annie."

"Go to hell!"

A weathered board proclaimed in faded letters: Broward's Rock Ferry.

Braking the Porsche in a swirl of gray dust, Max leaned out the window to peer at the sign. He could barely decipher days and times, but it did seem to indicate the ferry ran at 10:30 A.M. and 3:30 P.M. on Sundays. He looked around. Not a creature stirred in any direction. At least, not a creature in a New Yorker's vocabulary. No people. No cars. But the waterside teemed with life, and in the quiet after he turned off the throaty Porsche, he heard the rustle of the grasses in the on-shore breeze and the slap of water against the pilings of the ferry dock. Gulls skimmed just above the water and a *V* of brown pelicans expertly searched the water for mullet.

10:30. He had a little while. Max smiled ruefully at his pell-mell dash down the Eastern seaboard. Patience had never been one of his virtues. He picked up the *Mobil Travel Guide*, flipped open to South Carolina, then searched for Broward's Rock.

BROWARD'S ROCK ISLAND
Pop: 890   Area Code: 803   Zip: 29929
An all-year resort island, Broward's Rock was first settled four thousand years ago by hunter-gatherers. Traces can still be seen today of their descendants in the famous Indian Shell Mound, which contains oyster shells, animal bones, and clay pottery dating to 1450 B.C. White settlement began in 1724 with the arrival of Capt. Josiah Broward, who established the first plantation. Its ruins are visible today in the Island Forest Preserve. The island contains the remnants of Civil War fortifications. The sea-cotton economy of Broward's Rock was devastated by the War, and did not recover until the late 1960s, when construction began of a resort community patterned after its more famous neighbor, Hilton Head island. Two-thirds of Broward's Rock is a controlled access community with several hundred villas and condominiums. There are two golf courses, forty-five tennis courts, and eighteen miles of bicycle paths. The island is skillet shaped, seven miles long and five miles at its widest. It is home to deer, raccoons, alligators, and the endangered Atlantic loggerhead sea turtles, which can reach 400 pounds in weight. Climate is subtropical with more than 280 growing days a year. The island can be reached only by ferry, a 20-minute trip across Port Royal Sound.

Max slapped the guide shut and opened the car door. He stretched, welcoming the sea-scented breeze, then walked to the end of the dock and looked out across the Sound, shadowing his eyes against the bright morning sun. That must be it, that dark green, dimly seen hump low in the water to the southeast.

It sounded like Eden.

Annie thumped the door with her fist and contemplated disaster. Every penny Uncle Ambrose left her was invested in renovating this store. Her uncle would have approved. Under his steward-ship, Death On Demand had been a wonderful place, a pipe-smoky, dim, comfortable, welcoming center for writers, but she had taken the shabby, down-at-heels interior and fashioned it into a bookstore that even Carol Brener and Otto Penzler might envy, discarding Uncle Ambrose's functional steel shelving for the softer orange-brown gleam of gum, reflooring with heart pine, and creating, on the right, between the diagonal shelves slanting off the central corridor and the south wall, an enclave of American Cozy, a cheerful space scattered with rattan chairs with soft yel-low and red chintz cushions and cane-topped tables. Tangly green Whitmani ferns sprouted from raffia baskets. Onyx-based brass floorlamps spread golden pools of light, augmenting the high oval windows above the shelves along the south wall. In her heart, Annie knew this was what it would have been like in the sunroom of Mary Roberts Rinehart's three-story house on Massachusetts Avenue.

She smoothed the silky black feathers of Edgar on his pedestal just inside the door. Just past the raven, hanging beads marked the arched doorway that led to the children's corner, and its stock of all of the Nancy Drews and Hardy Boys, plus lots of nail-biters by two-time Edgar winner Joan Lowery Nixon. Annie had pined for just such a corner full of treasures when she was a kid.

She rattled the hanging beads, then started down the central corridor. The shelves that slanted diagonally on either side con-tained categories of mysteries. She didn't believe in lumping all the books together alphabetically. Cozy readers would never dream of picking up a horror story. Hardboiled enthusiasts would prefer the Yellow Pages to romantic suspense. The first case held all the Agatha Christies because, quite simply, these were and always would be Annie's personal favorites. She never tired of Dame Agatha's perceptive eye and clever plots. On the left side, the shelves held true crime books. These had been Uncle Ambrose's specialty. Everything from Lizzie Borden and Jack the Ripper to the Boston Strangler and Capt. Jeff MacDonald was represented here. Annie passed the spy novels and thrillers on the right and the caper and comedy mysteries to her left. From habit, she stopped to alphabetize the Craig Rice titles. Then came romantic suspense (all the Mary Stewarts) on one side of the aisle and psychological suspense and horror/science fiction on the other. The south wall held classic mystery books, John Dickson Carr through Edgar Wallace. Used books filled the shelving on the north wall. She must remember later to pull a copy of *A Judgement in Stone* off the shelf for Capt. Mac.

She paused at the end of the aisle and frowned unhappily at the coffee bar. This was where the Sunday Night Regulars always met. Not too much expense there. Five tables with straight-back chairs. Annie looked up at the east wall. This was her pièce de résistance, absolutely guaranteed to engender loud and sometimes acrimonious disputes. But it certainly brought in the customers, not only the mystery writers and readers, but the artists, too. Every month she huddled with an island artist, Annie providing the information, the artist creating the watercolors. The collaborations pictured scenes from famous mystery novels; the viewer's challenge was to recognize and identify book and author. This month, there were five paintings. In the first, a rosy-cheeked, white-haired old lady tumbled in front of a speeding car on a crowded London street. In that instant before oblivion, her pink face mirrored horror, fear, an awful knowledge—and a curious lack of surprise. The second painting featured a delightfully antiquated butler, who raised an arthritic arm to open the blinds in an ornate drawing room. The artist beautifully captured the rheumy fuzziness in the butler's pale blue eyes. The third watercolor was a still life, revealing the contents of a jumbled closet: two pairs of skis, a pair of oars, ten or twelve hippopotamus tusks, fishing gear, a bag of golf clubs, a stuffed elephant's foot, a tiger skin. In the fourth painting, a young man supported himself with a cane. His face twisted in disgust as he handed a letter to a slim, pale-haired young woman. In the final watercolor, a group of guests in formal evening clothes sat around a supper-club table, looking up expectantly at a middle-aged man who stood, a fluted champagne glass in his upraised hand, obviously ready to make a toast.

The first person every month to figure out which books the scenes represented received a month's free coffee and a new book. It wasn't quite in the same category as Edgar Wallace's £500 reward for the solution to *Four Just Men* in 1905. Still, it was unclear who enjoyed the contest more: Annie, or her customers.

And Elliot Morgan wanted to take all of this away from her. For a week, she'd known this coming evening held peril, but it had never occurred to her that she was personally vulnerable.

Annie paced slowly into the fern and rattan enclave, kicked at the rug, then sprawled in a cane chair. She wished she'd never come to the store today. On Sundays after early church, she usually jogged or swam. Now, she fervently regretted that she hadn't kept to her regular schedule. Normally, she loved Sundays, especially now that it was October and the island once again belonged to its own. She smiled at her calm assumption of belonging after three months in permanent residence. (Since it had taken Max three months to find her, he couldn't be too distraught at her leaving New York.) But she almost qualified as an old islander. As a girl, especially when her mother was so sick, she'd visited Uncle Ambrose every summer. That was when he'd introduced her to the delights of mysteries. Everything ultimately comes right in a mystery, and that made those uncertain teenage years easier for Annie. So she had a former summer visitor's approval for summer people, and now she had an islander's appreciation for their spending clout. But now that it was October, the summer people were gone. Their generous spending would be missed. Their penchant for dripping mustard from hot dogs or Coke from leaky cups would not. She had a sign at the front of the store, of course, that said No Food, No Drinks, Except for Coffee in the Rear. It was fascinating that people who seemed to be shopping for books were apparently selective in their reading skills. Her part-time helper, Ingrid Jones, never minded scolding, "No food, please, no food," but Annie found it difficult. After all, these were *customers*. And money was so tight.

She twisted in the chair. Time was running out. The Regulars would arrive on schedule at 7:30 P.M. unless she canceled.

Damn Elliot.

She was so proud of the Regulars. They had been her invention, too, although under Uncle Ambrose the store had long been the community center for area mystery writers. At first, Annie was astounded at their number, but Emma Clyde, doyenne of the mystery world, had explained.

"This is the only mystery bookstore this side of Atlanta, Annie. Of course we all come here."

Annie had looked at her in bemusement. "How can one little island have all these writers?"

"This isn't just any island, my dear."

Emma's point was well made. Broward's Rock wasn't just another low-slung swamp off the South Carolina coast. It was rapidly gaining in fame on Hilton Head and Kiawah Island.

As Emma said, most writers valued exclusivity almost as much as fame—but not quite. Annie's uncle had been quick to see the possibilities, and his beloved Death On Demand became *the* place for writers to meet, drink choice coffee, tout their latest novels, gossip, argue, and talk shop.

Uncle Ambrose. She was so very glad she'd come for her regular summer visit this year, since it was to be their last. When he was gone, and her visit drawn out because of the funeral and the need to settle his business affairs, every passing day had made New York seem farther away and less of a home. She had thought about her apartment, a one-room closet, actually, and her valiant but unrewarded efforts as an actress (seventeen tryouts without one callback). Then she had thought about Max and the future. The decision to stay on Broward's Rock was astonishingly easy to make, and she threw herself headlong into renovating her favorite bookstore in all the world. That was three months ago

Until now, she hadn't regretted it once. That wasn't to say that some moonlit nights didn't cause a twinge when she thought of Max, but she was nobody's fool, and she especially wasn't going to be Max Darling's fool.

Max Darling.

She'd accused him once of making up the name. He'd answered rather stiffly that the Darlings were a long-established family with illustrious antecedents, that it was his mother's maiden name, and that he used it in preference to his father's because he got damn tired of people either resenting him or fawning when they recognized his father's surname as that of one of the great financial clans of America.

Annie had answered sharply. "You don't need to change your name. You need to change your habits."

"You sound like my prep school counselors," he retorted equably. "And you're much too pretty for that."

"Don't be condescending. Look, you're smart and capable. Why don't you—"

He interrupted primly, "Live up to your potential?" He shook his head. "I've heard it all, Annie, chapter and verse. 'Maxwell, it's such a waste. Why don't you become a lawyer/journalist/doctor/foreign service attaché/stockbroker?' "

"Why don't you?"

"Lovey, my great-great-grandfather made enough money to buy anything the world has to offer." The laughter fell away. "The funny thing is, there isn't anything I want to buy. The world isn't clamoring for my services. I'm a fair writer, a competent actor, a damn fool at figures. I'm bored by business, I hate quarrels, and my interest in science stopped with a sixth-grade film about a turtle giving birth in the sand."

"What do you like?"

The grin was back. "People. People in all their wonder. I hawked sausages at the World's Fair in New Orleans. I've dived for pearls off Japan. Now I'm massaging talent as an off-Broadway producer. What the hell, Annie. Why can't you go with the flow?"

But she couldn't. She bunched a pillow more comfortably behind her. Damn him. Why did he have to reappear in her life?

Irritably, she slapped her hand against the chair arm. She had to decide what to do about Elliot and the Regulars tonight.

Tonight.

The Regulars.

There was no way she could afford another thousand a month in rent. Could Elliot really do that? Her lease expired in two months. She groaned. He probably could. The only shop presently vacant on the harbor front was much too small. He probably owned that one, too.

She couldn't lose her bookstore. It was the first thing in all her life that had been her own, and it was her only link with the happiest portion of her past, those idyllic summer days, curled up in a hammock behind Uncle Ambrose's tiny house, poring over the adventures of mousey Miss Silver, elegant Lord Wimsey, and gimlet-eyed Miss Marple.

Annie relished running Death On Demand. She'd loved mysteries since her first Nancy Drew. She loved mystery readers, who ran the gamut of society, with a small *s*. She enjoyed tipping readers to new, good writers, such as Jane Dentinger, Dorothy Cannell, and Charlaine Harris. She liked the way readers could surprise you: the wispy-haired spinster who never missed a Mc-Bain, the island plumber whose favorite author was Amanda Cross. Now, there was an accomplishment: to become a best-selling mystery writer and also win tenure at Columbia—the twin achievement of Carolyn Heilbrun, who writes as Amanda Cross.

She'd enjoyed meeting writers during her summer visits, but she'd never until now had a chance to know any of them well. She had to admit she didn't exactly love all these mystery writers. Still, she liked some of them a lot. Elliot was a stinker.

The phone at the cash desk rang.

Blast Max. He probably needed directions.

Steeling herself, she stayed put.

Would everybody come tonight?

Her Sunday Night Specials, when the store was open only to writers, were popular. At least, they had been until now. Every Sunday evening, one of the Regulars provided an informal program. One Sunday, the Farleys, who wrote children's mysteries, told the Regulars about Harriet Stratemeyer Adams, who built a mansion high above the Hudson with her profits from the Nancy Drew and Hardy Boys books and several other series which first her father, then she, authored. The Stratemeyer syndicate had worked under nearly fifty pseudonyms and sold over one hundred million books. During one session, Harriet Edelman, whose own hero was infamously clever, traced the history of the comedy mystery from Mary Roberts Rinehart's first injection of mild humor in *The Circular Staircase* through Constance and Gwenyth Little, Craig Rice, Donald Westlake, Stuart M. Kaminsky, and Joyce Porter to Gregory Mcdonald's triumphantly cocky and irreverent Fletch books. Another Sunday, Captain McElroy, or Capt. Mac as they called him, drew on his experiences as a former police chief to explain with stolid thoroughness how to avoid leaving fingerprints on almost any kind of surface. He was an unpublished author, but warmly welcomed by the group because of his expertise—he'd spent several years early in his career in the Miami Police Department. One thing he'd learned: In searching for a killer, try nearby cafes for descriptions of customers shortly after the murder. Killing makes people hungry.

Until now, the Sunday evenings had been special and a lot of fun. Until last week, when Annie realized something odd and ugly was happening to her Sunday evenings. That night, Harriet Edelman had arrived early and made straight for the coffee bar at the back.

"Give me some of that good Kona stuff."

Annie poured the dark, aromatic coffee into two white mugs and handed one to Harriet, whose battery of bracelets jangled musically as she took it. She stared down into the black coffee, then said savagely, "I swear to God, if you won't screw an editor, you can't get anywhere!"

"Surely it's not that bad. Besides, aren't most editors women?"

Harriet's mouth twisted. "Maybe, but I still say you can't get anywhere if you don't have pull—and you've got a lot better chance if you live in Manhattan and know the bastards." Her faded blond hair drooped across a high, domed forehead. Thick horn-rimmed glasses increased her owlishness. Oddly enough, Harriet wrote frothy mysteries which featured wryly funny heroes. Annie chalked it up as one of nature's jokes.

"Dropping sales, half-assed reviews, and if everything weren't lousy enough," Harriet continued bitterly, "some low-life wrote my editor and told her my last book had a stolen plot. Can you believe that?" Harriet's voice rasped up into shrill outrage.

"Oh, ignore it," Annie soothed. "Didn't someone once say there were only ten plots, and they've all been used?"

Harriet wasn't listening. Her sallow face glistened with anger. "Don't think I don't know who did it."

Annie looked at her with concern. The hatred in her voice was shocking, and horribly inappropriate against the snatches of conversation as the writers milled toward the tables in the coffee area.

"*Stick*'s his best. No doubt about that."

"No, no. *Switch* is tighter, tenser."

"I'll tell you who has the most original mind in crime fiction today—Tom Perry, bar none."

"Don't tell me you still read Dorothy Sayers?"

Bullish voices, didactic, perhaps, but none with the frightening edge of desperation in Harriet's.

Harriet's fingers dug into Annie's arm. "If it really is him—if he did it, I'll kill him."

Was it fate or irony or black humor that Elliot chose that moment to clap his hands for attention?

Annie looked up sharply and broke free of Harriet's grasp. What was Elliot up to? Emma was scheduled to speak tonight.

The writers settled swiftly around the tables at the back of Death on Demand. Elliot stood near the coffee bar, the customary spot for the speaker. He clapped his hands again. "I know every-one's eager to hear Emma tonight."

The Regulars looked obediently and expectantly toward Emma Clyde, whose fictional detective Marigold Rembrandt was second only to Miss Marple in readers' affections and earned Emma an astounding seven figures a year. Plump, motherly, and utterly down-home, Emma always seemed slightly bewildered by her fame, but Annie noticed that her mind worked with the precision of an IBM PC*jr*.

"No doubt Emma will be happy to share the secret of her enormous success," Elliot continued unctuously. "You know, I really felt pretty uncomfortable when I realized I would be follow-ing her next week. However, I've given a lot of thought to the program I plan to present."

Ego, ego, Annie thought. Elliot can't bear to spend a whole evening listening to another writer, so he's going to horn in on Emma. She got ready to move forward and cut him off before he did any more damage.

"I've been doing some investigating, some *real* investigating. You know, digging out those delicious little secrets people try so hard to hide."

"More true crime? Some shoplifter's memoirs?" Fritz Hemp-hill's thin voice was sardonic.

Elliot's head swiveled toward Fritz.

Annie was reminded unpleasantly of a snake.

Fritz wrote male adventure with blood, guts, and enough macho for a battalion of Green Berets.

"Not a shoplifter. No, I have something much more special in mind. My publisher and I are convinced this will be a best-seller."

"Like *Kiss a Stranger?*" Fritz asked sarcastically.

Oh, wow. Only Fritz would be courageous or crazy enough to say that aloud. Everyone knew Elliot's last book was a bomb and had been remaindered six months after it came out. It was a true-crime book, a horrific description of a Hollywood starlet's foolish and deadly passion for a hitchhiker.

Someone snickered, probably Harriet.

Elliot's face darkened, but his voice remained pleasant. "No, this little volume will knock their socks off. You know how the public has this enormous appetite to know all about their idols? Dirty laundry and all? Well, I've decided to tell everybody the truth about a very special group. Don't you agree it will make a hell of a book to tell all about some well-known writers? Mystery writers, that is."

The silence was absolute.

"The real truth—all the gritty, nasty little secrets." Elliot's eyes glistened with malicious pleasure as he scanned the frozen faces of his listeners.

"Sounds boring to me," Emma said lightly, but her light blue eyes sparkled angrily. "Not enough sex appeal, Elliot."

"I can assure you, my dear, there will be plenty of sex."

That was last week. Everyone had stayed for Emma's presentation, but they all scurried out afterward without the usual good-natured bickering and jousting. All week long Annie had procrastinated on deciding what—if anything—she could do to prevent tonight's explosion.

It was her shop. It was up to her.

But, after all, these people were adults. They certainly didn't need her to play Big Momma. They might even resent it.

It was her store—and she resented Elliot using her evening to poke and gouge at her friends. Moreover, she wasn't about to let him believe he'd cowed her with his threats to raise her rent.

Okay. She would . . .

Annie sat bolt upright in the cane chair and looked toward the central aisle. She couldn't see it, of course, not from her comfortable lounging spot on this side of the diagonal bookshelves. She didn't have to see the central aisle or into the coffee area to recognize that sound. When the back door to Death On Demand was pulled shut, a loose cupboard in the receiving room always snapped to with a sharp crack, like a .22 rifle.

She reminded herself that it was Sunday morning, she was

alone in her store, and the back door was locked. But she'd heard that sharp, unmistakable crack.

Annie slipped to her feet, skirted the table, another cane chair, a floor lamp, and the clinging fronds of a fern. The central aisle was shadowy. Afraid she might attract another Mrs. Brawley, she hadn't turned on the lights. She'd wanted peace and quiet to ponder her problems. So it was quite dim here in the center of the store. She could see a portion of the coffee area. It was utterly quiet, utterly still.

She opened her mouth to call out, but there was something so heavy and ominous in the waiting silence that her throat closed.

This is silly.

But that cupboard *had* slammed shut. She'd *heard* it.

Stealthily, feeling vaguely foolish, she edged down the central aisle, her eyes seeking out the shadowy corners, that dark splotch near the doorway to the delivery room.

A sudden wave of panic swept over her. She remembered something Capt. Mac had said in his talk. "Listen to your instinct. If you ever feel, even for an instant, that something is wrong, dead wrong, run. Run and scream."

Terrific advice. Except she couldn't scream. Her breath was bunched like a pineapple in her throat, and her legs wobbled.

Annie turned toward the front of the store and crouched, like a track athlete waiting for the starter's gun. Okay. As soon as she could force a deep breath, she was going to break and run for the front door and . . .

Annie blew out the bulge of air in a whoosh and felt like a fool.

She stood and walked a little unsteadily up the aisle and stopped to look into Agatha's languorous green eyes.

"You'd think I wrote mysteries, wouldn't you, Agatha? What an imagination!" She scooped up the sleek black cat from her basket, which rested on top of the Christie section, and stroked her gleaming fur, knowing Agatha would tolerate the effrontery for only a moment. A predictably independent feline, Agatha never stayed in the same room with a stranger. In fact, with few exceptions, she fled to hide beneath her favorite fern the instant anyone entered the shop. Obviously no stranger had come into the store-room. She'd probably imagined that noise. Perhaps it was the crack of a broken branch outside. In any event, it was time to stop behaving like a Barbara Michaels' heroine.

Agatha growled politely.

Laughing partly from relief and partly from embarrassment, Annie put Agatha gently back on the shelf. Agatha, of course, jumped down. Everything was okay; it was just another Sunday morning. How absurd to imagine anyone would break into the shop. After all, there was absolutely no reason for anyone to break and enter. It wasn't as though there would be cash in hand. She'd almost have to borrow money to buy lunch. The whole episode was just a product of her overly vivid imagination. Like reading *My Cousin Rachel* when she was fourteen and, for a doom-laden week, suspecting that Uncle Ambrose intended to do away with her.

Nevertheless, she checked the back door. It was locked.

There was nothing to worry about. As for the evening, she would fix Elliot's wagon. She would take the floor first and point out that the Sunday Night Specials were supposed to have pro-grams beneficial to the writers, and she felt there was a lack of interest in Elliot's program, and why didn't they take a vote on it? That would put Elliot in his place, all right.

Five

THE WHISTLE was frankly admiring and subtly erotic.

Annie didn't open her eyes. She didn't need to.

"How did you find me?"

"Dear Ms. Laurance, always so direct. I arrived on the ten-thirty ferry. Since there is only one ferry on Sunday morning, I was forced to count fiddler crabs while waiting. Fascinating creatures. When I reached your snug little island, I immediately rented a condo near the harbor and began my quest. I will confess I was surprised to find that the proprietress of Death On Demand is so slothful that she doesn't open on Sundays, but I recalled that said proprietress is tiringly vigorous and deduced that she would probably be found on the beach, either jogging or swimming. How disappointed I am to find her stretched out on a beach towel with her face covered by the latest issue of *Vogue*."

Annie yanked the magazine aside, opened one eye, and squinted. "I just ran three miles on the beach. How did you know it was me?"

"As has been said in perhaps another context, I would know that body anywhere."

She opened both eyes and laughed. He looked wonderful, of course. All six foot two inches of him. And she would know *his* body anywhere, every lean, muscular inch of it. To distract herself, she waved him down beside her.

Max flipped out a blue-and-white striped Ralph Lauren towel and dropped down, spattering sand.

"What took you three months?"

He shoved a hand through his thick, tangly blond hair, and rolled over on his elbow to stare down with ink-blue eyes. "Didn't your mother ever tell you it was rude to ask direct questions?"

She struggled to a sitting position and fished a sand-filmed bottle of Hawaiian Tropic from her beach bag. Studiously ignoring both Max's body and his eyes, she began slapping the coconut-scented oil on her legs, overlooking his appreciative "m-mm."

"Why three months?" she repeated brusquely.

"You didn't call to tell me where you were."

"No."

"Why?"

Annie looked up at him, and it was suddenly hard to breathe. "Dammit, Max, I was afraid you'd persuade me to come back to New York."

"Would that be so bad?"

This side of Broward's Rock faced out into the Atlantic. A clear, softly blue sky arched overhead. The air carried the pungent scents of salt water, tar, seaweed, and Annie's coconut-scented suntan oil. The water stretched endlessly to the east, as richly green as pea soup; a gentle surf strummed a seven-mile length of oyster-gray sand. There was a sprinkling of sunbathers and swimmers scattered up and down the beach, enjoying the eighty-degree day, but no one was near them. This stretch of beach was all their own.

"Max, it won't work. *You* don't work. Life is just a joke to you— a compendium of one-liners."

"So you'd like me better if I were earnest." He frowned, then the corners of his mouth twitched. "Let's see. What sufficiently important career could I pursue?" He leaned back on his elbows, staring pensively at the horizon.

Annie fought down a disquieting desire to touch the mat of hair on his chest, glistening a light gold in the sunlight.

Sitting bolt upright, he slapped his palm down and sand sprayed against her oiled legs. "I know. Annie, would you love me if I were a priest?"

"Max!"

He grinned. "Anglican, of course."

"Max." She used both hands to shove him backward, but he caught her as he fell, and they rolled together in the sand.

Max, who had helped brew the coffee, sniffed with theatrical appreciation when Annie poured him a mug. Lifting it to drink, he paused to look at the inscription in red cursive letters against the white background. "The Listening House. Do houses listen?"

"That's a title. If you looked on the bottom, you'd find the author's name."

Obediently, he raised the mug high enough to see the bottom. "Mabel Seeley."

Annie waved her hand abstractedly toward the rows of mugs shelved behind the coffee bar as she filled the cream pitcher. "Each mug has the title of a book which is considered important in the history of mystery novels." She put the cream pitcher beside the sugar bowl and reached for the corkscrew to open the bottles of sauvignon blanc.

Max moved behind the coffee bar and called out an occasional name that attracted him. *"The Mystery of Dr. Fu-Manchu, The Thirty-Nine Steps, The Rasp, The Tragedy of Y, The Cape Cod Mystery, Rebecca, Home Sweet Homicide."* He turned to look at her. "Where did you find these?"

"Oh, I did them."

"In your little home kiln?"

She laughed. "No, silly. I didn't *make* them. I painted the titles."

"Annie, I learn something new about you all the time. It never occurred to me that you could paint as well as act."

"I'm not exactly a threat to Van Gogh," she pointed out crisply.

He started to count the mugs stacked on the shelves behind the coffee bar but his attention soon strayed. "You haven't read all those books, have you?"

"Nope. But lots of them."

"A misspent youth, obviously."

"I suppose you were busy with Saint Augustine's *Confessions*?"

"Oh, in a manner of speaking. I suspect old Auggie would have been a *Playboy* man himself."

"The point is, he changed his ways."

"But not altogether for the better."

Since she wasn't winning this exchange, she concentrated on completing the ham, salami, and cheese tray. Agatha twined expectantly around her ankle. Annie held down a piece of cheddar for her. "Cats aren't supposed to eat cheese, silly."

Agatha demanded more, and, like a well-trained owner, Annie obliged.

"How many do you expect?" Max asked.

Among their other activities that afternoon, she'd told Max all about the Sunday evening sessions and Elliot Morgan. After all, it was something else to talk about besides Max's disinclination to toil and her determination to treat life in the serious manner it deserved.

She added them up, one finger after another.

"Elliot himself, of course. Then there's Emma Clyde. You know who *she* is. And the Farleys, Janis and Jeff. They write children's mysteries. Their latest is *The Secret of the Red Dragon.* Harriet Edelman does those clever Harrison Macintosh books. Fritz Hemphill wrote *Death in an Alley.* His heroes are always sleazy and very, very tough. You know, the guy busts open the villain's head with a tire tool, then gets beaned himself, slugs down some scotch, runs up a fire escape, and has sex on the tenth landing with a blonde he just met."

"That's six." Max paused teasingly. "Hey, maybe I could be an accountant."

Annie was dreading the coming session, but, somehow, that awareness couldn't dampen the bubbly sense of fun she'd felt ever since Max dropped down onto the sand beside her. Now he stood looking at her ingenuously, his thick blond hair carefully combed and dampened, his face fresh from a shower, his white broadcloth shirt crisp, and she thought he looked wonderful standing by the coffee bar at Death On Demand.

Sternly, she forced her mind back to her guest list.

"Okay, six. Oh yes, there's Hal Douglas. He writes caper novels like S. S. Van Dine but not as good. And Kelly Rizzoli. She goes in for psychological fiction à la Ruth Rendell. And Ingrid Jones, the woman who helps me out part-time, usually comes. That's every . . . oh no, I'm forgetting Capt. Mac. I told you about him."

"The somber sleuth."

Annie considered it. "No, not somber. I mean, he's extremely serious about everything, but he's really a nice man. He was wonderful when Uncle Ambrose died. Oh, Max, that night was so *awful*—"

"Annie, don't dwell on it. You can't undo the past."

"He must have taken ill, felt faint. Why, he spent more time in that boat than he did on land. He couldn't just have *fallen* off. If only I'd gone with him—" She stared down into her mug, face strained. "We found him floating only a few feet from the boat, right here in the harbor."

"You and Capt. Mac?"

"Yes, I phoned him when Uncle Ambrose didn't come home that night. I think I knew right from the start that something awful had happened, though Capt. Mac tried to persuade me I was being silly. He couldn't have been more wonderful when we found—Uncle Ambrose. He called the police and stayed with me the whole night."

"That was helpful." Max sounded faintly strangled.

She looked at him in surprise.

"How old is this noble Galahad?"

"Mmm. Fiftyish, I guess."

"The James Garner type?"

Max was jealous.

"Oh, I'd say more the James Bond type." Her voice fell seductively. "Absolutely irresistible to women of all ages."

Max's chin jutted out alarmingly.

"Actually, Max, he's built like a sumo wrestler, and his eyes look positively glacial, gritty and gray. But he *is* a very nice man, and he's invited me out for lunch a couple . . ."

The front door bell jangled. Agatha streaked past, en route to her special hiding place deep in the shadow of the largest fern.

The Sunday Night Special was about to begin.

The first arrival was Capt. Mac. He was, in a sumo way, attractive, his short black hair nicely frosted with white, his blunt, intelligent face softening as he looked down at his hostess. She glanced at Max and enjoyed his struggle between manners and immediate hostility.

"Max Darling," he said crisply as he thrust out his hand.

"John McElroy, but call me Capt. Mac. All these kids do."

Max's smile looked a little strained.

Emma Clyde and the Farleys came in next. Emma was carrying a covered bowl and two large bags of chips.

"I remember how these wolves devoured your food last time, Annie, and I thought I would pitch in. Shall I just put these things on the table?"

Emma wore a Hawaiian print caftan and looked like a wildly painted tugboat. Her hair sprouted in stiff bronze curls, and Annie was positive she'd paid a long visit to Island Beauty Inc. on Saturday. Emma neither looked nor sounded like a millionaire author, but Annie noticed her intensely blue eyes sweep the room. Was she looking for Elliot? But it was Max she fastened onto.

"A friend of Annie's! That's so nice. I'm delighted to meet you."

The Farleys stood at the edge of the coffee area. As usual, they gave Annie the creeps, which immediately made her inject extra warmth into her greeting.

"Jeff. Janis. I'm *so* glad you could come."

They looked at her unsmilingly. Jeff wore light blue slacks and a white crewneck sweater. He looked like an overage cheerleader despite his sleek blond beard and horn-rimmed glasses. Janis, slim and pale, stayed a pace behind him. Her large green eyes flickered nervously from Annie to Jeff and back to Annie. Janis had a quality of seeming more her husband's appendage than a person in her own right, a posture Annie found exceedingly irritating.

"Some coffee?" Annie urged. "Or would you prefer wine?"

Janis looked to her husband for guidance.

Even as the door bell jangled again, Annie had time to notice Max gravitating to Janis, who certainly did have a soft magnolia appearance. Trust Max. Jeff watched them, too.

Fritz Hemphill nodded a brusque hello. Ingrid Jones slipped in behind him, and in her self-effacing way began to help serve the wine and coffee. Her thin face flushed with pleasure at Max's friendliness. Ingrid was one of life's nicer surprises, a retired librarian who knew everything about books and genuinely liked to help. Moreover, she was content with part-time work at the minimum wage, which was all Annie could eke out of a slender budget. If the store ever made enough money to pay off the money she owed for improvements, an increase in Ingrid's salary was first on Annie's list.

Hal Douglas and Kelly Rizzoli came next, heads close together, which didn't surprise Annie. Instinct told her a romance was in the offing, if not yet in full bloom. Hal and Kelly were really the most normal of all the writers. They made an attractive young couple, Hal cheerfully chubby, Kelly slight, with dark red hair and an appealing air of vulnerability. There was almost always a genial smile on Hal's open, honest face. Annie liked Kelly but wondered a little at the force of her imagination. Her books focused on the dark and torturous impulses that drive decent people to evil. They were not good late-night solitary reading. Her most recent book uncomfortably reminded Annie of Margaret Millar's powerful *Beast in View*.

The room hummed with sound, the quick, insightful chatter of people who knew each other well. As she made sure everyone met Max, Annie felt grateful to him. His presence was helping. Maybe she had exaggerated the possibilities of disaster. Everyone seemed quite cheerful and animated, except, of course, for the Farleys, but Max's good-humored teasing was bringing a flush of excitement to even Janis's pallid cheeks. Jeff looked on darkly. It would be good for him, Annie decided virtuously, refusing to acknowledge any murky stirrings in her own psyche.

She began to enjoy her own party. Maybe Elliot wouldn't even show up.

"I told you there would be a good turnout."

He had come up behind her. At the sound of his voice, she managed not to jump. She turned slowly.

"Oh, Elliot, I'd like for you to meet Max Darling."

"Sure. I'd like to meet him. I know a lot about him." The ever-present cigarette dangled from Elliot's mouth. "Think I'd left you out of my research, darlin'?"

He might as well have thrown a red flag into a bull's face or dropped a match in gunpowder. Knowing her own proclivity for explosions, Annie normally kept a scrupulous rein on her temper, but too much had happened: Elliot's threats that morning, Max's unexpected arrival and all it might imply, the frightening, long moments when she'd thought someone was in the empty store.

Her control shattered like glass hitting concrete.

"That's the last straw. I've had enough of you and your insulting, obnoxious behavior, Elliot, and I'm warning you, I'm not going to let you ruin my Sunday Night Specials."

The room fell abruptly quiet. Heads swivelled, and Max started weaving his way across the room. The expression on his face, even in the midst of her fury, made Annie step forward to stop him. Dear Max. He looked *murderous*—and everyone else looked shocked.

Her face flushed. How could she have been so stupid? Elliot was an ass, a blowhard, a bully—and she was playing right into his hands by overreacting like this.

Everyone started talking at once, and Max was trying to push past her to Elliot when the string of bells at the door jangled, and a high-pitched voice shrieked: "My God, everyone, have you heard? Isn't it the most awful? What can we do?"

Harriet Edelman's wispy blond hair quivered, her light green eyes bulged. Leaning forward, she paused, savoring her moment in the spotlight. One hand was outstretched dramatically, and the large ruby on her hand winked like a cat's eye at night.

"She's dead, her head all bashed in. It's murder. Murder here on Broward's Rock."

A vocal melee broke out. It was Capt. Mac's stentorian bellow which finally brought quiet.

"The facts, Harriet," he instructed, with a former cop's authority.

With dreadful curiosity, everyone subsided and listened. In just such a fashion, Annie thought with a shiver, a Wentworth mystery began. She scanned the faces in the room.

Harriet's information was meager but grim.

"It's Jill Kearney."

There was a gasp from one of the circle, and Annie felt a pang of horror. She knew Jill. She *liked* her. Murdered?

". . . at the Island Hills Clinic. Her body was found this morning in the dispensary. Bludgeoned to death. Police are seeking information from anyone who saw her last night."

"Are any drugs missing?" Emma was crisp.

Harriet repeated blankly, "Drugs?"

"From the dispensary," Emma said, giving her tinted head an impatient shake. "Morphine, codeine, what have you."

Harriet's self-importance collapsed. "I don't know. I just heard about it a few minutes ago. I had on KM103, and they broke in with a news flash."

Capt. Mac moved toward the counter. "Annie, may I use the phone?" But he was already dialing.

They waited respectfully, avoiding each other's eyes. Capt. Mac got through immediately to Frank Saulter, Broward's Rock's aloof police chief. His questions were brisk and concise. But, when he hung up, he stared down for a long moment, and Annie could see the hard ridges in his face. Finally, he turned to face them.

"The body was discovered at 9:05 this morning by a boy who comes in on weekends to feed the animals. Everything seemed normal when he arrived, back door locked, no sign of forced entry. He unlocked the outer door, went in, and started to go directly to the kennels, when he noticed the dispensary door ajar down the hall. Shouldn't have been open. Walked in, saw Jill lying facedown on the floor. Said he knew she was dead, but he touched her anyway, and she was cold. Ran like hell to the phone, called Frank at home."

He paused and now not only his eyes looked glacial. His face might have been carved out of ice. Dirty ice.

"Was the dispensary rifled?"

Capt. Mac looked at Emma with respect. "No signs of it. They called in Dr. Foster."

Foster was Jill Kearney's partner.

"Damn funny place for a drug heist," Fritz Hemphill objected. "How about strangers? Jimmy Moon clock anybody in?"

The island residents understood the significance of that question. When the skillet-shaped end of the island was developed, the Halcyon Development Company set up a checkpoint past the old main street near Heron's Point. To reach any of the new condos, the golf courses, the tennis courts, the luxurious homes, the harbor shops, and, of course, the Island Hills Veterinary Clinic, cars traveled the single blacktop road that passed a checkpoint manned by a Broward's Rock resort employee. Jimmy Moon, an ex-Marine sergeant, had Saturday night duty. He knew everybody on the island. Strangers were admitted only with a pass from the Realty Company.

Capt. Mac's voice was uninflected. "Jimmy didn't admit any strangers Saturday night or Sunday morning." He didn't have to underscore it. "Looks like it happened early Sunday. M.E. sets the time of death after ten P.M. Saturday and before two A.M. Sunday. Her boyfriend, Si Whitney, took her home from the Island movies at shortly before ten. On their way, they stopped by the clinic for Jill's last check, but he said she intended to come back about one A.M., something about a dog that needed to be turned after surgery."

"Last ferry off the island leaves at ten," Fritz said, twisting a paper napkin.

They considered this in silence. Of course, someone could have come or left by boat, but it was a good twenty-minute boat ride to the mainland. Broward's Rock was a self-contained community. Casual marauders were unlikely. No, it had to be a resident or a visitor familiar with the clinic. Moreover, unless Jimmy Moon was mistaken, Jill's murderer had to be a member of the resort community because no stranger had passed the checkpoint.

"Why would anybody murder Jill?"

Capt. Mac shook his head. "It doesn't look drug-related. Foster checked the cabinets. All the morphine and codeine are accounted for."

"Was anything disturbed?" Emma Clyde's almost square face creased in thought.

"Nothing. Nothing at all."

"Was she assaulted?" Emma asked immediately, and Annie could almost see her mind tearing along, throwing up one scenario, then another.

"No. Nothing like that. Just the one blow to the head." He jerked out the next words. "Damn shame. M.E. said the girl had an unusually thin skull. Anybody else might have been knocked out and suffered nothing worse than a headache. Jill hemorrhaged. Damn shame."

"Some kind of maniac is loose on the island," Harriet hissed. "Nothing else makes sense."

"Something will make sense," Emma Clyde mused. "This doesn't have the hallmark of a senseless killing. Mark my words, when we know everything, there will be a motive."

"Any fingerprints?" Fritz inquired.

Kelly spoke at the same time. "What is known about Jill Kearney? What kind of person was she?"

Like sharks at feeding time, their intellects fed on Jill's death. Annie held up her hand.

"Hey, everybody, this is awful. I didn't know Jill well, but she was kind and—" Annie thought about Boots and what Jill had done. Oh, God. "Let's not talk about her like she's a lab report." With a pang, she realized that Jill was now just that. "Anyway, let's call it off for tonight. We can get together next week."

Harriet squealed. "Oh, I can't possibly go home now. I'll dream about it all night. Besides, maybe we can pool all of our brains." Her bony face was alight with greedy curiosity. "Don't you think we can solve it, if we try? Why, there can't be a better set of criminal minds—"

"For once Harriet's put her finger on it," Elliot interrupted.

He stood and moved toward the coffee bar. "*Criminal Minds,* that will be a wonderful title for my new book. Perfect." He bowed mockingly toward Harriet, who flushed an ugly crimson. "I have to thank you, Harriet. I wasn't pleased with any of the titles I'd come up with. *Criminal Minds.* Perfect."

He was leaning against the coffee bar, at ease, cigarette in his mouth, the noxious odor hanging heavily in the air.

"Come on, everyone, let's respect our little Annie's sensibilities. She doesn't want to talk about Jill's murder. Besides, I imagine we've exhausted all the information our police friend has, so why not take your seats? I promise to entertain you. In fact, I think each and every one of you will find my talk absolutely riveting, as they say in cover copy."

"Shall I boot him out on his ass?" Max hissed in Annie's ear.

She hesitated, but, with the harsh reality of Jill's murder, Elliot's swaggering suddenly seemed terribly unimportant—and so was her scheme to call for a vote on whether to hear him. Anything had to be better than sitting around talking about Jill.

"Oh, let him go on. It will fill up the time, then we can send them all home—and I don't ever want to see them again. This is my last Sunday Night Special."

Comfortably propped against the coffee bar, a half-smoked cigarette in his mouth, Elliot filled his *Puzzle of the Silver Persian* mug with steaming coffee.

Reluctantly, with muted murmurs, the Regulars took their places.

Thoroughly enjoying himself, Elliot smiled maliciously. "I can't provide a real-life crime—except, you know, maybe I can. No body, of course. That would be too difficult. But I can rattle a skeleton or two. My agent thinks I'm onto something hot, really hot. We writers spend a lot of time talking about motivation. Wouldn't it be fun to know what kind of crimes a few well-known mystery writers have been personally involved in?" He lit a fresh cigarette from the stub of the first, dumping the discarded butt in the tepid coffee in the *Unexpected Night* mug someone had left on the coffee bar. "We're talking big sales, maybe a fifty thousand first printing and six figures for paperback rights. This book has it all, blood and guts and some particularly nasty—"

The lights went out.

Dusk comes early in October. It was already dark when the first arrivals came. Now it was solidly black outside, and heavy clouds masked the moon. No light penetrated the stygian darkness in the back of the shop.

There was a squeal. Harriet. Then a flurry of movement. Someone bumped against Annie in the dark.

Capt. Mac called out reassuringly. "Annie, must be the power station. Where do you keep a flashlight?"

She was already resolutely groping her way toward the storeroom. A flashlight hung from a nail in the east corner. It was absolutely black, the only pinpoint of light the red dot of Elliot's Turkish cigarette.

Suddenly, there came a succession of sounds, a fluttering, a solid thump, a grunt, the noise of something heavy crashing to the floor.

A woman screamed.

Six

CAPT. MAC yelled for quiet.

"Sit down! Shut up! Stay where you are."

"What's wrong?" Harriet shrilled. "What was that noise? Somebody turn on—"

"Shut up, Harriet."

Hurrying, Annie smacked into a chair and yelped in pain.

"Who's that?" Emma asked sharply.

"Just me. I'm trying to get a flashlight."

"Annie's going to find a light." Capt. Mac's voice was reassuring, though Annie thought she could detect a faint undercurrent of stress. "Check the circuit breakers first," he instructed.

"Yes. Hold on, everybody. It will just take a second."

She moved as fast as she dared through the inky darkness. Reaching the door to the storeroom, she was surprised to find it ajar. Pushing it, she stepped inside the storeroom, and saw a pale oblong of deep blue light. The back door was open. She stared at it in surprise, then moved diagonally, sure of her course now, and reached up. Her fingers brushed against the rough cedar of the unfinished wall. The flashlight was hanging from a nail just about *here* . . .

She touched the wall, the nail.

The flashlight wasn't there.

It had to be there. She hadn't moved it. She'd seen it there, noticed it, at least peripherally, that morning when Mrs. Brawley was there.

At least she knew where she was now. The circuit box was just a couple of feet to her left. Unless it was an island-wide brownout, she should be able to turn the power back on. She couldn't imagine why the breakers should have flipped. Maybe the fault was in her wiring. She groaned. The cost of an electrician . . .

Her fingers found the circuit box—and its open door.

For the first time Annie felt cold.

She pulled the panel all the way open. The breakers were flipped to the right, all four of them, which would indicate some kind of massive overload.

One by one, she clicked them back to the left.

As the second breaker moved, the lights in the coffee area came on, and light spilled through the storeroom door.

Someone screamed again, but this time the scream began high and held and held.

Annie jerked around and ran across the storeroom to the doorway, then stopped short and clung to the frame.

There wasn't much blood, just a trickle. It was almost obscured by the dark, spreading pool of coffee.

Then Capt. Mac's stocky bulk came between her and Elliot Morgan's body, but she would always remember just the way Elliot looked as he lay lifeless, crumpled at the foot of the coffee bar. A smear of unbelievably crimson blood oozed around the shaft of the dart that protruded from the fleshy softness of his throat. *The Puzzle of the Silver Persian* mug lay empty beside him.

Annie started to shake. How many bodies had she viewed in her mind over the years, from Ruby Keene in Colonel Bantry's library to the blackened, unidentifiable lumps in *Ice Station Zebra?* But none of her reading had prepared her for this. She hadn't liked Elliot Morgan. She had even feared what he could do to the shop that she loved, but none of this mattered now. Elliot was dead. It was clearly, unmistakably murder. Not illness as with her mother. Not accident as with Uncle Ambrose.

But how could a dart kill someone? This was madness. First, they hear of the murder of a pretty young veterinarian. Then the lights go out, and a man falls dead from a dart in his throat.

Darts can't *kill* anybody.

Annie said it out loud.

"Darts can't *kill* anybody." She looked up to find Max at her side. His face was pale beneath its tan.

"I know, my love. But we just saw it happen."

"We didn't *see* it."

"Don't be so literal."

Capt. Mac, his face grimmer than ever, brusquely ordered everyone into a line at the far side of the coffee area.

"Don't touch anything."

"Why not?" Kelly Rizzoli asked politely. There were dark stains on her white linen skirt. She must have spilled her coffee when the lights went out, Annie thought automatically.

"This is the scene of a crime," the former policeman replied curtly. "Do as you're told, Ms. Rizzoli."

Fritz Hemphill grudgingly took his place in the line. "Look, McElroy, remember you're retired."

Capt. Mac ignored him and was already on the phone.

"I don't care where Saulter is. Find him, and tell him to get over to Death On Demand pronto. We've got another murder."

It was a tense wait.

Once Annie almost suggested they move away from the coffee area to the cane chairs grouped near the north wall, but there wouldn't be enough seats. Then she dismissed the thought. Clearly, she was no longer a hostess with guests. She was a hostess with murder suspects.

Annie looked at them in turn.

Emma Clyde stood a little to one side, as if disassociating herself. Her intelligent blue eyes moved from face to face, and Annie would have loved to know her thoughts. Then those vivid eyes locked with Annie's, and she was no longer certain she cared to know. Emma looked shrewd, tough, and frighteningly self-possessed.

Ingrid Jones's narrow little body seemed to have shrunk. She clutched her notebook, which she brought every Sunday evening, and stared determinedly at the horror section. The better, Annie guessed, to pretend she wasn't there at all.

Fritz Hemphill looked as comfortable as if he were waiting to tee off. He flicked an occasional impassive glance at the corpse, then picked up *The Bourne Supremacy* and began to read.

Capt. Mac made occasional forays around the coffee area; once he poked his head into the storeroom, then returned to the coffee bar and made notations on a napkin, his face creased in concentration.

An old firehorse, that's what Capt. Mac was. Annie felt reassured. Like Inspector Maigret or Steve Carella, he represented order.

Janis Farley clung to Jeff's arm. Her ivory complexion was tinged with green. Jeff stood stiffly, as if he were alone. For heaven's sake, his wife looked like she was about to faint. Why didn't the bloody idiot do something?

"Capt. Mac. Please. Let's get a chair for Janis."

He looked up, then nodded.

There was a little flurry: Ingrid Jones poured a glass of water, then brought some wine while Max dragged over one of the cane chairs and Annie helped Janis into it. She was shocked when she touched Janis's arm and found it bony and sharp like an underfed cat's spine.

Harriet's face was splotchy with excitement and terror, and her eyes shifted nervously between Elliot's motionless body and the others.

Hal spoke up suddenly. "My God. *Murders in the Rue Morgue. The Mystery of the Yellow Room. He Wouldn't Kill Patience. Death in a Top Hat.*"

Harriet enthusiastically moved from the general to the particular. "A classic locked-room situation. He's standing in front of a room facing—" she counted "—eleven people, the lights go out, presto, he's dead. The murderer has to be one of the eleven."

Emma Clyde's forehead puckered. *"Death in the Air."*

Jeff Farley swung toward Harriet, high spots of anger burning in the gaunt cheeks above his beard. "Be careful what you say. Nobody's going to call me a murderer."

"I'm not calling you a murd—"

"She's just saying you have to look at the obvious," Hal explained earnestly.

Kelly Rizzoli's dark red hair swung in gentle negation. "Nothing is ever obvious. Certainly, this will not be."

"The back door was open."

Annie's quiet declaration created immense interest, and Hal was starting for the storeroom to investigate when Capt. Mac summoned him back.

Emma Clyde spoke authoritatively. "That answers the question, then. There's no question of a locked-room murder—if the back door is open."

The murder maven was looking at Annie with approbation. Then, as clearly as though she'd actually said it, Annie realized Emma believed she'd opened the door herself!

A siren sounded in the distance.

"Nutty," Frank Saulter muttered in disgust.

Capt. Mac rubbed his jaw. "It would take a damn writer, wouldn't it?"

Saulter ignored him. "Wonder if he had a weak heart? We'll have to call on the county for help. The boat picked up the Kearney corpse two hours ago. Now they'll have to come get this one." He took a deep breath. "I guess we'd better get started."

He turned to study the assembled writers.

Dislike was instantaneous on both sides.

Saulter was humorless, dogmatic, religiously read *Sports Illustrated* in the barber shop, and liked Broward's Rock better before all *those* people came and moved into the elegant beach houses. The summer tourists were the worst, but he didn't much hold with the year-rounders either if they talked funny and drove those expensive cars. He especially didn't like ex-cops who'd made money and thought they were too goddam good for plain people anymore, like Hemphill with his fancy-dan golf clothes and McElroy with a saltwater swimming pool. When had they ever dropped by the station to visit? Now McElroy was acting like he was the only cop in the room. Saulter's ulcer burned like melting tar in August. It hadn't helped when he got the call on that vet, though the way she drove her car, he'd always expected to find her dead someday anyway. But not with her head bashed in. By God, he could handle it. And he didn't appreciate any off-island cops—or former cops—telling him how to run things.

Saulter pursed his mouth into a miserly line. "It's pretty clear what happened."

They'd all been standing on one foot then another for almost an hour. This pronouncement got everyone's attention.

"One of you people killed him."

Emma Clyde drew herself up and managed to look imposing, despite her five-foot-three stature and the flowing, outrageously colored caftan.

"My dear man, that is an unwarranted assumption."

"You people were sitting in this room. Eleven of you. The lights go out, and somebody tosses a dart. So who else could have done it?"

Annie stepped forward. "When I went to check the circuit box, the back door was open." All eyes scrutinized her, some avidly, others skeptically. "Someone must have come in that way because no one left the tables, so none of us could have turned off the lights."

"How do you know nobody left the tables?" Saulter demanded. "You left—and nobody saw you, did they?"

"I went to see about the breakers."

"So *you* moved," Saulter said icily.

Max stepped closer. "Somebody else could have moved, too."

Saulter took one look at Max and decided to ignore him. He concentrated on Annie. "You went to put the lights on. How did you know you could do it by flipping the breakers?"

"I didn't know it," Annie said reasonably.

Saulter's eyes were accusing.

She straightened and met his gaze directly. "I knew that was the first thing to try. I figured there'd been a power failure, so I was going to get the flashlight. But it was gone."

"Where did you keep the flashlight?"

"On a nail in the storeroom."

"So when the lights went out, you were the only person here who knew where the circuit box was and where to find a flashlight. Right?"

"I suppose so—"

Capt. Mac interjected, "I found the flashlight, Chief. It was on the floor by the storeroom table."

The back of Saulter's neck reddened. "Did you touch it?" he snapped.

"Of course not."

Saulter didn't pursue it. Instead, he swung again at Annie. "Pretty convenient that the flashlight was in the wrong place. It had to be if you were to have some extra time—"

Max interrupted sharply, "That's an unwarranted assumption, Chief. If the murderer rigged the lights to go out, he could easily have moved the flashlight, and anybody here could have gone back to the storeroom earlier in the evening when everyone was talking and milling around here."

"But what made the lights go off?" Saulter's narrowed eyes were still on Annie.

For Pete's sake, did he think she had a device rigged to cause the blackout?

"Let's go look . . ." Max began, but Saulter and Capt. Mac waved him back and moved toward the circuit box.

Everyone waited tensely, leaning toward the storeroom in order to unabashedly eavesdrop.

"Look, Chief, there's thread tied to the breakers," they heard Capt. Mac say.

"Don't touch it," Saulter growled.

"Wouldn't matter. You can't lift prints from a surface that narrow. At least you can print the box. Somebody tied that thread to the breakers."

"I don't need you to tell me what to fingerprint." Saulter's voice bristled.

The two men moved back into the coffee area, eyes scanning the floor. "Probably ran the thread in here somewhere and left it on the floor," Capt. Mac theorized. "To cut the lights, the murderer gave a yank. That pulled the breakers, and it was absolutely dark."

Saulter looked skeptical. "Totally black?"

There was an enthusiastic chorus of assent.

"Then how the hell did the killer get Morgan with the dart?"

"That was easy, Chief," Emma offered, her cornflower-blue eyes disdainful of official slow-wittedness. "Elliot was a chain smoker. All your killer had to do was grab the dart and throw it at the lighted tip of his cigarette."

"Jesus," Saulter snorted. "That's the craziest goddam thing I ever heard of."

"It worked," Capt. Mac said drily.

"Yeah." Saulter sourly surveyed the survivors standing around the coffee area, as if he wished them all dead, too. "Okay. I want to know where everyone was. Exactly. Take the places you had when the lights went out."

Harriet shuddered and pointed a skinny, beringed finger toward the lifeless bundle that had once been Elliot Morgan. "Are you just going to leave that there? This seems exceedingly distasteful to me."

"It won't hurt him," Saulter answered laconically.

Reluctantly, they drifted back toward the tables where they had been sitting when the lights went out. Ingrid Jones came along with Annie and Max to the farthest of the tables. Max spoke softly to Ingrid and Annie watched her hand him her tablet. He remained standing, his pencil flying over the page. Peering around his shoulder, she saw the bookstore take form on the tablet page.

As Annie watched, Billy Cameron, one of Saulter's assistants, began taking photographs of the murder scene. The second assistant, Bud Jurgens, dusted the circuit box and, Annie was glad to see, the back door, with fingerprint powder. Cameron and Jurgens constituted Chief Saulter's entire force. Annie thought of the well-trained men of the 87th Precinct and felt distinctly unimpressed.

Kelly Rizzoli and Hal Douglas sat at the far right table. Kelly's delicate face looked surprisingly untroubled, and her eyes were bright with curiosity. Hal picked up his coffee mug and swished the liquid around as if hoping it would still be hot.

Fritz Hemphill and Emma Clyde had the center table. Fritz looked frankly bored. Annie wondered if that were not perhaps the ugliest response of all. Emma, as usual, appeared confident and capable. Her stubby hands lay open and relaxed on the table in front of her.

Janis and Jeff Farley were at the next table. She huddled miserably in her chair. Jeff continued to be oblivious to his wife's discomfort. Angry patches of red stained his cheeks.

Capt. Mac and Harriet silently took their places at the table nearest the back wall. The retired policeman surveyed the coffee area thoughtfully. Harriet, of course, was enjoying herself, however much she might protest their proximity to the corpse.

Saulter shuffled from one table to the next, sighting toward Morgan's body, obviously figuring a possible trajectory for the dart. It looked to Annie as though the dart had caught Elliot almost dead center.

"The murderer could have moved the minute the lights went out," she pointed out. "In fact, there was a sound of movement."

Capt. Mac nodded. "She's right. There was definitely a feeling of movement. I sensed it, too."

Saulter scowled, but walked over to stand beside Annie's chair. It was, she realized with a sinking feeling, almost directly in line with the body.

His artistic assistant trained his Polaroid on all of them in turn, then Saulter ordered fingerprints taken, a messy and subtly dispiriting chore. No one objected, not even Emma Clyde. Somehow, Annie didn't think Emma Clyde relished ink on her fingers, but even she kept her mouth shut.

When the fingerprints were made, Saulter brusquely gave everyone permission to leave as soon as Billy Cameron wrote down

TABLES: 1—ANNIE, MAX AND INGRID
2— CAPT. MAC AND HARRIET
3— FARLEYS
4— EMMA AND FRITZ
5—KELLY AND HAL

MAX'S SKETCH OF DEATH ON DEMAND

their names and addresses. They stood in line by the coffee bar, uncomfortably close to the now sheet-shrouded form.

"Hey, Chief!" It was Capt. Mac, and his voice vibrated with intensity. Annie thought of the high, keen baying of a blood-hound.

"By God." The stocky policeman crouched beside the wicker wastebasket by the far end of the coffee bar. "This answers some questions, all right."

Everyone surged toward him, but Saulter barred the way. "Stand back." Then he hurried to McElroy.

Once again, they all bent forward to listen.

"I don't see—" Saulter began.

"Smell it, man."

Saulter, too, hunkered down beside the wastebasket.

Capt. Mac pulled a couple of quarters from his trouser pocket and used them as pincers to lift out a sodden ball of white cotton.

Saulter sniffed. "Fingernail polish remover." He stared blankly at Capt. Mac.

"I've only run across it once before," the former policeman explained, "but I'll bet my pension on it. The murderer covered the tips of his fingers with clear fingernail polish to keep from putting prints on the dart. I can see it now." He pointed toward the coffee area and the tables. "The lights go out, the murderer has the dart hidden nearby. Probably on the floor by the wall. The murderer grabs the dart and throws it. While Annie's going to see about the lights, there's time to use the cotton drenched in polish remover to wipe off the polish, then drop the cotton into the wastebasket. Saulter, there won't be a damn print on that dart. By God, that's clever."

The two men stared at each other, then slowly rose to face the watching suspects.

"Fingernail polish remover," Saulter repeated. He looked at the women in the room one by one, then his gaze locked on Annie.

Perhaps she should have kept quiet, but she was getting tired of his not so subtle suspicion.

"We all paint our fingernails, Chief."

"But nobody knows this room as well as you do," he retorted.

"We've all spent a lot of time here," Capt. Mac said quickly. He cleared his throat. "Chief, I'd be glad to lend a hand with your investigation."

"Thanks. We can take care of *our* job. For now, you're all free to leave. We'll be in touch with everyone tomorrow."

Everyone started up the central aisle toward the front, but McElroy hung back. "I'd hate to see anybody get off on the wrong foot," the retired policeman said. "Why, Annie couldn't possibly have killed anybody."

Harriet Edelman stopped and slapped her hands on her hips, and her bracelets clanged gratingly. "So you think little Miss Pretty Face shouldn't be considered a suspect? I happen to know she and Morgan had a hell of a spat this morning."

Saulter wanted to hear all about that, of course.

"I was going by on my bicycle when she slammed the door on him. I saw it with my own eyes."

Annie hadn't seen Harriet, which wasn't too surprising. At that point, she had been so furious with Elliot she wouldn't have noticed an audience of dancing tarantulas.

Saulter gestured impatiently for them to keep moving toward the door. "Don't worry. I don't give a damn about pretty faces, and I'll be interviewing everybody tomorrow, including Miss Laurance, about their relationships with the deceased."

"That's reassuring." Emma looked sardonic.

"Or pots of money, either."

Agatha chose that moment to leap up on the Christie section and hiss.

Janis clutched at her husband.

Fritz Hemphill laughed.

"She wants out." Annie opened the front door, and Agatha shot out into the night. Annie was right behind her. When she looked back, she met Saulter's eyes. Now she knew how a fox felt when sighted by the hounds.

□ □ □ □

For once Max drove at a reasonable speed.

"I don't understand why he sent us all home," Annie mused.

"What else is he going to do?" Max peered through the night. "The Black Hole of Calcutta can't hold a candle to a country lane on Broward's Rock. No pun intended."

"No street lights," she replied absently. The tourists always complained, too.

"No lights of any kind. Not even moonlight." The beams from the headlights scarcely pierced the gloom beneath the spreading live oak trees whose branches met over the roadway. The pleasantly cool night air, drifting through the open windows, smelled of marsh water. "Are you sure Hansel and Gretel don't live down this way?"

"I guess it's a little daunting at night."

"I'd take Central Park after dark anytime." He abruptly slammed on the brake, and she jolted forward, restrained by the seat belt.

"Good God, what's that?"

The thick, low-slung creature darted swiftly across the dusty dirt road, clearly illuminated by the headlights. "That, city slicker, is a raccoon."

Max eased the car forward.

"He didn't even ask any questions."

"Like, 'Miss Laurance, did you do it?' "

"All right, smartass. Turn to the right, down that lane."

Max slowed and swung the Porsche to the right, scowling. "This isn't a lane. This is a bloody footpath."

"Actually, it's pretty rustic. Now, slow down. I live in that second tree."

"The second tree. You did say *tree*?"

"It's a bargain. Some developer got the notion everybody would want to live like Robinson Crusoe, and he built a half dozen houses that are really platforms up in oak trees. Unfortunately for him, they didn't go over very well."

The Porsche's lights illuminated the tree house now. Wooden

steps curved gracefully up from the ground to a circular house
built around the main trunk.

"That is really homey," Max commented drily. "Just you and
the earwigs."

"The realty company sprays every month," she said severely. "I
am bug-free."

Max braked and clicked off the lights, but Annie was already
opening her door. "That's okay. You don't have to get out."

"I know I don't, but behavior patterns are ingrained. I do not
drop a girl off at her front door, especially when it is up in a tree
in the middle of a swamp."

"The South Carolina Tourist Association would frown on the
term swamp."

But he came around to take her arm and gallantly insisted on
coming inside and checking every room.

Annie stood quietly in the center of her circular living room,
waiting for Max, who was on his knees at the base of her bed,
peering beneath it, to return. "Now, why did you do that, Max?"

"Because I've got the wild suspicion the island air isn't too
healthy right now." He glanced around at the hexagonal living
room. The walls were eleven-foot-tall sheets of glass, which, in
daylight, bathed the room in light and warmth. Now, with the
blinds up, the night pressed against the glass, threatening, dis-
turbingly inimical.

Annie quickly lowered the slatted, tropical blinds, and leaned
down to turn on a Tiffany lamp. With the night closed out, she felt
a good deal more secure. The room was familiar again, the comfortable rattan furniture, fortunately so appropriate for a seaside
dwelling, and so affordable. Here, too, as at Death On Demand,
bright cushions provided splotches of orange, burnt sienna, and
Texas red clay. Her latest photographs were pinned haphazardly
to a square bulletin board in the center of the bookcases that
filled the wall between the living room and bedroom. She was
especially proud of the shot she'd taken at dawn near Moccasin
Creek of a Little Blue Heron, his feathers slate blue on his body
and purplish red on his neck. Her Nikon lay on an end table, next

to her trophy for being the winning pitcher for the Island Dolphins. The colorful paperbacks stuffed into every inch of the bookcases added another note of cheer. Her favorite books: all the Agathas, the wonderfully funny Leonidas Witherall books written by Phoebe Atwood Taylor as Alice Tilton, the Constance and Gwenyth Little books. Her room, safe and friendly.

"Nobody would want to hurt me."

"How do we know that?"

Annie dropped down on the largest wicker couch, and Max settled right beside her. There would have been room left over for several others to sit. She scooted over a few inches. He followed.

"Look, Elliot was begging for trouble. He was threatening to talk about—well, you heard him—he was going to rattle skeletons. Somebody didn't want his or her bones disturbed."

"What about the lady vet?"

Annie sighed. "I can't imagine. Oh, Max, she was such a lovely person. Right after I came here to visit Uncle Ambrose this summer, Boots was hit by a car."

She would never forget how Boots had dragged himself to her uncle's house, his back legs useless, his fur matted and streaked with dirt and blood. The memory still hurt.

"Anyway, I took Boots to the Island Hills Clinic. I didn't know Jill then, and Dr. Foster took a look at poor Boots. He was nice enough but disinterested. He told me the only thing to do was to put Boots down, there was no hope. I asked what they would do, and he said they'd give him a shot of succinyl-choline, and he would be out like a light. A girl came in while Foster was talking, but I didn't pay any attention to her. Foster left, and I was saying goodbye to Boots when a boy came to get him. She spoke up and said, 'Don't give him succinyl-choline. Use 5 cc.'s concentrated sodium pentabarbitol.' Of course, I wanted to know what the heck, and then she told me. Foster was old-fashioned and a lot of vets might use succinyl-choline, but she didn't advise it. She said the animal suffocated. She said it was cruel." Tears filled Annie's eyes. "So you see, it couldn't be a *personal* murder with Jill.

Maybe it will turn out to be something like a drug robbery, after all."

Somehow, Max's arm was now tightly around her shoulders.

"I don't have a glimmer why anybody coshed her, but two murders on an island within twenty-four hours! They're connected, or I'll eat that raccoon."

"It isn't our problem," she objected. She was unbelievably tired. "It's that unpleasant man's problem. But I still don't understand why he sent us all home. He did say nobody was allowed to leave the island, but there isn't a ferry until morning anyway. He didn't even *try* to find out anything."

"I imagine he's busy doing that right now, my dear. And they have to examine the crime scene. Your old chum was still hanging around as we left."

Her old chum. Max meant Capt. Mac. Suddenly, Annie wished fervently that Capt. Mac were in charge of this investigation.

"Max, did you see the way Saulter looked at me?"

The floor creaked.

Annie swam up from the depths of sleep, rolled over, and stifled a scream. She bolted upright, her hair tousled, realized her nightgown was more than drooping low, and hastily yanked a sheet up to her chin.

"What the hell are you doing here?"

"You are at risk," Max intoned sternly.

Annie yawned and started to rub her eyes, then grabbed again at the sheet. "Let's start over," she said patiently. "*I* am in bed. *I* am asleep. Perhaps *you* could tell me what *you* are doing in my bedroom at the crack of dawn?"

"Anybody could get in this house. I spent the night in my car— and I've got a stiff neck." He milked a pause for sympathy and tried to rotate his head. "Ouch."

"You rented a condo. Why don't you stay in it?"

"Because there is a double killer somewhere on this island . . ."

"Not in my bedroom," Annie objected.

"He could be."

"Or she."

"Annie, listen to me. This house is as full of holes as Swiss cheese. Do you know how I got in?"

Annie was stubbornly silent.

"I picked up a stick at the foot of the steps, tiptoed up, and pried open a window in the kitchen."

"I didn't hear you."

"You sleep like an elephant, my lovely. The point is, this place isn't secure. So I'm going to get my stuff—"

"No."

"There's plenty of room. I can curl up on the couch."

"You won't have a stiff neck, you'll have a rigid spine. No, Max. I appreciate it, but I'm a big girl, and I am perfectly capable of taking care of myself."

They squabbled about it all the way through breakfast.

Annie poured each of them a second cup of coffee and watched with fascination as Max wolfed down his fifth sugar-covered doughnut. They sat on the airy porch outside the kitchen. The soft air was fragrant with pine, marsh, and tar; sunlight slanted through the tall sea pines. A blacktopped path disappeared into a dense clump of palmettos, southern red cedars, yuccas, and bayberry shrubs. The beach was only a ten-minute bicycle ride away. For a fleeting moment Annie wished that today could be a holiday for her and Max, that they could go walk down a dune with an October splash of flowering herbs, violet, magenta, yellow and cream, to the long spread of gray sand with nothing more to think of than sun and water and play.

"I guess I'll open the store as usual."

Max nodded, his mouth full, then said indistinctly, "That's the best thing to do. Act completely normal." He swallowed and said clearly, "Besides, I bet a buck they'll all come by, one by one, to see if you know anything."

"Who'll come by?"

"Our suspects."

"God, I hope not."

"Hey, Annie, don't be silly. This will be our chance to pump them."

"I don't want to pump them. Why should I?"

"Saulter is a dummy. Anybody can see that. We can solve it."

"Oh, no. Count me out. I don't want any part of it."

Max licked a trickle of sugar from the corner of his mouth, and rattled the empty doughnut bag. "We need to do some grocery shopping. Don't you ever eat at home?"

Uncertain which argument to pursue first, Annie opted for anti-detection.

"Max, listen carefully, because I am only going to say this once. I am not a detective. I am not even a mystery writer. I just happen to run a bookstore where a man got murdered. I intend to scrub that floor and rearrange the coffee area and forget it ever happened. Mysteries are a business for me, not a vacation. This is not a game. There is no way I am going to get involved in this investigation—and I mean it, absolutely, positively, and without any shadow of doubt. Period."

Max grinned.

Seven

THE ARGUMENT continued on the stairs of the tree house.

"I'm going to work just as usual. I do not want to talk about murder."

"Murders."

"It has to be a coincidence," she said mulishly. "Jill and Elliot didn't even know each other. He didn't have any pets."

"How do you know?" Max barred her way down the steps.

Since she didn't want to go into that, she ducked under his arm. "Look, I've got to hurry, or I'm going to be late." She'd already informed him in no uncertain terms that he was not coming to the store with her. To divert him, she offered, "I'll have lunch with you. Come to the shop about one, and we'll go have a mango sundae."

Max took a childish delight in new tastes, and Annie was pleased at her skill in deflecting him. This was not the time to admit that she'd dated Elliot a couple of times and had once been invited to dinner at his house. That evening was enough to frost any interest on her part. Elliot collected West Indian art and artifacts, including voodoo dolls from Haiti. Her appetite had been seriously damaged by his long-winded and ghoulish description of the walking dead.

Ugh.

Annie ran on down the steps, then realized her car was still in the crushed oyster-shell lot near the plaza, the closest parking place to her store. Of course, Max had brought her home last night.

Since he drove this morning in the old mode, fast and hard, there was no time for conversation.

Annie's home was on the fringes of the developed part of the resort area. The tree houses had been a builder's short-lived fancy. She loved living in a remote area, and delighted in the daily surprises of marsh life. Her tree house overlooked the high marsh, and from her sun porch she could watch the never-ending play of light and wind on the thick cordgrass. Salt myrtle, marsh elder, and southern bayberry flourished. A single narrow road snaked inland through palmetto palms and sea pines toward the populated area. Spanish moss shrouded the glossily green live oak trees. Alligators sunned on the banks of shallow green ponds, and turtles, frogs, and snakes slipped silently through the water. The soft air shimmered a paler shade of green beneath the tree limbs.

When Max's red Porsche plunged out onto the blacktop that circled the island and ran past the luxuriant green of a sleekly mowed golf course, he commented, "From the boondocks to the country club."

"Part of the charm."

The blacktop served the access roads to the islands' mansions, which overlooked the fairways of the Island Hills Golf Club. The three-story Tudor-style Club House glistened in the morning sunlight. Ornate, twelve-foot-tall bronze gates were already open to admit early morning foursomes.

She pointed toward an imposing home on a gentle rise near the fourteenth green. "That's Emma's house."

Max grinned. "Her little place in the country."

Annie nodded. "Right. I saw a feature on it in *American Country Homes*. That little cottage is valued at just under two million."

"Crime does pay."

"For her."

Max squinted against the sunlight and upped his speed to sixty.

They flashed by more magnificent homes, some barely glimpsed through the spreading live oak trees.

Max decreased his speed almost immediately because they were already upon the harbor area. Red-tiled roofs marked the beginning of the condos, Swallows' Retreat. The stores and cafés bordering the basin gleamed a soft gray, the natural wood exteriors weathered by the sun. Max pulled into the crushed-shell parking area.

"She could have done it."

Looking ahead to Death On Demand, Annie didn't make the connection.

"Who could have done what?"

"Emma could have murdered Elliot. She's smart enough."

"Max."

"Somebody did it," he said virtuously.

"Somebody did," she agreed. "And that charming Chief Saulter can figure it out."

To Annie's surprise, Max didn't even attempt to come into the shop with her. In fact, he dropped her off at the edge of the plaza, promised to meet her for lunch, and waved goodbye with an annoyingly cherubic smile.

Curving around the natural harbor that served as the marina, the plaza was the social hub of Broward's Rock. Since it was well past the summer season, some of the sailboats were battened down for winter, but most were moored by the wooden docks, ready for island owners to enjoy on idyllic October days. On the far side of the harbor were yacht slips. There were only three big yachts left now, and one of these was Emma Clyde's, *Marigold's Pleasure.*

Annie loved the little harbor. It was as elegant as a Fabergé egg. From her front windows, she could watch sailboats scud into the sound and sea gulls swoop and hover near pier's end in hopes of free fish. All of the shops built on the curve of the plaza were open, but now that the tourist season was over, the atmosphere relaxed perceptibly. The occasional shoppers were more likely to be year-rounders. It was a good time of the year to inventory, to decide on new stocks for next summer, to savor the relaxed hush.

As she crossed the plaza, she was thoughtful. Why was Max so easily dissuaded from accompanying her? And what was happening in the investigation into Elliot's death? A *dart*? That still seemed impossible—and contrived. The more she thought about it, the crazier it seemed.

She walked up on the verandah that fronted the shops and stopped at her own storefront. *Death On Demand* marched in square gilt letters in the center of the south window. The north window carried the information painted in bold scarlet: Mysteries, Suspense, Horror, Adventure, New and Old.

She looked appraisingly at the display behind the north window. The *Murder Ink* mystery companions took pride of place. Hard to imagine a true mystery aficionado without them. Her latest and most prized old books, first editions all, lay enticingly in front of the trade paperbacks: *Dog in the Manger* by Ursula Curtiss, the eight volumes of complete Sherlock Holmes published by Collier, and a rare $110 copy of Elizabeth Lemarchand's first book, *Death of an Old Girl*. New hardcovers, with splashily bright covers, filled the south window. Annie nodded approvingly. It was always a plus when she could offer a new Martha Grimes or Ken Follett. Readers flocked. All right. She couldn't stand there forever and put off going inside. No matter what had happened last night, she was determined to erase the memory of Elliot's murder. She had work to do.

Annie was fishing her key ring from her purse when woodpecker-quick steps tapped up behind her. Ingrid Jones, her springy gray head bobbing, swooped up, waggling the key. "Decided it would be a good morning to shelve those books from that Texas estate."

Ingrid usually worked only on Saturdays and during lunch hours in the off-season. Annie wasn't sure what prompted her early arrival, but she knew darn well it signaled support, and she felt a rush of affection. How nice it was to have friends! Then, insidiously, she wondered what made Ingrid decide it was time to rally round the flag.

Ingrid unlocked the door, and led the way inside, flicking on the lights and chattering nonstop about the snowy egret she'd spotted that morning over near McAlister's Point. Annie followed

slowly, not really listening, but very grateful for human—and animal—sound. Agatha streaked inside, meowing imperiously. Annie stopped by the cash desk and looked down the main corridor
toward the dark coffee area.

No one was there.

She had almost expected to find that corner cordoned off and a
policeman in residence. But that was ridiculous. With a police
force of three, and two murders taking place in less than twenty-
four hours, Chief Saulter could hardly spare the manpower.

She tucked her purse in its accustomed place beneath the cash
register, then walked down the central corridor, flicking on lights.
Agatha loped silently ahead. At the coffee bar, Annie stopped.

A wobbly chalked outline marked the long oblong where Elliot
had fallen. She looked quickly away and went around the bar to
open the refrigerator and get out Agatha's milk. When it was
poured, she shook some cat food into the blue ceramic bowl that
was inscribed in white script, *The Grande Dame*.

The bell jingled. Annie jumped up to peer down the central
aisle, then struggled to look normal as Ingrid welcomed Sam
Mickle, the postman.

"Good morning, Sam."

"Morning, Ingrid. Miss Laurance."

Annie murmured for a moment to Agatha, who expected saluta-
tions along with provender, then moved unhurriedly up the aisle
to glance through the pile of mail Ingrid had stacked on the cash
desk. Despite everything that had happened, Annie was beginning to relax. It was a marvelously normal Monday. She thumbed
through the material, dropping junk into the wastebasket, bills
into a pile to her left, *Publishers Weekly* to the right. She would
read *PW*, then . . . She held a small square package between
thumb and forefinger and stared at the bold, slanted writing of the
address.

There was no doubt in her mind who had written her name in
thick, dark strokes.

But why would Elliot Morgan have mailed a small, square

package to her? Shades of *The List of Adrian Messenger,* she thought miserably.

It didn't take Max long to figure the layout of Broward's Rock. Of course, it wasn't very big, seven miles long and five miles at its widest. One blacktop road circled the island, beginning and ending at Heron Point where the ferry landed, and funneling into the resort area through the checkpoint. The guard on duty nodded respectfully at the Porsche as it scooted by. The ferry office was part of a tin-roofed beer joint and bait shop owned by Ben Parotti, who could chew tobacco and guzzle Schlitz concurrently. When Halcyon Development Company decided to create a rich man's refuge, it bought the skillet end of the island, intending to leave the narrow handle with its old, weathered homes, some of them shacks, for "support personnel," as the developers delicately phrased it. However, Halcyon Development found the smelly bait shop and dank beer joint by the ferry landing unappetizing. Since rich prospective residents would arrive by ferry, Halcyon decided to buy the ferry service and its accompanying office/baitshop/beer joint, planning to build a tasteful cottage by the terminal. Square, stumpy Ben Parotti, who also captained the ferry, intended to continue his life as it had always been, and no sum could budge him. It was a singular experience for the young Halcyon lawyer from Atlanta, whose credo until that moment had been that enough money could buy anyone.

Max took the three wooden steps in one stride and pushed open a creaky door. Inside, he paused, his eyes adjusting to the rank dimness, his nose crinkling at the mixture of smells, chunks of bait, stale beer, sawdust. A bottle-scarred wooden bar ran along the wall to his left. The mirror behind it might last have been polished just before Pearl Harbor. Two round wooden tables with kegs for seats completed the hospitality area. Straight to the back were the cash register and coolers holding chunks of black bass, grouper, snapper, squid, and chicken necks. To Max's right, a worn, golden oak desk that might once have stood in a country school provided office space for the Parotti Ferry Service.

Max tried to look genial while not inhaling too deeply. "Bud Light."

Parotti squinted at him with interest.

"Summer folk don't drink beer this early. And you ain't no boozer." He frowned at Max's crisp blue-and-white seersucker suit. "You another damn lawyer?"

"God forbid," Max said piously.

Parotti chuckled. "That's good. But you want somethin' besides beer."

"Information."

Parotti fastidiously pulled the tab off a can of Schlitz. "Funny. You're the first rich dude to ever pay me the time of day."

Max looked at the bent but still recognizable sign of a Flying Red Horse, which hung crookedly on the wall back of the cash register. "You've been here a long time. I figure you probably see everything that happens on this island."

"Maybe."

"The cops ask you how many people came on the ferry yesterday—and Saturday?"

"Sure. Told 'em four. You're one of them. You were the only stranger."

Max drank the cold Bud Light with relish. "That's what I figured." He nodded companionably at Parotti. "That means I need to know about some people who live here."

"Why should I tell you?"

"The hell of it." Max drank more of the beer, then smiled his most winning smile.

Parotti chuckled, looking like an amused but slightly sinister and very tatty leprechaun. "I like you, young fella. Who do you want to know about?"

"You know a fellow named McElroy? They call him Capt. Mac."

Parotti nodded and tilted his can of Schlitz. "Keeps to himself pretty much. Comes by here for beer, bait. He was a police chief some place in Florida. Gets a lot of packages on the ferry, picks 'em up here."

"What kind of packages?"

Parotti shrugged. "Electronic stuff, I think. Maybe he has one of those computers. Most of them do."

"Most of them?"

"The writers. The ones you want to know about." The shrewd blue eyes were amused.

"So you already know all about me?"

"You're friends with the new girl, the one who took over Ambrose's shop."

"What do you know about the rest of them?"

Parotti took a paint-stained rag from his back pocket and noisily blew his nose. "I'm not in the business of talkin' about people."

"You know Saulter?"

The old man's face twisted. "Always tryin' to pick trouble with me, he is. I won't tell him nothin'."

"He's trying to pitch the murders on Ambrose's niece."

"Yeah?" Parotti rubbed his nose. "He's a dumb bastard, all right." He hitched closer to Max along the dingy bar. "Listen, what did happen last night?"

Max described it all. Then concluded, "So, you see, I've got to find out about all the writers who were there. One of them did it." He ticked their names off, one by one, starting with Emma Clyde.

Parotti muttered under his breath a couple more times about Saulter, took a large gulp of beer, and made up his mind. "Yeah, I can tell you lots. Now, that Emma Clyde, she's a tough lady."

"How do you mean?"

"Had a husband, younger than she was. Everybody said he was slipping around with a Cuban girl. Now, he's not around anymore."

"What happened to him?"

"Fell off her big boat. Late one night. Accident, they say."

"You think it was an accident?"

Parotti pursed his mouth. "Most rich folks are smart enough not to fall off their boats when they're anchored." He drowned a snigger in his Schlitz.

"What about Fritz Hemphill?"

"Keeps to himself. Plays a lot of golf. I did some work for him once, digging for a sea wall. He tried to cheat me. I told him what happened to the last man tried that."

"What happened?" Max asked dutifully.

"Funny thing. His car blew up one morning when he started it." Parotti's rheumy blue eyes were as cold as an early frost.

"Hemphill pay what was due?"

"Yep."

"Know anything about the Farleys?"

Parotti jerked his head eastward. "They live a couple miles from here. One time I ran out of gas near their place. Heard somebody screaming."

"Screaming?"

"A woman. I went up to the house, called out, and in a minute he came to the door. I asked if there was anything wrong, told him I heard screams. He said his wife had burned herself, spilled hot grease on her hand."

Max remembered Janis's air of tension and the way she looked constantly to her husband for support. Hot grease.

"Do you know the middle-aged blonde, Harriet Edelman?"

Parotti grimaced. "I stay away from women like that. Reminds me of my first wife." He shuddered in loving reminiscence and gulped down the rest of his beer.

"How about Hal Douglas?"

For a moment, Parotti looked blank. "You mean the fat one that lives on Blue Magnolia, grins a lot? He seems all right. Another newcomer. Just been here about a year."

"There's one more, a pretty redhead, Kelly Rizzoli."

Parotti opened the refrigerator door and surveyed the contents before taking out another can of Schlitz.

"That's a funny one. Saw her one night, streaking down the beach like a crazy woman. Turns out she was chasing another female. Caught her on a dune not far from my cabin. They were kickin' and rollin' around in the sand, and I almost went out to see what the hell, then the first woman kind of gave up and started bawling, and the redhead led her away down the beach."

Annie hadn't been in the store fifteen minutes before she understood why Ingrid had shown up. It was a deluge. Twenty-seven customers before lunch. She didn't even have time to do more than open Elliot's package, see that it was a floppy disk with a folded note, and slip it behind a package on the storeroom table.

It took only a few more minutes for her to realize that half the curiosity seekers believed this was their big chance to rub elbows with a Lizzie Borden—her. Typical was Mrs. Porter Fredericks, who bought six hardcovers while watching Annie with walleyed fascination. The woman didn't even know the books she'd grabbed up, which included one first edition Mike Hammer and two James Bond titles. Annie was tempted to offer to cut off a sprig of hair and price it at fifteen dollars. Ingrid worked grimly and fast, saying once out of the corner of her mouth, "By God, if they come in, they're going to buy something!" Annie would have been delighted at the constant ring of the register, but the price was pretty high. More than one customer jumped back perceptibly when she approached. Ingrid finally shooed her off to the storeroom. "I can handle this." She resembled a militant sparrow, darting up and down the aisles coercing the sightseers into purchases. Annie was absurdly grateful for her support.

Mrs. Brawley squeezed down the central aisle at one point and poked her head into the storeroom. "Miss Laurance, I hate to bother you—"

"The Pollifax is not in."

"Oh, I know that, but I wondered if you could just give me a *little* hint on that picture with the butler in it." She fluttered her bejewelled hand toward the watercolors pinned to the back wall. "I think I have all the rest of them."

Annie was impressed at this evidence of singleminded devotion to the hunt, but she shook her head chidingly. "Now, now, Mrs. Brawley. That would be cheating, wouldn't it?"

Grudgingly, Mrs. Brawley turned away. She was still posted in front of the watercolors twenty minutes later, and Annie heard her muttering to herself, "Just one more, and I can get my Mrs. Pollifax free!"

The only fellow suspect to come in was Harriet Edelman, whose arrival almost caused a traffic jam on the verandah when people realized they could see *two* of the people who were *there*.

Max drove fast. He had time for just one more stop before he met Annie for lunch.

He tossed the names up in his mind like confetti, then glanced down at the crude map he had drawn with Parotti's help.

Max squealed onto Sandpiper Terrace. Number Eleven was the third house on the left, a yellow two-story stucco with a long clear pane of glass in the front foyer. The largest hanging fern he'd ever seen glistened in the sunlight on the front porch. He parked and strode up the manicured gravel path past crisply trimmed monkey grass. Summer marigolds and zinnias still bloomed. Mauve and gold chrysanthemums flooded a square plot by the front steps with autumn colors.

He stepped up on the recently painted porch and rang the bell.

A voice boomed, "Come on around here. I'm out in the garden."

Turning, Max saw Capt. Mac. He wore khaki slacks and a tattered pale blue polo. Max's mouth turned down. James Bond. Then he managed a smile.

"Glad I caught you."

McElroy led the way down a flagstone path past the house to a tiled patio beside a swimming pool. He waved Max to a white, webbed patio chair. The air carried the scent of honeysuckle and crape myrtle from the back stockade fence.

"You wanted to see me?" McElroy's voice was friendly, but his gray eyes were wary.

Max tried butter. "Annie tells me you were a super cop."

"Really? I don't remember ever talking about my work with Annie, Mr. Darling."

Strike one.

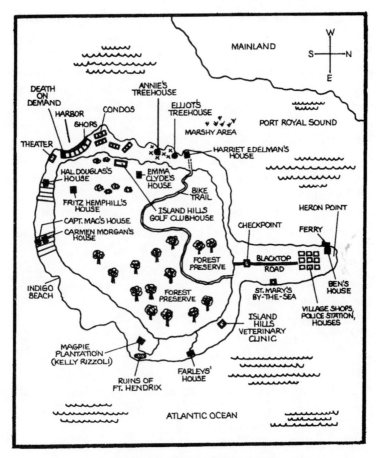

MAX'S MAP OF THE ISLAND

"I guess someone else must have told her. You were a police chief in Florida?"

"Chief and assistant chief. On the Gold Coast. Before that, I was a cop in Miami. The Gold Coast is a good deal more pleasant."

Max glanced up at the house. It wasn't large, but it was nice. Very nice. And the figure-eight pool was a beauty.

"You retired to the same kind of place."

"Right. The only difference is, I don't know all about everybody here."

"You didn't like that?"

"A police chief in a high-class resort gets to know more than he wants to sometimes." Capt. Mac's face was no longer genial, and Max suddenly had a glimpse of a tougher, harder persona than the retired man usually revealed.

"Is that true of Saulter?"

"Ask him." Not unpleasant, but not exactly forthcoming. Capt. Mac sat solidly in his deck chair, his posture almost military.

"I'm surprised you aren't lending a hand."

"Lending a hand?"

"Helping out. I don't suppose Saulter's ever handled two murders in one weekend. Or maybe even one."

"He knows the drill." But was there in that dry comment just a hint of disbelief in Saulter's ability to properly run such an investigation?

"You keep on top of it last night?"

McElroy leaned forward in his chair. The polo shirt fitted him snugly, revealing the strength of his upper torso. "Saulter didn't quite want to throw me out, so I hung around. He did okay. He secured the area, made a list of all the physical evidence. Photos. Dusted for fingerprints."

"What did he come up with?"

Capt. Mac squinted. "What's your interest, Mr. Darling?"

"Call me Max."

McElroy waited.

Finally, Max said baldly, "My interest can be summed up in one word: Annie."

The deeply tanned face softened. "That I can understand." He scowled. "I'm a little worried there, too."

Max had an uncomfortably empty feeling in the middle of his chest. If this ex-cop were a little worried, Max was a lot worried.

"Why?" he asked sharply.

McElroy picked up a cigar from a humidor on the glass-topped patio table and offered one to Max, who declined. He rolled the cigar in his fingers. "I don't want anybody to think I'm critical of another cop."

"Of course not."

He took his time putting the cigar in his mouth, lighting it. He didn't look at Max.

"Thing about it is, Saulter thinks the simple answer is the best." He blew a thin stream of smoke that hung in the soft, pine-scented air. "Of course, that's how cops are trained to think. The simple answer usually is the right answer."

"So what's the connection between the simple answer and Annie?"

McElroy tapped the ash from the cigar. "Let me tell you how a cop thinks. One, who had the best opportunity to set up the kill? Two, does that person have a motive? Saulter's worked it out.

"Who could rig the lights to go out?

"Whose fingerprints are all over the circuit box?

"Who could hide a dart at her leisure?

"Who had an argument with Elliot Sunday morning and was obviously furious with him on Sunday night?

"Who faced financial disaster if Elliot raised the rent on her shop?

"Who was the champion pitcher and batter on the Island softball team in August?"

Capt. Mac took a deep breath and frowned significantly.

"There's one name that fits—and that's Annie."

"What about the writers?" Max demanded hotly. "Didn't you tell him what was going on? That Elliot was about to dump everybody's inmost secrets out on the floor? Did you tell Saulter about that?"

"Sure, but that's too fancy for Saulter. Besides, how much dirt could Elliot possibly have on these people? If they'd done something criminal, how could Elliot know about it and not the authorities? No, I'm telling you, Max, Saulter sees this as an open-and-shut equation: Annie fought with Elliot, Annie was mad, it's

Annie's store. Who did it? Annie. All he's doing now is looking for proof."

Max felt like someone had kicked him in the stomach.

But Capt. Mac wasn't through. He gripped the cigar so hard it dented. "And there's something you don't know, son. Something bad. Saulter's got another damn fool idea—"

Eight

ONE OF ANNIE'S first purchases for Death On Demand was an Apple computer to keep track of inventory and sales. It was a wonderful, almost miraculous timesaver which could balance her books, churn out a mailing list, keep an appointment book, and check her spelling.

What it couldn't do was read the disk Elliot Morgan had mailed to her.

Okay. She understood that. Elliot used a different computer. She remembered one evening when the writers had discussed their machines. Elliot had an Epson. Some of the machines were compatible if you had the right software, but she didn't have the right software or the right machine.

Elliot knew that. So he mailed this disk to her with a snide note:

Dear Annie—I figure you are the only one of the Sunday Night Regulars who can be trusted not to destroy this on receipt, so be a good scout and keep this for me for a few days. Your wearisome honesty must be a result of your provincial upbringing. Don't you see how the wages of sin are infinitely more rewarding? I have the goods on everyone on this disk. I'll share it Sunday evening. Yours in sleuthing, E.M.

Of course, he'd been far too arrogant to expect that he was going to be murdered. Obviously, however, he was uneasy. Why else would he send her a copy of the disk? Had he intended to safeguard himself by telling someone that another copy of the information existed? What was on that disk?

She set to work unloading the used books she'd bought from the Texas estate sale and tried to ignore the sounds of shuffling feet and whispers outside the storeroom. She briefly considered going out to help Ingrid, then furiously decided to deny those sensation-seeking eyes their afternoon treat. She lifted out the seventh Phoebe Atwood Taylor novel, a first edition. What should she do with the damn disk?

This would drive Max crazy. He had pestered her for information on the Sunday Night Regulars. With any luck, the disk contained whatever dirt Elliot had managed to scrape up on all of them.

But someone had killed Elliot to prevent him from revealing what he knew. That information absolutely had to go to the police.

Still, she argued, she didn't know for a fact that one of the writers had murdered Elliot. Sure, it was a reasonable assumption, but the back door to Death On Demand *was* open last night. It would be unspeakably cruel to throw everybody on that disk to Saulter. At least, not until she knew what was on it. Max wouldn't hesitate: he was dying to investigate the whole mess anyway. Personally, she didn't want to have anything to do with it. But she did have that damn disk.

Did anyone else on the island have an Epson?

She ran through them in her mind. Writers are inordinately proud of their word processors, each convinced his own is best. No, the only Epson belonged to Elliot.

The only way to read the disk, then, was to use Elliot's machine. Which brought up an interesting question: Was Elliot's house being watched?

She frowned. Probably not. After all, Saulter only had two men on his force. The house would be locked up, but Elliot lived in a tree house, too, and Max had already demonstrated how easy they were to enter. On the island, no one worried about security. At least, no one had until now.

The storeroom door began to open. Annie's heart lifted. It was

almost lunchtime. Lunch with Max. Despite everything, she began
to smile. Max. Why did he have to be such a bum at heart? If
only . . .

"Miss Laurance."

Annie's smile vanished. Not Max.

There wasn't a vestige of warmth on Chief Saulter's face. He
stood only a foot or so from her worktable, a bigger man than
she'd realized. Last night she'd wondered about the look in
Saulter's eyes. Now there was no question about it: he was clearly
hostile. He had a bony, worn face with faded brown eyes, sallow
skin, and a tight, thin mouth. She was excruciatingly aware of the
revolver that rode in a shiny black leather holster high on his hip,
emphasizing the power behind the tan uniform shirt and pants.

She felt her hackles rise, but she managed a pleasant "Good
morning, Chief Saulter."

He didn't bother with pleasantries, but pulled a small spiral
notebook from his pocket, flipped it open, then looked at Annie,
his eyes as lifeless as agates.

"I'm interviewing the people who were present last night." He
looked around. "Could we bring a couple of chairs in here?"

He did help move the chairs from the coffee area to the storeroom. The customers ostensibly in search of horror reading shifted
their attention from the chalked outline on the floor and watched
them with avaricious delight. As Saulter closed the storeroom
door, Annie heard a woman say, "I've heard there's going to be an
early arrest. Do—"

Those cold eyes bored into hers, but he spoke in a monotone.
"I'm advising you, Ms. Laurance, that you are a murder suspect. I
am also advising you of your rights. You have the right to remain
silent. You have a right to have counsel present when you are
questioned. You may waive these rights. Do you wish to remain
silent or will you consent to be interviewed?"

The Miranda warning. For her.

"I don't have anything to hide," she said hotly.

"I'm advising you further that at any time you may refuse to
answer my questions or you may request counsel."

"Yes, I understand." Her tone was combative. Did that surprise him a little? Well, he wasn't going to find her easy to push around.

"All right, Miss Laurance. Tell me about yourself."

The apparently innocuous question surprised Annie. It seemed irrelevant, but Saulter's tone of voice was deadly earnest—and cold.

"What do you mean?"

"Where you're from. Your parents. Where you went to school. Why you came here last summer."

Once started, it was fairly easy. After all, she'd put together so many resumés these last few years.

"I was born in Amarillo. My mother was Claudia Bailey Laurance. She divorced my father when I was three. I don't remember him. She died of cancer when I was a freshman in college. I went to SMU, received a bachelor of fine arts degree in acting."

Saulter stolidly took notes.

"After college, I went to New York and tried to get work as an actress."

"You didn't succeed." It wasn't a question.

"I did all right."

"You came here because you were down on your luck." Saulter's bony face jutted forward.

"No. I came to visit my uncle, just as I had every summer since he retired and moved here twelve years ago from Fort Worth."

"You didn't have any money."

Okay, her bank balance was $35.21 when she arrived on Broward's Rock. "I had enough."

"You could stay for free at your uncle's."

"He didn't charge rent," she agreed sarcastically.

"He was your mother's only brother."

"You seem to know all about my family. Why are you asking me?"

Saulter studied her as if she were a particularly repugnant piece of flotsam.

"Suppose you tell me how you killed your uncle, Ms. Laurance."

Annie felt her shoulders press back against the hard ridges of the straight chair. There was a funny roaring in her ears, but she heard distinctly every word Saulter said.

"Ambrose Bailey was a good man." Saulter's voice changed. The chief had truly liked her uncle. But then who hadn't? Ambrose Bailey *was* a good man, a devoted friend, an implacable enemy, determined always to see justice done. That had been his reputation as a man and as a prosecuting attorney in Fort Worth. "A fine man. And you came down here and shoved him into the harbor so you could inherit his store. That's what happened, didn't it? Elliot Morgan found out and threatened you—and we see what happens when anyone threatens your security. Morgan died. And you cleverly did it in a way to throw suspicion on all the people who came to your bookstore. But no one else there had a quarrel with Elliot Morgan. Only you."

"Uncle Ambrose—it was an accident."

"Is that what you claim? Is that what you're going to tell the jury? Did you see him fall, Ms. Laurance?"

"How dare you!" she exploded. She was on her feet, glaring furiously at Saulter. "He went out about nine. He was by himself. I guess he went to check on his boat since he was leaving town the next day." Poor Uncle Ambrose. He'd been looking forward to his trip, a combination of research and fun. He'd been so pleased that she'd come to visit and could look after the store. She'd watched the Johnny Carson show. It was almost midnight before she began to worry. "When he didn't come in—"

"You dialed McElroy. I guess you thought that would be a good way to have the body discovered."

"Nobody *killed* my uncle."

Saulter's thin face flushed, and he rose to loom over her. "Oh, yes, Miss Laurance, somebody killed Ambrose Bailey. I should have known it at the time. Last night, I rechecked that autopsy report. There was a small contusion behind his right ear. Maybe it happened in a fall, but now that two other people are dead, I don't believe it."

Annie watched him with sheer fury in her eyes and in her heart

—but the words rang terrifyingly true. Uncle Ambrose knew boats, and he had been well that night, that last night.

"My God."

Saulter's mouth twisted. "A big surprise to you. Is that how you're going to play it? Maybe you should have stayed an actress, Miss Laurance. Well, you damn well can't do that over Doc Kearney. It's pretty clear why you had to get rid of her."

It was like standing in the shadow of an erupting volcano and watching tons of burning debris and roiling mud sweep down toward you.

"You didn't play that one too good. You told too many people how swell the doc was, how she didn't use succinyl-choline to kill your cat. Too damn cruel. Wasn't it pretty cruel to watch Elliot Morgan suffocate?"

"A dart killed him," Annie said stubbornly.

"Sure thing. A dart with a wad of cotton that'd been dipped in Succostrin. That, little lady, is the trade name for succinyl-choline. And who on this goddamn island ever heard of the stuff until you went around blabbing about it?"

Annie felt a surge of adrenaline. Her body recognized danger. In a flash, she remembered the boarder in *Mrs. McGinty's Dead.* If it hadn't been for Poirot, the boarder would have been hanged for a murder he didn't commit. Circumstantial evidence could kill you. But she wasn't like that boarder. Saulter had a fighter on his hands this time.

"Maybe if you told me all about it, you would feel better. Why don't we start with your uncle's murder? Tell me how you did it, Miss Laurance."

Anybody with sense would keep her mouth shut. She knew it. But she absolutely throbbed with anger. This big-mouthed galoot wasn't going to sit there accusing her of murdering her uncle. By God, she was going to tell him in no uncertain terms exactly what—

"My client has nothing further to say."

Both she and the chief jerked around. Max stood in the open door of the storeroom.

Annie's mouth closed.

"Your client?" Saulter demanded.

Max nodded, and his eyes warned Annie to keep on keeping quiet. "She is entitled to the advice of counsel, and my advice is to say nothing more."

"She can talk, Mr. Darling, or she can come to the station."

Max didn't yield. "Ms. Laurance isn't going anywhere. Do you have a warrant for her arrest?"

Max loved Annie's eyes. Usually. He could get lost in her eyes, dark gray eyes with golden flecks. Sometimes they were as sensuous as a Rubens painting, and sometimes as laughter-filled as a picnic afternoon. But, right now, they glinted with fury and reminded him of bright flashes from target pistols.

"Cool it, sweetie. Never lose your temper. That's always an advantage to your opponent."

"I'm too mad to be careful."

"Honey, when you are dangling from a hair-thin lifeline over the side of a precipice, it's time to be careful." It worried him to see Annie so visibly angry. At all costs, she had to avoid provoking Saulter. He pushed down his own impulse to pound something hard with his fists, preferably the doltish face of a certain police chief. Dear Annie, his stubborn golden girl, with her sun-streaked hair, freckle-spattered cheeks, and prickly, independent, explosive nature.

"He's not going to get away with it." Then she jammed her hand through her hair. "My God, Max, somebody *did* kill Uncle Ambrose." Her face compressed into a stern frown. "And Saulter's pitched on me. That means we have to find out what really happened."

"Sure. We'll do it. But, Annie, don't hassle with Saulter."

"That man is not going to bully me."

"Of course not, but you keep your lips buttoned, Laurance. Okay?"

Diverted for a moment from the object of her ire, she said

briskly, "Listen, it was great of you to try and help me. But I wouldn't suggest pretending to be a lawyer. You'll end up in jail."

"It would take Saulter a hell of a long time to do a fifty-state check to see whether I've passed the bar."

"But one phone call to the American Bar Association would take five minutes. Max, this isn't a laughing matter. Although, I'd bet he's a lot more interested in putting me in jail than in running checks on you."

"Right."

Anger glinted in her eyes.

Max could have kicked himself. If she got mad again—

"Look, our job now is to figure out what the hell's been going on before either of us ends up in jail. We need to check up on your uncle. Why would anybody murder him?"

The catamaran tilted a little, and Max adjusted the tiller.

Annie steadied herself. There was something nice about the delicately cut white swimsuit that emphasized the tawny richness of her skin.

Mmm. Mmm. Mmm. Max wanted to . . .

"Uncle Ambrose murdered— It's absurd!"

The catamaran lifted on the port hull. Spume rose over them like a gauzy curtain. They hung between sea and air, skimming the water like a hungry pelican, until Max moved the tiller, and the sail eased down.

Beads of water clung to Annie like seed pearls. Max knew just how it would feel to slide his hand gently over her soft skin.

"If somebody killed Uncle Ambrose, that same person killed Jill and Elliot—and Saulter's convinced I did all of it. So we've got to solve it ourselves." In her excitement, she scrambled up on her knees.

He shoved the tiller out of the way. The cat jerked, whipped, then started to tip.

Max reached out for Annie as they began to fall, and he felt her long, warm length against him. It was, he discovered, quite possible to choke on salt water and smile at the same time.

Nine

"HOW OLD were you here?" His finger rested on the black-and-white picture of a scrawny, pigtailed girl standing in front of a palmetto.

"Eleven. That was my first summer on Broward's Rock. See, here's Uncle Ambrose."

Oh, and she remembered that magical summer so well, the way the hot sand felt on her bare feet, how it smelled sitting on the end of a dock with her first pole in her hands, not expecting a thing to happen, the excitement when something yanked on her line, and her delight when Uncle Ambrose helped her haul out a toadfish.

The photograph of Annie and her toadfish was on the next page. It had curled a little with time, but it clearly showed the slimy brown, large-mouthed fish and Annie, grinning through a filigree of braces.

"Mouthwise, you and that fish were neck and neck."

But she was looking at the pictures of Uncle Ambrose. His hair was still a chestnut brown then, only lightly touched with white. Uncle Ambrose, who taught her so much more than how to cast a line or dig for clams. Because she never knew her father, she felt shy and uncomfortable around men until this gruff old curmudgeon given to long silences took the time to spend his summer days tramping the beaches with his niece and summer evenings pointing out the constellations that glittered in the southern sky like diamonds against black velvet.

"He made all the difference in my life," she said simply. "When Mother died, he helped me with school, and he always made it clear I had a home with him."

She flipped to the last page of the album, then reached out and gently touched the photograph of a distinguished-looking elderly man standing on the deck of a sailboat, the *Sleuth*. The aquiline face looked amused, skeptical, fiercely intelligent.

"A hell of a guy, huh? So why would anybody kill him?"

"He was a hell of a guy—to me, to his friends. But there were people who would have feared him at one time. Remember, he was a prosecuting attorney for years in Fort Worth, and he hated crooks. He had a passion to catch lawbreakers. He called them renegades, and he had no pity for them. He said pity should be for victims, not abusers."

"So somebody out of his past, somebody with a grudge, comes to Broward's Rock twelve years after the guy retires here and shoves him off of his sailboat?"

"I know, I know." Annie thumped a pillow in frustration. "It doesn't make a lot of sense. But people can hold grudges. Think about *The Count of Monte Cristo.*"

"But he was the guy who'd been screwed. You're talking about a crook wanting revenge for going to jail."

"High Noon."

"That wasn't twelve years later. No, it has to be something immediate, something urgent."

"Something here on Broward's Rock," she said thoughtfully.

Max closed the scrapbook. "You said he had a passion for justice. Right?"

Annie nodded emphatically.

"If he spent his life putting the baddies in jail, he'd find it hard to ignore it if he ran into something criminal on Broward's Rock." Max's shoulders hunched forward. He looked like an All-American tackle ready to spring.

She was concentrating on her uncle's life, trying to think, but she did take pleasure, purely aesthetic, of course, in the animal grace so close to her.

"Don't you see," he continued earnestly, "if Elliot could come up with stuff serious enough to get himself murdered, what're the odds your uncle had picked up on the same information?"

Annie clapped her hands to her head. "My God, true crime. That's it. That has to be it! Uncle Ambrose's book."

"He wrote books, too?"

"Not like the others. He'd been collecting material for years for a different kind of true-crime book. He was fascinated by the ones who got away, always on the lookout for accidents or suicides that might really have been murders."

"A shove down those attic stairs for dear old Grannie Whipple? Or over the cliff with Cousin Alice?"

"Or the side of a boat. Like Emma's husband—and, oh, Max, Uncle Ambrose himself!"

"Better wait until after dark," Max urged.

Annie disagreed. "I can't see in the dark. Besides, there are snakes and things. No, I'll pretend I'm out getting some exercise. I can see if anyone's lurking around. I'm going to go now."

"I'll come with you." He did look wonderfully like an anxious Mountie, stalwart and true.

"We don't have time. You do as we've planned. I can take care of this by myself."

"Dammit, I don't like it."

He continued to frown reprovingly as she rolled her bike out of the shed. She dropped the neatly folded towel in the white vinyl basket, then turned to beam at Max.

She maintained the smile until she was out of sight, a matter of riding six feet, then dipping down into an aquamarine world. The late afternoon sunlight filtered through the trees in a green and gold haze. The three-foot-wide bicycle path wound through luxuriant swamp growth. Live oak trees, pines, palmetto palms, and flowering shrubs vied for life in the spongy, wet ground. Thick vines hung from trees, wrapped around trunks, snaked along the ground. As she pumped the old-fashioned bike, twigs skittered from beneath the wheels, and her approach disturbed the seen and unseen inhabitants of this peculiarly private domain. A flock of blue-green tree swallows circled noisily, looking for their last insect snacks before dusk. Three sunning turtles slipped into dark green water. An alligator raised his head.

Annie pedalled harder. It was eerily silent on the bicycle path. In the summer, families wobbled through the damp heat, and daredevil ten-year-olds rode fast enough to imperil anything in their way. But now, late on an October afternoon, the sunlight already waning, it was pleasantly warm but isolated.

She was pleased she had decided not to turn the disk over to Saulter. There was no reason on earth to put the innocent writers at risk. But Capt. Mac had made it clear to Max that Saulter wasn't impressed by Elliot's threat to reveal some nasty truths about his fellow writers. For the chief, that was entirely too fancy a motive for Elliot's murder. Instead, Saulter saw her as a killer driven by purely financial fear. That was an understandable motive. Money mattered. Saulter knew it, and Annie knew it. Still, she thought, reputations mattered, too, especially to the Sunday Night Regulars.

The disk. Annie's only hope was to load it, read the information it contained, and, armed with this knowledge, face down each suspect. If she were lucky, it might shed some light on what had happened to Uncle Ambrose.

She and Max would discover the murderer before Chief Saulter came to arrest her. Max was on the phone right now, seeking information about the Sunday Night Regulars, seeking some lever to help them break through a false face of innocence. Emma Clyde, Janis and Jeff Farley, Harriet Edelman, Capt. Mac, Fritz Hemphill, Hal Douglas, Kelly Rizzoli. One of them had a secret that must be kept—whatever the cost.

Annie braked and let the bike coast to a stop. Here the path curved, crossed over a short wooden span, then melded into the dusty gray road that led to Elliot's tree house. She dragged the bike down the short incline, keeping an eye out for snakes, and put the bike beneath the wooden bridge. Carrying the folded white towel, she climbed back to the path, and peered over the railing. Good. The bike wasn't visible.

She stopped in the shadows of a towering pine and stood there for at least five minutes, listening to the occasional honk of a frog, the slither of a woodland animal, the sibilant rustle as leaves slipped down through the green and gold air to land on the road and among the underbrush. It was so beautiful and peaceful on the island. It seemed impossible to believe two people had been murdered there. Three, if the chief were right about her uncle.

Even though Elliot hadn't been dead twenty-four hours, his tree house had already acquired a deserted air. The blinds were closed. There was a dusting of sand on the steps. Leaves bunched along the walk, already carpeted with pine needles. On Broward's Rock, the swamp didn't take long to reclaim its own.

Satisfied that she had his tree house to herself, she stepped briskly onto the road and walked swiftly, the gray dirt scuffing up beneath her tennis shoes. She stopped once and looked sharply around, nagged by an uneasy sense of being watched, but no one moved on the rutted, uneven road, so she hurried the last few yards to the steps and ran lightly up them, the towel in her hand. She tried the front door. Locked. She moved around the porch. She stopped at the kitchen window and pushed. It moved grudgingly, caught, then, after a hearty shove, screeched sharply and rocketed up.

Annie's heart thumped. She looked frantically around, but nothing disturbed the silence.

Knowing Tessa Crichton had never hesitated in search of clues, she balanced awkwardly on the sill, stepped into the sink, then jumped to the floor.

In Elliot Morgan's living room, a microphone taped to the underside of a chair picked up the sound of the opening window and Annie's arrival, recorded them, magnified them, and carried them to a receiver in another living room on Broward's Rock.

The occupant of that room was lifting a glass to drink, but the sounds halted the movement of the hand. So someone had come.

That bastard Morgan must have been telling the truth: he had given a copy of that damned disk to someone.

Too much curiosity killed cats—and people.

Harriet Edelman wore baby blue jogging pants and a yellow t-shirt. She hadn't been jogging, but she was comfortably dressed for a long vigil on her widow's walk. She'd waited most of the day, eating her lunch here, carefully staying in the shadows, but always keeping her field glasses trained on Elliot's tree house. She'd been certain someone would come. It was too much of a coincidence for Elliot to be killed on the night he was going to reveal all the garbage he'd gathered about all of them. Somebody was bound to come searching for what Elliot knew.

Her thin mouth twisted. Served him right. Such a know-it-all, such a busybody. She smiled grimly. Not a busybody now. The smile turned to a grimace. To claim she'd stolen the plot to *Deadly Diamonds*. She hadn't even read the manuscript that idiot woman had sent her to critique. She'd mailed it back without looking at a single page. It was coincidence, that was all. Coincidence.

And let anybody try to prove differently.

But it could have been awkward, Elliot having an affidavit from that woman and threatening to send it to her publisher. Publishers were so antsy, scared of their shadows.

Shadows . . . My God, look who was here, creeping around the side of Elliot's porch, breaking in. If that wasn't the damnedest thing. She'd never expected it to be Annie. Not pretty-faced Annie Laurance, of all people. Why, she wasn't even a writer. What could Elliot possibly have known about her?

Harriet picked up her Minolta, removed the lens cover, and focused it. She snapped two pictures as Annie climbed in the kitchen window. That ought to be enough proof the girl was up to no good.

She could just envision the newspaper headlines: *Mystery Writer Solves Crime*. That ought to jack up her sales. Grimly, she trained the camera again on Elliot's tree house, took two more pictures, then lowered the camera and snatched up her binoculars to watch another familiar figure walk up the steps.

A dull flush suffused her face.

She was the one who had watched all day. By God, she was going to get the credit. Dropping the binoculars and the Minolta on the wooden seat, she hurried to the ladder. It would only take her a minute by bike path to get to Elliot's house.

The phone rang. Annie jumped three feet, her heart thudding. The phone rang and rang and rang.

Frozen in the doorway to the living room, Annie thought, *Lord, this room gives me the creeps!* The last shafts of sunlight glittered on Elliot's collection of steel drums. One entire pane of glass in the hexagonal room was covered by carnival masks—several shaped like bats, one of the Devil with horns, a tail and spear, another of a red-haired Viking. A massive painting of an old black man, his face fierce and threatening, rested against an easel. Papa Bois, the spirit of the forest. He protected animals, Elliot had told her. Any animal in his right mind would take one look at Papa Bois and head for the city. The furniture, blood-red leather chairs and ebony black tables, contributed to the aura of unhealthy darkness.

She steadied her heartbeat and tiptoed across the uncarpeted living room floor. From the evening she had dinner with Elliot, she remembered that his office was in the second bedroom. She was, obviously, alone. That phone call would have roused anyone. Moving with more confidence, she opened the door into the second bedroom. She didn't turn on the lights, though. No point in advertising her presence.

Elliot had worked on a table in front of the window. Again, the blinds were closed. Annie left them closed. The CPU, monitor and keyboard were neatly covered with a clear plastic hood. Annie removed the hood and sat down. She studied the set-up and found the on-off switch on the right side of the CPU toward the back. She turned it on. Red lights flashed on the keyboard, then green letters centered against the black screen: *Insert Diskette.*

Her hands were sweaty. "What do you expect," she scolded herself wryly, "for a first-time housebreaker?" She unfolded the towel and lifted out the disk. Slipping it out of its white jacket, she put it into the right-hand disk drive and pushed it in. The operating software was already in place in the left-hand drive.

The cursor flashed in the upper left corner, then green letters centered on the black screen: *Initial system checks satisfactory. Please wait for system to load.*

A clock ticked somewhere across the room. Outside, a sea gull shrilled. A dripping noise obtruded. Just a slow leak in the bathroom.

An odd, uneven creaking sounded behind her.

Annie jerked around.

A faint bar of sunlight edged into the bedroom.

Must be from the kitchen. Those window curtains were open. Dust motes swirled.

God, she was jumpy. There was no one here. She had an oppressive feeling of danger. But that was easy enough to understand. After all, she had broken into a dead man's house. If Saulter found her here, he'd carry her off to jail for sure. The sooner she looked at the disk and got out, the better.

The terminal hummed with on-screen commands: *Fonts loaded. Loading Valdocs system. Loading interrupt and background support modules.*

It was taking forever.

Finally, the message flashed: *Press any typing key to enter editor.*

Almost there. Only seconds away now.

As the document window appeared, Annie studied the keyboard. She pressed the index key.

The index listed all the files stored on the disk. This was pay dirt, all right.

There were eight files.

1. Emma Clyde   10/8:03
2. J/J Farley   10/8:01

3. Harriet Edelman   10/9:02
4. Fritz Hemphill   10/9:01
5. Hal Douglas   10/9:02
6. Capt. John McElroy   10/10:03
7. Annie Laurance   10/10:02
8. Kelly Rizzoli   10/10:01

She studied the dates. Elliot was killed on Sunday the thirteenth, so he'd finished working on the files on Thursday. That figured. He must have dropped the disk into the mail to her on Friday for arrival Monday.

Should she take the files in order, beginning with Emma Clyde?

She pushed back a curl from her forehead. The tiny house was incredibly stuffy. She looked longingly at the air conditioner in the rear window. It wouldn't do any harm to turn it on. She reached over, switched it on, then turned back to the screen and punched the command to retrieve a file. The cursor blinked by Emma Clyde's name. Annie almost pushed return, then, remembering Elliot's taunt about all the information he had on Max, tapped the down arrow until the cursor blinked by her name. It would only take a second to see what Elliot had put in her file. She punched return.

Within seconds, the sentences began to form, fluorescent green against black.

Good grief, how did he know about that week in Santa Fe? He must have talked to Richard.

He had the goods, all right. When Elliot claimed that he could ferret out information, he wasn't kidding. Yes, here was the stuff on Max.

Her eyes widened. Well, for God's sake. Max had never told her . . .

The blow caught her completely unaware. A streak of fire flared on the side of her head, then nothing more.

□ □ □ □

Max groaned and massaged the back of his neck. He'd never before appreciated the fatigue associated with constant phoning. Somewhere in all of this jumble there had to be the one fact they needed. Figuring out which fact mattered, that was the rub.

Absently, he picked up his glass, finished the last of the Bud Light, and ignored its faint warmth. Time to organize.

He rolled paper expertly into Annie's portable Olivetti. He'd mastered a fast hunt-and-peck when he worked as a reporter one year. He typed quickly, and, when he was finished, he reread the compact bios, ignoring typos.

Emma Clyde—Doyenne of American mystery writers, author of 76 classic mysteries. Born Jan. 18, 1922, Billings, Mont. Graduated from Cincinnati Heights School of Nursing, 1942, U.S. Army Nurses Corps, 1942–45, discharged as 1st lieutenant 1945. First mystery, *Murder in Casablanca* (1946). Married same year to Harold Caston, owner of several Memphis boat stores. They met on a troop transport returning to the U.S. from N. Africa. Surgical nurse, St. Jude's Hospital, Memphis, Tenn., 1945–1950. Five more mysteries published. Divorced from Caston, Aug. 13, 1950. No children. Moved to NYC as full-time writer. Active in Mystery Writers of America, serving three times as Chairman of Book Awards, recipient of two Edgars for Best Mystery of the Year, winner of Grand Master Award. Married June 8, 1982, to Enrique Morales, prop. Horizon Villas in Boca Raton, Fla. Purchased resort home on Broward's Rock, July 15, 1982. Morales drowned in boating accident fifteen months later. Morales and Emma returned after midnight that evening by motorboat to her yacht, *Marigold's Pleasure*. Morales decided to smoke a cigar by the stern. Emma went to bed. She discovered him missing the next morning, alerted authorities, and search began. Body was found floating 50 yards from the yacht. Coast Guard theory is that Morales became dizzy, lost his balance, fell overboard, and drowned because his heavy sweater became waterlogged and he was a poor swimmer. *Marigold's Pleasure* was anchored far out in the bay to avoid public notice, as Emma was often besieged by fans.

Emma Clyde. It might be fascinating to take a peek at the police report on Morales's death. Max rubbed his nose. Funny. She was apparently never known as Mrs. Morales. The bare bones suggested that Morales stopped running his resort (motel? vacation apartments?) as soon as he married and took up a cushy residence on Broward's Rock. Of course, his drowning might have nothing to do with the murders now. Emma's secret could go back as far as her days as a surgical nurse.

Hal Douglas. Harold Clifton Douglas, born March 18, 1955, in Wiesbaden, W. Germany, son of career Army officer. Grew up on Army posts in Europe and the United States. BA from Washington University at St. Louis. Married to Lenora Harris 1978; writer with Hallmark Cards, Kansas City, 1976–79; publicist, Sierra Leone Films, Hollywood, Ca., 1980–82. First novel, *The San Bernardino Heist*, a 1983 best-seller. Bought home, Robber's Nest, on Broward's Rock, March 12, 1983.

Max frowned and reread the paragraph on Douglas. Annie had mentioned Douglas and Kelly Rizzoli as a twosome. So where was Lenora Harris Douglas?

Harriet Edelman. Born July 5, 1948, Carlisle, Pa. BA from Penn State, 1969. Lived in Nice, France, 1969–75. Immediate success with Macintosh series, the first two, *Ride a Wave* and *Gentleman's Smile*, set in Nice. *Ride a Wave* Edgar winner for Best First Mystery. Contributor to *Armchair Detective*. Purchased a home on Broward's Rock in 1976.

Zero on weaselly-faced Harriet. The net hadn't fished up anything useful. But Annie'd mentioned that Harriet'd been mad as hell at Elliot, because he was hinting she'd cribbed somebody else's book.

Jeff and Janis Farley—Jefferson Allen Farley, born Feb. 3, 1953, St. Louis, Mo. Foster child. Married Janis Corey 1970, BA in journalism University of Missouri, 1974. Collaborated on their first book, *Danny's Delight*, in 1975, Jeff plotting and writing, Janis drawing the pen-and-ink illustrations. Jeff employed as a crime reporter on the *St. Louis Post-Dispatch*, 1974–1984. Purchased island home Sept. 22, 1984.

Janis Corey Farley, born April 11, 1955. Foster child. Married Jeff Farley 1970. Illustrator.

Jeff and Janis Farley. Could be volumes there. Both of them foster children and marriage at a sadly young age for Janis. It helped explain her utter dependence on that stiff. No schooling for her, but lots of talent with pen and paper.

Fritz Hemphill—Born April 16, 1945, in Long Beach, Ca. Graduated from Long Beach City (Jr.) College, 1964; U.S. Army, pfc., 1964–66, Ft. Ord, Saigon, V.N.; BA, Loma Linda University, Loma Linda, Ca., 1968; LAPD, 1968–80, patrolman, sergeant, detective; married Doreen Norris 1968, divorced 1980. One child, Alice, now sixteen. First police procedural, *The Agony Chain*, published 1972. Third novel, *Kerrigan's Heart*, runaway best-seller, sixteen weeks on *The New York Times* best-seller list. Purchased Broward's Rock harbor condo Sept. 1, 1980.

Max wiggled his shoulders and stretched. Without losing his place, he rose and used peripheral vision to cross the living room to the kitchen, open the refrigerator, and pick out another Bud Light. This time he settled on the couch, feet propped on the rattan coffee table, took a double gulp, and continued to read.

John McElroy, police captain (ret.). Born April 24, 1930, in Ft. Walton, Fla. Attended Jacksonville University, 1948–50; OCS U.S. Marine Corps, 2nd. Lt., 1950–52, Camp LeJeune, La., Korea; Miami PD, 1952–60; Asst. chief, Silver City, Fla., 1960–80; capt., Silver City police, 1980–84. Married Thelma Farris 1954. Three children: John, age 30; Theodore, 28; and Michael, 26. Divorced 1962. Purchased home on Broward's Rock, July 20, 1984.

Kelly Rizzoli. Born Aug. 26, 1959, Ft. Smith, Ark. Attended College of the Ozarks, 1977–78. BA in psychology, University of Arkansas, 1983. First novel, *The Shuttered Mind*, a paperback best-seller in 1983. *Sad Song* sold 55,000 in hardcover two months after 1984 publication. Bought Magpie Plantation on Broward's Rock in July 1984.

Max pulled a legal pad closer, sighed, and rubbed his face, then downed the rest of the tepid beer. Damn, he was getting hungry.

He looked up. For a moment, his tired eyes refused to focus, then they noted the open living room windows, the slatted, tropical blinds not yet closed for the night.

For the night . . .

Darkness had fallen. He looked at his watch, and an empty, sick feeling moved inside him. 7:15. Annie had left for the five-minute bike ride to Elliot's house a few minutes before six.

Where the hell was Annie?

Ten

ANNIE MOANED. The sound came from her, but it seemed separate and far away. She tried to lift her head, and pain seared down into her shoulder. She moaned again and rolled her head. The pain caused her to cry out. She opened her eyes. And saw nothing. An instant of panic flared. Her heart thudded erratically, and she fought down the nausea.

Elliot's house. The disk.

She was lying on her back, her hands outstretched. Something heavy lay in one hand, her left hand. Something heavy and nastily sticky.

Unsteadily, Annie rolled on her side. She let go of the horrid thing, whatever it was, and propped herself up, then attempted to get up.

She stood and swayed as if the floor moved beneath her feet.

She was going to be sick.

Moving heavily, one hand clasped to her mouth, she reached the doorway. Elliot's tree house was built to the same pattern as hers, the only difference was his second bedroom. She turned left toward the bathroom, flicked on the light and made it just in time to heave violently into the toilet. Sick. Sick. Sick. Finally, clinging to the edge of the lavatory for support, she knew the sickness was past.

Breathing unevenly, she stared down into the basin.

Then she saw the reddish stickiness on her left hand. Slowly, she turned her hand, looked down at the palm, at the blood smeared across it. Blood streaked the whiteness of the lavatory where she had gripped it.

Blood.

Her head.

Annie looked up and saw her face in the mirror. A smeary face. Blurred vision. Clumsily, she moved her right hand up to her head, gingerly touching her scalp behind her right ear. The swelling felt spongy. But her fingers located no cut or fresh wet blood. She turned the spigots and thrust her hands under the cold rushing water, ridding them of the unpleasant stickiness, then patted water on her face. She used a pale yellow towel to dry her hands. It was pink where she had touched it.

Her head. Somebody hit her. That's what had happened to Jill Kearney. But Jill had a skull like an eggshell. Annie's head felt like hell, but it must be as thick as Max had always maintained it was. No blood. Where had the blood on her hand come from? Must have been a little cut, already dried.

Dried. God, how long had she been here? She'd better get—

The disk. She was reading the disk.

Annie moved like a drunken june bug, misjudging distance. Swaying unsteadily, she reached the hall, started up it toward Elliot's office.

She saw the blood first, spatters of it dark and ugly against the ridged bamboo wall. As if blood had sprayed upward, clots of it, then finer particles . . .

The head was shattered, unrecognizable. Blood and tissue were smeared across the back of the pale yellow t-shirt. One hand was outflung. Even in the dim light, Annie recognized the large red ruby ring that Harriet always wore.

Bludgeoned. That's what Harriet had said had happened to Jill Kearney. Harriet was wrong. Jill had been struck once. Harriet had been bludgeoned, the entire side of her skull was a pulpy mass—bone, tissue, blood, and hair indistinguishable.

Annie jolted around and again made it to the bathroom just in time.

Harriet dead. Why? Crazy, crazy . . . Saulter called it nutty when Elliot was killed. Elliot was dead, and Saulter suspected her of his death and of Uncle Ambrose's. Now here she was at the scene of another crime. Good luck, Annie Laurance. Who would believe she hadn't done it? Just like Pam Frye in *Octagon House*. But she didn't have Asey Mayo to save her. Then the fiery pain in her head gave a measure of relief. Her own head. That was it. Someone had struck both her and Harriet down.

Resolutely, Annie once again faced the hall. This had gone too far. This time she had to call Saulter. She moved sideways down the hall, like a reluctant crab. God, she couldn't get past Harriet, get past all that blood. Elliot's office. There would be an extension in there.

She stepped into the office and turned on the light. She was stumbling across the room, her hand outstretched to pick up the telephone when she saw the blackjack. Her shoulders hunched.

A blackjack. And then she knew. Someone had killed Harriet with that blackjack. There was blood on it and hair. The black-jack lay where she had been. Heavy. Blackjacks were heavy. The blood on her hand. She had awakened with the blackjack in her hand. Her fingerprints would be on it. She remembered what Capt. Mac told them, that Sunday evening. Leather holds finger-prints very well. Very well indeed.

Moving in a thick gray fog, the only reality the pounding ache in her head and the thick crimson spatters on the bamboo wall, Annie returned to the bathroom. Her movements were slow and clumsy. She used the towel hanging on the rack and carefully scrubbed the toilet, the lavatory, and the light switch, pausing occasionally to retch.

What else had she touched there? Nothing.

She rubbed the walls in the hall, then went to the kitchen. She leaned out to wipe the window, the sill, and the area around the sink.

In Elliot's office, she took time to turn on the monitor. At first she was hopeful. There was a disk in the right-hand drive. It took only a moment to discover it was blank. It must have taken her attacker forty seconds to erase the files forever. Annie wiped the disk, the disk jacket, the side of the CPU, the keyboard, the chair.

Her head throbbed and furious tears burned in her eyes.

What else had she touched?

The doorframe, the floor where she had lain, the light switch.

Although nausea threatened again, she used one end of the towel to pick up the bloodied blackjack, and the other to wipe it clean. She bent down to pick up the towel she'd brought to cover the disk.

A thunderous knocking erupted at the front door.

Beneath the low-flung skirt of a pine, Max crouched. The whirling red light atop the police car threw scarlet flashes around the clearing and against the dark masses of foliage.

Max strained to see. Saulter thumped again on Elliot's door, then waved a hand behind him. Max lifted his head. Another man waited on the other side of the clearing, and Max understood. Saulter thought someone was in Elliot's tree house, and he intended to flush out the intruder for his deputy to grab.

From his vantage point, Max could see the deputy waiting near the police car, Chief Saulter at the top of the steps, and a slender form outlined against a window on the side of the tree house.

Saulter couldn't see Annie. But if the deputy turned his head, he would.

Max reached down, scooped up a large pine cone, and heaved it as hard as he could. It splatted against the back of the police car.

The deputy immediately dropped out of sight on the ground.

"Halt, or I'll shoot!"

Max smiled. That shout would forewarn Annie nicely. He scooped up five cones, nice solid ones, and, wriggling backwards, began to move toward the bike path he knew she would take.

The second and third cones landed on top of the tree house.

"Come out with your hands up," the deputy yelled frantically, and ran, crouching, toward the back of the house.

Max moved to intercept Annie, a slight silhouette momentarily limned by the flashing police light.

He hissed urgently, "Annie—this way."

She was moving oddly, a kind of drooping shamble. He caught her as she stumbled and fell.

A shower and a clean cotton nightgown helped. But best of all was the double whisky Max thrust in her numb hands.

"What if I have a concussion?"

"Best thing in the world for it."

It did ease the throbbing pain. But not even telling Max eased the horror of that evening.

Max looked as grim as she had ever seen him—and that was scary.

Annie rested against the bright cushions of the wicker divan, a patchwork quilt across her knees. She shivered, though her blue terrycloth beach robe was warm and soft. "He'll arrest me, won't he?"

"Hell, no."

It had a hollow ring. Max managed a smile. "Look, Annie, this is the truth. We were here all evening. We never left the place." His dark blue eyes narrowed in thought. "The phone rang once, maybe about six-thirty, but we didn't answer. We didn't give a damn about the phone. Come on, Annie, stop brooding about it. We've got to figure out how to solve this."

He handed her the notes he'd made from his calls while she was at Elliot's, then rolled up his sleeves and fixed ham sandwiches and brewed fresh coffee, black and strong. He brought her a tray, then plunked down in the easy chair next to her and fussily insisted she eat every bite as she read the bios. This wasn't her old, familiar, cavalier Max. There were dark shadows under his eyes, a stubble of beard on his chin. He stayed very close and occasionally reached out to touch her, but his voice remained crisp.

"All right. Let's go at it from the first—from the murderer's side."

"The murderer's side?"

"Sure. Let's figure out what the killer did when and why and fit that against the suspects. We know Elliot's murder was premeditated, of course."

"Because of Jill and the poison?"

"Right. The murderer needed to do several things. Get a dart, steal the poison, and set it up so the lights would go out at precisely the right time Sunday night."

Annie shot up straight, then winced. "Max, the murderer is a woman."

"Why?"

"Because the dart had to be carried into the store Sunday night. A woman could bring it in a purse, but there's no way for a man to get a four-inch dart in the store."

"No. I don't see it that way. That would be too risky. The dart would already have the wad of cotton soaked in succinyl-choline on the end. That would leave traces. No, I see it this way. The murderer got into the store sometime Saturday night or Sunday morning . . ."

"Sunday morning," Annie interrupted.

"What time?"

Annie figured for a moment. "About nine forty-five. I heard the cabinet slam, and that meant someone had closed the back door. I was all set to beat it out the front door, then I saw that Agatha wasn't upset, so I thought it was some other noise. That means that Agatha knows and likes the murderer."

"If Agatha could only talk."

Max grabbed a sheet of paper and scribbled out a timetable:

Sunday

1 A.M.—Jill killed, poison stolen.

9:45 A.M.—Death On Demand entered, string tied to switches, dart hidden.

7:45 P.M.—During cocktail chatter, back door opened, storeroom door left ajar.

8:10—Lights out.
8:12—Dart thrown.

Monday

6:10 P.M.—Annie knocked unconscious.
6:15 P.M.—Harriet murdered.

Annie took the sheet. It didn't help a hell of a lot, though Archie Goodwin would probably have deemed it a creditable effort. But Archie was awfully good-humored.

"How did the murderer get in?"

"How?"

"How? I had the place locked."

His face crinkled in thought. "Okay. Keys. Presumably the Island Hills Clinic doesn't leave its doors open for the world to enter, so the killer had keys there. It isn't hard to come up with keys, and there's nothing special about the locks at either place."

The idea that a killer could come and go in her shop at will wasn't exactly a cheering one.

"The killer came into my place about nine forty-five. The phone rang about ten minutes earlier, but I ignored it. Whoever called figured the place was empty."

"You wouldn't normally be there Sunday morning?"

"No. I was trying to decide what to do about the Sunday evening session."

"It would only take a couple of minutes," Max reconstructed. "Nip into the store, hide the dart on the floor by the wall, then tie thread to the breaker switches, and run that along the floor into the café area. Presto, the stage is set for a murder."

Annie couldn't help admiring the plan. "Whoever did it was damn smart. It was beautifully plotted. You know, I told Elliot those cigarettes would make him sick someday. And they really did, because the murderer counted on the red tip of his cigarette to serve as the target for the dart. Hell of a throw."

"Avoid talking about good throws," Max cautioned. "Let's hope Saulter doesn't dwell on your softball prowess."

"I skunked his pitiful team, eleven-zip."

"Poor planning." Max absently rubbed his bristly jaw. "Unlike our murderer. It all went like clockwork. During the confusion of the blackout, all he had to do was yank on the thread until it broke and reel it in. When the lights came on, he could drop it unobtrusively into the wastebasket, along with the cotton soaked in polish remover. Voilà: one corpse and nothing to link the murderer to the crime."

Annie pulled the quilt up to her shoulders. "I'll bet Dr. Thorndyke could have found some traces if he'd been there with his small green box."

"He didn't have to trifle with search warrants, *et al.*"

"Lacking the good doctor's expertise, let's try to ratiocinate, like Sherlock Holmes. Okay, Dr. Watson, why was the back door open when I came to check the circuits?"

"Just a little bit of insurance. It would have been easy for the murderer to slip into the storeroom and open that door while everyone was squabbling over the coffee and snacks. That open door was to make sure Saulter considered the possibility of an outsider."

"But Saulter didn't look past me," Annie said bitterly, "much less outside."

"Well, you have to admit it was brilliantly thought out." He sighed and got up to pour himself a drink. "And we don't have an iota of proof to show Saulter."

Annie gingerly massaged her temples. If only her head didn't ache quite so much. Words jiggled in her mind: scraps, proof, papers . . .

"My God, Uncle Ambrose's book. Max, his *book*!"

"You told me about it," he said soothingly. "He was working on a book about accidents that just might have been murder."

Annie threw back the quilt, pulled herself to her feet, and wobbled, but her words came fast as shotgun pellets. "Don't you see? We said Elliot might have picked up on what Uncle Ambrose suspected. Well, somebody beat us to the disk at Elliot's, but we can go through Uncle Ambrose's papers!"

□ □ □ □

When Annie unlocked the front door and turned on the lights at Death On Demand, Agatha rose, stretched leisurely, and focused two luminous, quizzical eyes on them. Annie scooped up the cat from atop the bookcase and rubbed her cheek against the ebony fur. "Who came in Sunday morning, Agatha?"

But Agatha wriggled free and stalked down the center aisle. It wasn't the proper time for Annie to be in the shop, and her tail indicated her disdain for Annie's unprofessional hours.

Her nagging headache was forgotten. They were nearing the end of their hunt. She felt almost lightheaded as she led the way to the storeroom. The chalked outline was no longer in front of the coffee bar. Dear Ingrid. She was holding down the fort in every way.

"I gathered up most of his stuff and put it in the two back cupboards," she chattered to Max. "There were folders and photographs and news clippings, along with his manuscript pages. I never had a chance to go through any of it, I've been so busy with the store."

Max hauled out two huge cardboard boxes.

It took almost an hour to wade through it all.

When they were done, Annie stared soberly at the heaps of materials. "Oh, Max, he *was* murdered. There isn't a single page of his manuscript here. Not a page."

"Are you sure he had actually written any of it?"

"Of course I am. He never talked much about it, but he worked on it at home in his den. He typed on an old Smith Corona and used yellow second sheets for copy paper."

"Are you sure the manuscript was in this stuff when you packed it all away?" He waved his hand at the materials spilled across the worktable.

"I'm sure." She looked grim-faced at the empty cartons. "Some bloody thief took it out."

It could have happened at any time in the three months since Uncle Ambrose died.

Without a great deal of hope, Annie went to the front desk and dialed Capt. Mac.

"The cases Ambrose was interested in?" Capt. Mac paused. "Let's see. There was the explosion in the Armbruster plant in Montana, killed Old Man Armbruster. Supposed to have been a labor dispute, but he had a worthless son who inherited six million. And Ambrose was suspicious of the Vinson suicide in Hawaii. You remember that one? And, of course, the Winningham case. That happened when I was at Silver City, but I was only assistant chief, and the chief played investigations pretty close to his chest, so I didn't know much that was helpful to Ambrose. That's all I remember. You know how close-mouthed your uncle was. A great one for letting the other fellow talk."

"Did he ever mention a case that involved anyone here on Broward's Rock?"

"Oh. I see where you're going. No, he didn't, and frankly I don't see any connection with the three cases I mentioned. That Armbruster heir lives in New York, and Mrs. Vinson's husband stayed in Hawaii. As for the Winningham case, everybody involved is dead. Cale Winningham went down in a plane crash not long after he 'accidentally' shot his wife. If Ambrose was onto something close to home, he never let on to me. Sorry, Annie. I wish to hell he had."

She walked down the central aisle back to the coffee bar, scuffing her feet in mounting disappointment. Max was making a diligent foot-by-foot survey of the entire store.

She called after him. "Capt. Mac doesn't know whether Uncle Ambrose was onto a lead here, but, dammit, I know it in my bones —it all goes back to him. I'll bet the store he found out something, and somebody pushed him off his boat to keep him from making his research trip."

Max was moving from table to table, then turning to sight where Elliot had stood. Annie looked at each table in turn, mentally placing the Sunday Night Regulars on the fateful evening. Elliot had been standing just there. Surely, it should be possible to figure where the dart had come from its angle of entry. Dr. Thorndyke would have been able to do it. But not, apparently, Chief Saulter. Annie wasn't geometrically talented, but she gave it a try. She and Max and Ingrid were at the table nearest the storeroom, and the Farleys at the table opposite theirs. Capt. Mac and Fritz Hemphill had the table nearest to the watercolors on the west wall. Emma Clyde and Harriet sat next to the central corridor, and Kelly Rizzoli and Hal Douglas nearest to Elliot and the coffee bar. Of course, Elliot could have turned just the moment the dart was thrown. She gave up, and turned back to Uncle Ambrose. Had any of these people ever been involved in a case of accident or suicide that could have been murder? Annie recalled Max's typewritten notes, and Emma Clyde's name flashed in her mind like a six-foot neon sign.

She whooped and told Max.

"Yeah, that's a real possibility. Of course, there's the question of Hal Douglas's wife. Where is she? It's really too bad you didn't have a chance to read Elliot's disk."

"The killer's too smart for us. He must have destroyed my uncle's manuscript months ago, slick as a whistle. Now he's wiped out Elliot's disk. How the heck did he know I was at Elliot's house?"

"I don't know. If we knew that . . . Think back, Annie. Did you hear anything? Was there a noise or a smell, anything that might give some hint to the murderer's identity?"

"Nothing. I was sitting there, reading . . ."

Max looked at her sharply. "You actually started reading the disk? Did you find out anything?"

"I certainly did. Max, why didn't you ever tell me you had a law degree?"

For an instant, he looked absolutely blank, then he began to shake with laughter.

"Annie Laurance, for shame. There you are, inches from discovering a murderer's identity, and do you call up one of the suspect's files? No, you call up Annie Laurance's file."

She tried to brazen it out. "I thought it would take only a minute."

"It merely proves you are human, my love, succumbing to that feminine weakness for gossip before duty."

"I may be weak, but you are deceitful. And chauvinistic."

"Did I ever tell you I *didn't* have a law degree?"

"Max, be serious. Why didn't you say you did?"

"Oh, that was filed under miscellaneous information. You already know all the important things about me: I'm wondrously handsome and charming, sinfully rich, exquisitely perceptive, staunchly devoted to the intellect. I have three sisters and an enormous summer house on Long Island. I'm—"

"You are evading the issue. You are perfectly well qualified to practice law. You can have a *serious* career."

"I'll tell you what, Annie. After we find the maniacal killer who is rampaging across wee Broward's Rock, I will give every consideration to pursuing what you term a *serious* career."

"Do you mean it?"

"Of course. Now look, you called up the index, and decided to check out your own file. You didn't perchance look at anyone else's?"

"No. And when I came to, the disk had been erased."

"Rats." He scowled darkly. "You are looking at the screen, somebody comes up from behind and biffs you." Max paused. "Why did he—or she—just *biff* you?"

"That was the only Epson on the island, and anybody looking at the index would know I had only looked at my own file."

"How?"

"Every time a file is stored, the machine records the date."

A green expression flitted across his face. "Thank God for your curiosity."

Annie pondered it for a moment, then felt a little sick, too. "If I'd looked at the wrong file, read the killer's, then . . . It would have been like Harriet."

"Harriet must have walked in on the killer."

Thank God, indeed, for her curiosity. Then, as her head twinged, she felt a flash of her old temper. "By God, I don't like being slammed. Okay, so I didn't get to read the files. We'll still figure it out."

"You bet we will." Max pulled the typewritten bios out of his pocket. "Come on, let's get to work."

"What are we going to do?"

"Prep you."

"Prep me to do what?"

Max bent forward to tell her.

Eleven

ANNIE FELT THE ARM on her shoulder, shaking, shaking. She blinked and struggled to turn her face away from the piercing light.

"Come on, Annie. Open your eyes. I have to check your pupils. My God, I think you do have a concussion. This is like trying to wake a South American tree sloth."

"Go away," she mumbled, thrashing out blindly. "You've checked every bloody hour on the hour all night long. Go away."

"One eye open. Just one."

Finally, miserably, she opened one eye, glared, closed it, and sank back on her pillow.

Annie breathed in deeply of the hot, swirling air in her shower.

"Need any help?" Max caroled just outside the shower door.

"I'll call if I do," she sang back sweetly.

"Always ready to help out my fellow man."

When she'd dried off with the thick, fluffy blue towel Max had thoughtfully draped over the wicker clothes hamper, Annie slipped into a yellow-and-blue patterned skirt and a soft yellow cotton pullover. She brushed her hair very carefully to avoid the swelling behind her right ear, wiped the steamed mirror and peered at her head. Well, she looked normal. No visible bumps or bruises. She probed the skin behind her ear and winced. It still smarted, but she couldn't help smiling as she listened to Max bustling cheerfully around the kitchen. When she came in, he waved her to a seat.

"Chef Darling at work. Observe and enjoy, Madame."

Potatoes and onions sizzled invitingly in the skillet, and Max whipped the eggs to a froth.

"One exquisite frittata coming up."

They carried their plates to the wooden-planked table on the balcony outside the kitchen.

As Max poured the coffee, he stooped to kiss the top of her head. "Just a preview of *one* of the myriad pleasures of connubial life."

"Oh, Max, why aren't you willing to invest this kind of effort and energy into a job?"

His coffee cup paused midway to his mouth. His eyes widened. "What an obscene thought."

"I'll have you know I'm serious."

"I know. That is both your great charm and your great failing, my sweet. You are very serious." He sighed. "Annie, don't you believe in fairy godmothers?"

"Not really. I believe in hard work and devotion to duty."

He sighed lugubriously and tried again. "Annie, what if I—or your fairy godmother—slipped a freighter ticket to Singapore under that four-leaf clover? Couldn't you take it and run away with me?"

"No."

"Why not?"

"I wouldn't have earned it."

"Look. Think about it this way. You know the guy who won thirty million dollars in the New York raffle?"

"What about him?"

"Is it immoral for him to accept his winnings from a raffle?"

"Well, no, I guess not."

"Annie, look on me as a great, big, loving raffle ticket!"

She was fashioning a withering retort when the police car pulled up in front of the tree house. She slowly put down her coffee cup.

"Remember, we were here all night," Max said calmly.

Chief Saulter walked heavily up the steps. He looked tired, and Annie wondered if he had been up most of the night. She rose to meet him.

The police chief looked at her intently, then past her at Max.

"We're having breakfast," she offered.

"I want an account of your movements last night."

"My client has nothing to say, Chief Saulter."

"Innocent people don't need that kind of advice."

"Innocent people need the protection of angels, Chief Saulter."

Annie and the chief both looked at Max in amazement.

He smiled fatuously. "Did I understand you to ask for Miss Laurance's movements last night?"

"That is correct."

"Then I can tell you very simply. She was here. I was here. We were here all evening." He couldn't have been more insouciant ice skating at Rockefeller Plaza.

"All night?"

"Most of it. We went to the bookstore for a few minutes about eight. Why?"

"Any phone calls? Anybody come by to visit?"

"One phone call. We didn't answer it. Nobody came by. Why the questions about last night, Chief?"

The chief's chilly eyes turned to Annie, who was pretending to nibble on her toast. "You know Harriet Edelman well?"

"Moderately," Annie answered pleasantly. She repressed an image of the bloodied mess she'd last seen in Elliot's living room. "I had an autograph party for her a couple of weeks ago."

"She was murdered last night."

"Oh my God . . ."

"Where? What happened? Do you know who did it?"

"She was found in the living room."

Annie saw the trap, and skirted it. "She lived alone. Who found her?"

"It didn't happen at her house." The chief spoke grudgingly, his suspicious eyes intent on Annie's face.

"Where?" Max asked dutifully.

"At Elliot Morgan's house."

"Good grief," Annie exclaimed, "what in the world was she doing there?"

The Porsche jolted up a sandy track. "At least he didn't arrest me. Max, did you get rid of that towel?"

"That towel is well-wrapped around a heavy rock and resting at the bottom of a lagoon on the opposite side of the island. Even if it floated up, there's nothing to connect it to you."

"Right. But I wonder if my bike tires left a track under the bridge."

"Anybody could have used your bike. The shed is never locked."

She glanced at him grimly. "Is that counsel's argument for the accused?"

"We are going to make sure somebody else stands in the dock."

That sounded like a swell idea to her. This morning she intended to ask a hell of a lot of uncomfortable questions in her search for the real killer. Philip Marlowe, look out.

The red Porsche curved through the twelve-foot-tall bronze gates of the Island Hills Golf Course. The crack of a cleanly hit ball carried through the fresh morning air. Annie thought regretfully of her own clubs and wished she and Max could be walking down the broad wooden steps at the Club to the first tee. Max, of course, was a scratch golfer. A club tournament tennis player. An expert scuba diver. A fixed-wing pilot. Talk about a misspent youth!

"Nice," he commented laconically as they drove past one imaginative home after another: a modernistic two-story gray house built on four levels, the highest flat-roofed and topped by a deck; a modern version of an antebellum mansion, with slender Doric columns supporting two verandahs; a California Mission stucco in the palest of pinks. "My God—"

Annie laughed. "This is the one that drives the local homeowners crazy, but it's the natural outgrowth of not being able to have your cake and eat it, too. The zoning laws here are very particular about how many square feet, maximum height, things like that. But the local board very proudly fixed it so that there could be 'imaginative variety with artistic integrity.' They said they didn't want everything to look alike like Hilton Head, where all homes are built of wood and weathered to a natural gray."

The Porsche crept to a halt as Max craned for a better view. It was a two, no, three, could it be four stories? The building materials alternated between chrome, bronze, and quartz. Rooms thrust out at eccentric angles, and the whole was topped with a thirty-foot round tower of gleaming aluminum.

"I'd like to meet that owner," Max breathed.

"So would everybody else. It was built by Marguerite Dumaney."

He whistled softly. The aging Hollywood star's name was legendary. Checkout counter tabloids had whispered in recent years that she was a female Howard Hughes.

The Porsche moved ahead, curved around a bend, and arrived at the entrance to 603 Cormorant Road.

This home was, quite simply, lovely. Perfectly suited to the landscape, it was constructed of the unassuming native pine, softly weathered to a dusky gray. But it still had an unmistakable aura of elegance. The three-story entryway had a glass panel running from ground level to the roof beside the nine-foot front door. Beautifully tended beds of white-topped asters, tall goldenrod, and camphorweed fronted the path.

As she got out, Max gave her a thumbs-up. Then he called after her, "Remember—keep at least two feet from each subject, don't hesitate to use the mace, and make sure they know I'm waiting."

Emma Clyde wore a pink-and-white seersucker skirt and blouse and looked like summer candy. She was surprised to see Annie but gracious. Her lips, carefully painted a bright coral, parted in a smile, but the smile didn't reach her cornflower blue eyes.

"How nice of you to drop by, dear." A pause. "You know, I do write in the mornings."

They stood in the main entryway. The green and gilt terrazzo floor glinted in the flood of morning sunshine through the roof-high glass pane. Water fell musically from a corner fountain, artfully constructed to look like a miniature Hawaiian waterfall. Sprays of orchids filled crimson-and-gold Chinese vases. Annie remembered reading about Emma's prize collection of orchids. Shades of Nero Wolfe.

"I'm sorry to intrude, but I had to see you."

It was like being a kid and going up to the top of a slide that rivaled the Empire State Building. She felt that same mixture of utter exhilaration laced with fear. Was this how The Saint felt when he began an exploit?

"You *had* to see me?"

"You see, I really don't know what to do," Annie began.

Emma waited, blue eyes alert and calculating.

"Elliot sent me the material he was going to use Sunday night."

Emma continued to wait. She might look like summer candy, but she emanated an unyielding, icy solidity. The entryway had seemed warm and sunny when Annie first began. Now she felt as if she'd stepped into a deep freezer.

"I don't know what to do about it."

"Why ask me?"

"Some of the information concerns you." Did she intend to stand there like a sphinx all morning? Damn the woman, why didn't she react?

Emma's face looked like a mud mask in a beauty salon.

One more try. "Look, Emma, I don't want to go to the police with this. I thought if you could explain it to me, I wouldn't reveal the information about you. After all, surely what Elliot wrote can't be true."

"Of course, it isn't true," Emma responded. "The Coast Guard ruled it was an accidental drowning."

So that was it, the death of her second husband. What was it Max had picked up from the man who ran the bait shop? Rumor had it that Enrique Morales was secretly meeting a Cuban girl.

"Did the Coast Guard know about the Cuban girl?"

If it seemed chilly before, the atmosphere dropped to glacial in the elegant foyer. The soft splash of the waterfall was the only sound for a long moment.

Emma asked harshly, "How much do you want?"

"Want? Oh no, Emma, I don't want money. I'm just trying to understand what happened."

"It's all in the Coast Guard report." Emma's voice was clipped. "Ricky and I had a few drinks after dinner at the Sans Souci Club. When we came back to the boat, he said he wanted to stay on deck for some fresh air. I went below to bed."

"You didn't hear anything? A splash? A cry for help?"

"As I said, we'd had a few drinks, and I'd worked hard that day. I was tired. I fell asleep immediately, and I didn't realize anything was wrong until the steward brought my breakfast. I asked him to call Ricky for me, and he came back and said his cabin hadn't been slept in."

So they didn't share a cabin.

Emma had asked the steward to call her husband. Why didn't she call him? Was it because the very rich avoid all possible exertion? Or was it that she knew his cabin would be empty and wanted to get the search under way?

"Why did you want to talk to him so early in the morning?"

For just an instant, that smooth mask shifted. No one had ever asked her that question.

Annie knew then, just as surely as if she'd seen it happen, that Emma Clyde came up behind her non-swimmer husband on the early morning of Sunday, October 16, and pushed him over the low railing to drown.

"I wanted to talk to him about some investments."

On Sunday morning?

Her immediate assumption that Annie had blackmail in mind seemed to indicate she was accustomed to blackmail. But Elliot must have had more than suspicion if he were blackmailing Emma: Blackmail had to be based on more than speculation. There had to be a threat, something concrete Elliot had learned that could cause the investigation to be reopened, perhaps lead to a murder charge against Emma.

"The steward must not have been aboard that night."

"That's right."

"Did he normally have Saturday evenings off? What about the rest of the crew?"

"Only the steward and the cook remain aboard when we are anchored. I'd given them the evening off because Ricky and I had plans on shore."

"But the steward didn't go ashore, did he?" Here was Elliot's source, the steward or the cook. Someone heard cries or saw Ricky and Emma on deck together. Elliot had found a witness to the murder of Enrique Morales.

Emma didn't change expression, but there was a sudden relaxation of tension. Annie's question must have revealed that she didn't possess the critical piece of information.

"It's always heartbreaking when such a dreadful accident occurs. Isn't it, dear?"

Those shrewd blue eyes dissected Annie now, probing, weighing.

The silence between them was ugly, freighted with unspoken meanings.

"I'm sure you know exactly how I feel. And how upsetting it is to be the subject of vicious gossip. You, of all people, should understand that."

It couldn't have been plainer if she'd shouted it. Emma saw a special kinship between them. Emma believed that she had pushed Ambrose Bailey to his death.

Annie clenched her hands. "Does everybody think I killed my uncle?"

"Hell, no. That's just her guilty conscience in action."

"She meant that everyone was talking about me." Annie felt as if something slimy had touched her. She had been so happy on Broward's Rock, confident of her place in her own version of St.

Mary Mead. Instead, smiling faces hid ugly suspicions. The reality was a Ruth Rendell world.

As the Porsche ran beneath the interlocking branches of the yellow pines, Max reached over and squeezed her hands. "Don't let an old battle-axe upset you."

"I thought I had a lot of friends on Broward's Rock."

"You do. Lots."

Annie recalled the sensation seekers at the shop yesterday, and Chief Saulter. "Who?"

Max scrambled. "Ingrid Jones. And Ben Parotti. And Capt. Mac. Me. Look at it. Your very own four musketeers."

She knew who pictured himself as D'Artagnan. She managed a bleak smile.

"That's a girl. Don't let the bastards get you down. Come on, you're one up, not Emma Clyde. You got a lot out of her, and what you got is damn interesting."

She twisted in the seat. "Max, this changes everything. Elliot must have been a blackmailer."

The Porsche slowed for a stop sign, and Max turned back onto the main road. He glanced at his map and drove past the harbor shops off to the right, then followed the curve of the island to a sign pointing to beach houses. He turned right on Blue Magnolia. As he braked, he said abruptly, "No, that can't be right."

"Why not? I'd bet my first edition of *The Murder of Roger Ackroyd* that Emma's been blackmailed."

"What's the point of blackmail?"

"You pay to keep someone quiet."

"Right. But Elliot was going to stand up and reveal all to the world—or at least to the Regulars."

Annie got out of the car slowly. Then she poked her head back inside. "Maybe this was Elliot's fancy way of putting on the pressure for a bigger payoff."

She mulled that over as she walked up the oyster-shell path, then she brought herself in hand. She'd better play this next interview better than the last.

A battered station wagon stood in the drive. The zinnias in the front bed were choked with weeds and the weeping willow beside the porch desperately needed a trim. Yesterday's newspaper rested unopened next to an empty bait bucket, which still smelled like chopped squid.

Her reception this time was warm if puzzled. Chunky Hal Douglas, unshaven, wearing a soiled t-shirt and torn tennis shorts, offered coffee, beer, or a drink. Unlike Emma's elegant home, Hal's was furnished with happenstance furniture, a shabby maple sofa, mismatched easy chairs, and a card table in one corner stacked with old magazines, *Geo, Esquire, Playboy,* and *Omni.* He tried frantically to straighten the litter as he led her to the den, sweeping a pile of newspapers onto the floor and grabbing up a damp beach towel, tennis shoes, and a racquet.

He was boyishly friendly, and she hated going into her spiel. What a way to kill a friendship. How do investigative reporters manage? The thrill of power had to outweigh the human need for approbation. A trade-off.

Annie took a deep breath. She'd be as forthright as Dagliesh. "No, Hal, thanks. Nothing for me. Actually, I hate to be here."

That was true.

His round face compressed into a worried frown. "What's wrong? Can I help you? Is that cop bothering you?"

"That's the problem. And the thing is, I've got some information that could get him off my back, but I *hate* to give it to him."

"Don't hesitate, Annie. You can't protect anyone in a murder investigation."

Every kind word he uttered made her feel more like a louse. Another word and she would turn tail and run, but if she didn't see it through, she'd find herself in the island jail with the centipedes and roaches.

Annie blurted, "Elliot mailed a copy of his talk to me."

Hal's open face abruptly looked a good deal less pleasant.

"I don't want to tell Saulter the stuff about you. I thought maybe you could explain it away and then I won't have to."

For the first time, she realized how big a man he was—tall, powerfully put together, with bearlike shoulders and arms. He was maybe twenty pounds overweight, which gave his face disarming roundness. He might be soft, but he was clearly strong. She slipped a hand into the pocket of her skirt and gripped the oblong, two-inch container of mace.

"I don't want Kelly to know." He lifted those massive hands and rubbed his bristly jowls.

"I can understand that," she murmured.

Hal lifted his head, his eyes intent. "Does anyone else know?"

Careful, Annie.

"Just Max."

He whirled around, stepped toward the mantel. One hand swept out, knocking off a half dozen books. When he turned back to face her, he was breathing heavily.

She braced herself. If he took one step toward her, she'd pull out the mace. Surreptitiously, she flicked off the safety guard.

"Goddammit." Hal spoke jerkily. "She left town. That's all there was to it. Lenora left town."

"People said you'd been fighting."

His head wobbled on its thick neck. He no longer looked like everybody's nice guy. He looked like a fighter who'd taken one punch too many. "Elliot got that wrong, the sorry bastard. There wasn't anybody to see. We were at the cabin in the mountains. No neighbors for miles, but she'd been into town a lot, picked up guys, like she always did. I went fishing, and, when I came back, she was gone. No note. Nothing. Some bastard came by and got her."

There was nothing good-humored about that pudgy face now. It was twisted with remembered pain and hatred.

"You say Lenora went away. Surely you've heard from her since then?"

Hal smoothed out his face, evened his breathing. "No reason for her to get in touch. I'd told her, one more man and we were through. One more and that was it."

"Where was the cabin?"

"Near Tahoe." He moved restlessly, rubbed his hands against his thighs.

"Have you ever told Kelly any of this?"

"I don't want Kelly to know." There was a plea in his eyes. "And it doesn't matter, not for the two of us. I got a divorce in Tijuana. I'm all finished with Lenora."

"Where did you meet Lenora, Hal?"

"What the hell difference does it make?" Hearing the edge in his voice, he said, "In St. Louis. At school. But what difference does it make? It's all over with her." He forced an ineffective smile. "Annie, this was all no big deal. And it's been over for ages."

"Sure, Hal. I just wanted to hear it from you, not the way Elliot had written it."

Hal's eyes bored into hers. "What did he say about Lenora?"

"That nobody's seen her in years."

It was quiet for a long moment. Annie could hear his breathing, see the pulse pounding in his throat.

"Hell, Lenora's having a ball somewhere. Like she always did." But his eyes were so empty.

"Sure," Annie said again. "Sure."

As she walked down the path toward the Porsche, Annie wondered how hard it had been to dig a grave miles from that lonely cabin.

They took the container of Kentucky Fried Chicken to the beach. Max looked suspiciously at each piece as Annie emptied the barrel onto a paper plate.

"Perhaps we aren't compatible," he mourned, setting up camp chairs from the Porsche's trunk. Trickling sand through her fingers, Annie thought of Mary Roberts Rinehart and a trip she had made in 1925 into the desert near Cairo. At night her party rested in tents decorated with scenes from tombs. Oriental rugs covered the sand in their dining and bedroom tents. Dinner included soup, appetizer, roast with vegetables, salad with quail and dessert. Then fruit, Turkish coffee and candy. Gourmet picnicking. Max would have fit right in.

"I love Quarterpounders, too."

He winced.

Annie bit into the lushly crusted half-thigh, half-breast while Max turned an oddly shaped piece around uncertainly.

"Was this chicken double-jointed?"

"It provides variety—and surprise," Annie retorted, mouth full.

With an air of incalculable bravery, Max began to eat.

By meal's end, they had admitted to irreconcilable culinary tastes.

Max liked sushi.

Annie adored fried pies. Peach, not cherry.

Max admired nouvelle cuisine.

Annie was passionate about Texas chili.

Max detested pretzels.

Annie loathed quiche.

Then they walked, hand in hand, up the beach, stopping to look at sandpipers' tracks, turning over a shell-encrusted piece of driftwood and skirting the tendrils of a Portuguese man-of-war.

It was great fun, but it couldn't last.

Already Annie was looking ahead. "Time to get back to the fray," she said brightly. "Sherlock Annie continues in relentless pursuit of wrongdoers." Her voice was lighter than her mood. It was a good deal more fun to read about bearding suspects in their lairs than to track them down.

"That's a girl. And, remember, I'll be there, if you need me."

Just like Tommy and Tuppence.

Sort of.

Twelve

JEFF FARLEY stood unsmiling on the porch. The two-story, weathered wooden house on pilings overlooked a dune bright with October color, the pale violet of butterfly peas and the shimmering gold of camphorweed. Beyond the dune, the beach stretched two hundred peaceful yards to the ocean. No other dwelling was within view. Annie stood halfway up the wooden steps, clinging to the railing, and the wind off the ocean touched her with the light fresh scent of salt. This was a choice beachfront exposure on a perfect autumn day, yet there was a sense of darkness and isolation here. Did it come from the almost feral gleam in Jeff Farley's light brown eyes? He didn't look much like an overage cheerleader now, though he wore white duck pants and a white knit V-neck pullover with navy trim. He stood rigidly, his arms tight against his sides.

"I need to talk to you, Jeff." Annie raised her voice against the rumble of the surf.

"We're busy." His voice was flat and hostile. He was turning away to close the door on her.

"Then you want me to give Elliot's information to Chief Saulter?"

Jeff stiffened, then jerked around to face her. He lunged toward the ladder.

"What the hell are you talking about?"

"Look, Jeff, I've come out here to give you and Janis a chance to explain. If you can't or won't, I don't have any choice but to go to Saulter. You must see that."

The screen door behind Jeff burst open, and Janis rushed to the railing.

Annie's eyes widened. The right side of the girl's face was painfully swollen. A reddish-purple bruise spread from cheekbone to jawline, hideously distinct against her pallid skin.

Jeff glanced distractedly toward his wife. "Get back inside."

Janis looked at him fearfully, but she took one step, another, then ran to the edge of the stairs. "Oh, Annie, please don't tell. He can't help it. He doesn't mean it, it just happens sometimes. He gets so mad, and that's what they did to him when he was a little boy. That and worse. They burned him—"

Jeff caught her from behind and whirled her around. The back of his hand hit her face with a stinging slap.

Janis screamed as the blow struck that inflamed skin.

Annie yelled, "Stop that! Stop it!" Pulling the mace out of her pocket, she charged up the porch steps.

He was using his fists now, raining blows on Janis's bent back as she huddled against the wall of the beach house.

A stream of spray from the mace container caught the side of Jeff's face. He staggered back, his hands clawing at his face. A spasm of coughing and choking convulsed his body.

Janis, blood trickling from her mouth, turned toward Annie, arms flailing, and lunged vengefully at her, screaming incoherent curses as she rained blows on her astonished protectress. Max shot up the steps and caught Janis by the arms, imprisoning her.

"It's just mace. He'll be all right. My God, Janis, I had to stop him. He was hurting you!"

"He didn't mean it. You've got to understand. He doesn't mean to hurt me. He loves me," she whimpered brokenly. "You can't know what he's endured—"

"Did Jeff threaten Elliot when he knew Elliot was going to tell everyone?"

"That wouldn't matter," Janis said desperately. "It doesn't matter what he said—or what he does to me. Jeff wouldn't kill anyone. That's crazy. He wouldn't kill Elliot—or Jill or Harriet. Never."

"But he beats you," Annie said wearily.

"He doesn't mean it." Janis held out trembling hands. "Please, please don't tell anyone. If you do—"

"Shut up, Janis. Don't be a bloody fool." Jeff's face was mottled with rage and pain.

"Janis, don't stay here with him. Come with us. You can stay with me," Annie offered.

Janis wiped the blood away from her chin. Her eyes filled with tears, but she shook her head. She wouldn't come with them no matter how they protested.

"You'll have to get him to a doctor," Annie said urgently, "or one of these days, he will kill you."

But Janis wouldn't leave him.

"We'll have to tell Saulter," Max said grimly as they drove back to the main part of the island.

"If it gets in the papers, they'll be finished."

"Finished? What do you mean?"

"As writers."

"What does wife beating have to do with writing?"

"Probably not much—except in their case. They write for children. Do you think a children's publisher is going to keep an author who regularly bloodies his wife? Think again, Mr. Darling."

"Oh. So they have a hell of a motive. Both of them."

"Not her. She can't do anything without him."

"May I remind you that she was ready to tear your eyes out when she thought he was threatened. What do you think she would do to somebody like Elliot who was going to spread all this out for the enlightenment of the Sunday Night Regulars?"

"Punch him. At the least. Still, I can't believe Janis would have the gumption to figure out such a clever plan. But Jeff could—and she'd never give him away."

As the Porsche zoomed away from the beach house, Annie said tightly, "You know, I'd almost give Elliot's murderer a gold star— if it weren't for Jill and Harriet and Uncle Ambrose."

They were soon arguing over their next stop, Max plumping for Kelly Rizzoli, Annie preferring Capt. Mac, when a siren shrilled behind them.

Max pulled over. "Thirty miles an hour. I swear, I was going thirty miles an hour."

But Broward's Rock's only motorcycle cop was having a Mannix day. He wasn't thinking speed limits.

He dismounted and leaned down to look past Max.

"Chief Saulter wants to see you, Miss."

Chief Saulter didn't want Max there, but Max wouldn't budge.

"You can talk to my client only if I am present, Chief." Max folded his hands across his chest and looked immovable.

"I can put your client in jail, Counselor."

"What charge?"

"How about first-degree murder?"

"I'll have her out on bail in two hours. You don't have a scrap of evidence."

The police chief clenched his jaws and built a teepee with his fingers. With a wrenching effort, he tried conciliation.

"Ms. Laurance, I just want some cooperation out of you. If you didn't kill the vet and Morgan and Edelman and your uncle, you should want to help the authorities."

"Four people. You honestly think I killed four people!"

"Somebody did, and you profit, young lady. You profit."

"Actually, Chief, Ms. Laurance doesn't have a financial motive." Miraculously, Max sounded casual and good-humored.

"Sure she does." Saulter ticked it off on his fingers. "She's broke. She inherits her uncle's estate, including the bookshop—and you know how she feels about that bookshop. Goodbye, Uncle. The rest of them are protection. Somehow Morgan figures out she shoved Ambrose into the drink and that spelled finish for him. Plus Morgan is threatening to run her out of business with a rent she couldn't pay. The vet is knocked off to get the medicine, and that damn Edelman busybody poked her nose into a buzz saw."

Max ran a hand through his hair and shook his head placidly.

"Nope. You're off base. See, if Annie wants money—or needs money—all she has to do is marry me." His dark eyes glinted. "And, after all, Chief, that's a lot easier than going around slugging, darting, and bludgeoning—and guaranteed to be more fun."

Saulter opened his mouth, and Annie knew he intended to ask tartly just how much money Max had. As his eyes moved from Max to the window with the red Porsche in view, he abruptly closed his mouth.

"I intend neither to kill for money—nor marry for money," Annie said acidly. Her counselor was finding this altogether too amusing for her taste.

"You never told anybody here on Broward's Rock about this fellow?"

"No, but—"

"Annie, tell the man truly. Could you marry me anytime you want to?"

"Yes, but—"

"So no motive." Resting his case, Max lifted his hands, palms upward. Annie glared.

"If you two can direct your minds back to the murders, and away from me, we might get somewhere. Chief, we believe the same person who killed Elliot murdered my uncle. Somebody has stolen his manuscript."

Saulter stiffened like a dog on point. "His book about the murderers who got away with it?"

For the first time since the lights went out in Death On Demand, Annie felt a glimmer of hope. Saulter knew about Uncle Ambrose's book. Surely he would understand the implications of a missing manuscript. She longed irrationally to present him with a copy of *The Bay Psalm Murder.*

"Exactly. Max and I figure that he found out about a crime involving somebody here on the island and—"

"Naw. I'd talked to Ambrose about his murders. He was interested in the Armbruster case." Saulter's forehead wrinkled. "And the Vinson suicide, so-called. And he mentioned the Winningham thing." The sudden flash of interest in those agate eyes faded.

"None of that has a thing to do with anybody here. That's a false trail."

"The manuscript is missing."

"Sure." He might as well have said, "Good try."

"Look, Chief, you aren't going to pin this on me. If you won't help, I guess Max and I will have to find the murderer by ourselves. But you can at least listen to what we've discovered—"

Max was semaphoring messages with his eyebrows, but she was too angry to pay any attention.

"To begin with, Emma Clyde, Hal Douglas, and Jeff and Janis Farley all had terrific motives to get rid of Elliot."

"Is that so?" Saulter's tone wasn't encouraging, and Annie knew he was thinking in particular of Emma Clyde's considerable wealth and power. A leading citizen like Emma could do a lot to influence next year's elections.

"That *is* so. Emma Clyde killed her second husband. She pushed him off her boat and let him drown. And Hal Douglas killed his wife and buried her in the mountains in California, and—"

"Young lady!" Saulter boomed.

"Annie, my God!" Max cried.

She raised her voice resolutely: "And Jeff Farley beats his wife."

Saulter's palm thumped on his desk and the in-box slewed sideways. In the silence that followed, he scrutinized Annie with chilly contempt.

"Just how do you know all this, Ms. Laurance?"

Abruptly, Annie understood Max's semaphore. Oh, what an incredibly appropriate word "dumbstruck" is. She stared at Saulter. She wished she'd been born a deaf-mute. No, look what happened in *The Spiral Staircase*.

"Come now, Ms. Laurance, you're helping us quite a lot. But how do you know this?"

Annie picked words as carefully as footfalls on a canyon ledge.

"I keep telling you. Elliot Morgan had his big scene all planned, and everyone knew it was coming. Sunday night he was

going to tell about a lot of very unpleasant things that people
didn't want known." She described Elliot's planned book. "You
see, the things he was going to talk about were criminal activities."

For the first time, she had Saulter's attention. "Criminal activities by all these people?" Saulter leaned forward. If he had been a
dog, his nose would have twitched.

"The people who were at your bookstore—Mr. and Mrs. Farley,
Emma Clyde, Hal Douglas, Kelly Rizzoli, Capt. McElroy, Harriet
Edelman, Fritz Hemphill—and you, Ms. Laurance."

The last, her name, had a full, rolling sound like a tumbril on a
cobbled Paris street.

That night in Santa Fe. Emily had been wrong—as the law sees
right and wrong—but Annie had never regretted helping her. And
she'd do it again without hesitation.

"No, sir. Not me. Or Capt. McElroy. We were the only people
there, besides Ingrid, who aren't writers. And Max, of course. But
Max doesn't count because he only happened to be there by accident that night. Elliot made it painfully clear to all of us that his
book was going to expose the criminal minds of some well-known
mystery writers."

"So you expect me to believe these accusations you've made
are part of what Elliot intended to say?"

"Exactly."

"So what did Elliot have on the rest of them?"

Wham.

Annie opened her mouth, closed it, and remembered the last
fish she'd hauled gasping out of the Atlantic. Brother, talk about
empathy.

Max cleared his throat. "My client isn't at liberty to disclose
that information at the present moment, Chief."

Saulter's head swung irritably toward Max. "Why the hell not?
She couldn't wait to unload on the others." He swivelled back to
Annie. "Come on, what's the dope on the rest of them—Edelman,
Hemphill, Rizzoli?"

Annie shook her head decisively. "No, Max understands. I can't give you any further information until I have verified it."

They both looked at her blankly.

"It's a matter of principle." Hildegarde Withers could not have been more priggish. "Elliot was not trustworthy. Therefore, I can't possibly reveal the information he gave me until I have the opportunity to interview the accused person and confirm or deny Elliot's accusations. In our system of government, in our world view, all are innocent until proven guilty. Well, that's the way it is with me." A ringing speech, worthy of Perry Mason. Annie stood up. "So Max and I will get back to work. That's what we were doing, Chief, when your motorcycle cop so rudely stopped us."

Alas, Saulter wasn't quite that easy or that dumb.

"Ms. Laurance, just one more thing."

She paused at the doorway.

"You said Elliot gave you this material."

The sinking feeling swept Annie again. One peril past and on to the next. It was like surviving a ten-foot wave and looking up to see a fifteen-footer.

"When did he give it to you, and where is it?"

"When?"

Saulter didn't pong. He waited.

If she admitted the disk came in the mail on Monday, the chief could attack her for hiding evidence. Hiding it? He could accuse her of losing it, because that's precisely what she had done. And she couldn't claim to have a typewritten copy, or she would have to account for that. She had *nada* to show Saulter. If she told him about the disk, he'd want to know what happened to it—and if he ever had any hint that she'd been in Elliot's house when Harriet was killed, Annie was one plucked goose.

She took a deep breath. "He didn't exactly give it to me."

"No?" The question was chillingly genial.

"My client has nothing further to say," Max interposed.

Saulter shook his head. "Oh, no, Mr. Darling. She's going to answer this one. Or I'm going to arrest her as a material witness."

Desperately, Annie glanced around the chief's office. A battered old Remington sat on a typing table. She remembered the outer office. Two secondhand desks for his two policemen, one desk for his secretary. Not a VDT in sight.

When in doubt, tell some of the truth.

"Elliot mailed me a floppy disk. You know, he was used to working on computers." She carefully did not suggest the disk had been produced on his own computer, and maybe, God willing, even in this electronic age, Chief Saulter might not realize that the material recorded on a floppy disk using one particular program and machine could not be read by any incompatible program and different machine. "Anyway, I read the disk—and I was so outraged by what he'd put down that I erased it."

"You what?"

"Erased it." She looked at him inquiringly. "Do you have a computer, Chief Saulter?"

When he shook his head, she felt Max's sigh. She leaned forward. "This is how it works . . ."

Max came out of Parotti's store bearing two Bud Lights.

"Parotti says no strangers came across yesterday."

Annie took the beer and looked puzzled.

"Just making sure," Max explained. "Whoever killed Harriet was already on the island by Sunday or came by private boat."

"Whoever killed Harriet was here Saturday night because the person who killed Harriet also killed Jill—and Elliot, of course."

"I believe it, but a defense lawyer could make some argument if some strangers arrived Monday."

Annie choked on her beer.

"Pretty weak defense."

Max shook his head. "Annie, did anybody ever tell you that you have mouthitis?"

"It sounds scaly."

"It can be terminal," he said bitterly. "And what the hell are we going to do when Saulter finds out that any disk Elliot produced could be read only on his machine?"

"I read it on my machine," she said stubbornly. "So Elliot must have had access to an Apple."

This time Max choked on his beer.

Annie sipped hers daintily.

"All right, Miss Clever Tongue. What are you going to tell the chief when he discovers that package arrived in the mail on *Monday* morning *after* Elliot's unfortunate demise? I mean, while he's busy charging you with destroying evidence."

Would Saulter check with her mailman? Would he begin to wonder about the accuracy of everything she'd said? Would he talk to somebody like Capt. Mac, who liked to repair computers for fun?

"How much time do you think we have?" she asked grimly.

"The rest of today. Maybe tomorrow."

"Then I suggest we get started."

Thirteen

A GREEN LIZARD clung to the side of the house. The drapes were closed against the sliding glass doors that opened onto the deck. Afternoon sunlight flooded the deck with light and deepened the shadows beneath the eighty-foot sea pines. The only sounds were the occasional rustle as squirrels scampered from limb to limb, the soft thud of falling cones, and the tap of fragrant pine needles against the pitched roof of the house.

Sweat beaded Annie's face, slid down her back and thighs. Actually, it wasn't terribly hot, a pleasant seventy-eight degrees and not humid. The last time she broke into someone's house, the results—for her—were catastrophic. Think of what nearly happened to Grace Kelly in *Rear Window*. But this time she wasn't alone.

She turned her head slightly and whispered, "It looks okay."

Max put out a restraining hand. "I'll scout in front. If I don't see anybody, then I'll knock. You stick tight here and wait for me."

They'd agreed that Harriet's house deserved a once-over. After all, something must have prompted Harriet to show up at Elliot's house at—for her—just the wrong moment.

Had Harriet been suspicious of a particular person? If so, would there be anything in her desk or diary to reflect it? Annie knew she kept a diary. Harriet bought the blank-page books from Death on Demand, never failing to mention each time she did so that all *real* writers had the compulsion to record their thoughts and feelings for posterity.

Ho hum.

But now it might matter.

Annie crept forward and touched the low limb of a live oak. The warm air lapping against her was as soothing as a hot tub.

Today and maybe tomorrow. They had so little time. They still needed to talk to Fritz Hemphill, Capt. Mac, and Kelly Rizzoli. But what good would any of it do? What if they came up with a motive for everyone, but not a single shred of evidence linking a particular person to the murders?

Somewhere there had to be evidence. Real, physical, concrete evidence. How could anyone move unseen and commit three murders? Had Saulter checked to see if anyone out late had seen a car near the Island Hills Veterinary Clinic? But, of course, he would have. He was probably asking all and sundry if they had seen her 1982 blue Volvo.

There wouldn't be any fingerprints at the Clinic, not after that evening when Capt. Mac had so thoroughly demonstrated just what did and did not hold prints.

Would there be fingerprints at Death On Demand? Of course there would be, and everyone could shrug them away. After all, they'd been there many times. All Saulter cared about was her prints on the fuse box.

As for Elliot's house . . . She had that empty feeling that precedes awful knowledge. Had she left prints on the window sill or the floor? She'd scrubbed everything she thought she'd touched. She could always say she'd been at Elliot's for dinner a few weeks earlier. Still, her prints in a hard-to-explain site would be all that Saulter needed to clap her in leg irons. Once again, she felt a terrible impatience to be active. Surely if they looked long enough, hard enough, there would be a clue to reveal the murderer. Where the heck was Max? As if in answer, she heard his rattling knock on Harriet's front door. There was a pause, followed by another loud round of knocking.

In a moment more, he rounded the corner of the house. Annie gestured at him impatiently. He responded with a thumbs-up. Obviously, he was enjoying himself. She could see it in the glint in his dark blue eyes. He probably read *The Saint* as a boy. She'd have to ask him later.

"All clear," he whispered.

They crept across the flagstoned patio, Max in the lead. Annie was irresistibly reminded of playing Cowboys and Indians as a child.

Max tugged on the patio door.

Annie touched his elbow, pointed at the broomstick wedged inside in the door track.

"Was the front door locked?" she asked softly.

"I didn't try. There's a house across the street. It didn't look as though anyone was home, but I thought we'd better try back here."

The McGuires, Annie knew, lived across from Harriet. Mildred McGuire was a Sara Paretsky freak who had given copies of *Deadlock* to all her friends and had named her parrot Boom Boom.

Annie nodded, then motioned to him to follow. Feeling extremely conspicuous, she moved around the side of the house and tried the first door they reached. It opened, and they stepped into a laundry room. Light from the opened door illuminated a windowless, square utility room. Two concrete steps beside the washer and dryer led up to a door into the house.

"I'll bet the kitchen door is open. Hardly anybody locks up."

"Broward's Rock—robber's delight," Max commented drily.

"Until now, we've never had to worry about robbers—or murderers."

The kitchen door was unlocked.

Yesterday afternoon Harriet had left her home with no idea that she would never return. Ivy glistened in the kitchen window in a ceramic gingerbread house. The drainboards were immaculate. Harriet didn't litter. Annie thought regretfully about her own kitchen and the haphazard piling of bags of Fritos, pound cake, and cookies when the breadbox was full.

A recently vaccumed peach-and-cream oriental runner ran the length of the main hall. The living room, shadowy because the periwinkle drapes were drawn, reflected a warmth and taste that seemed oddly at variance with Harriet's abrasive personality. Obviously, she had treasured loveliness: Oil paintings of the Riviera coast hung above an unstained pine mantel holding matching cut glass vases. An ornately carved rosewood grand piano took pride of place before the closed French windows. October issues of *Antiques* and *Architectural Digest* lay on the square rose marble coffee table. The pale blue-and-gray oriental rug repeated the colors in the patterned wallpaper.

Harriet's housekeeping skills were evident throughout the house. No dust marred the butler's table in the entry hall or the mahogany desk in the library. Annie paused before the extensive collection of books on France, Impressionist painting, French cooking, wildflowers, and, of course, mysteries, and admired what appeared to be a complete collection of Rex Stouts. One even looked like a first edition—maybe even autographed—but she resisted the impulse to check.

In Harriet's office, her ITT was neatly hooded, her desk top clear.

Max eagerly pulled open the drawers. Check stubs and bill receipts in the first drawer, insurance policies in the second, publishing records in neat folders in the third.

Annie promptly located a row of cloth-backed books on the bottom shelf of the office bookshelves. Harriet's diaries, neatly numbered on the spine and dated.

She reached down confidently, then paused. The last diary in the row was dated June 23–October 1 of that year.

Obviously Harriet had begun a new diary October 2– but it wasn't on the shelf.

They looked in all the bookshelves. They checked the closets. They peered beneath the furniture and scanned the kitchen.

"Let's try upstairs," Annie suggested. "She probably wrote in it every night when she was ready for bed. That's where it will be."

She started up the stairs. Oyster-gray carpet on the treads. Harriet must not have expected much traffic. Annie, now excruciatingly aware of fingerprints, was careful not to touch the railing, which still glistened from its last polish with lemon oil. Her feeling of intrusion mounted. It seemed obscene for them to be here, poking their noses into Harriet's private domain. They bypassed the two guest bedrooms. Harriet's bedroom was dominated by a white, four-poster French provincial bed with a pink silk spread. A bisque-faced doll with delicate features and painted blue eyes —remarkably like Emma Clyde's—sat atop the matching white chest. Who had given the doll to Harriet? Was it all that remained of her childhood? The doll's delicate white lace dress looked freshly laundered.

Harriet's bedroom was as scrupulously tidy as the rest of the house. Only the warm-up jacket carelessly dropped on the pink silk bedspread indicated anything out of the ordinary. Harriet must have been in a hurry, tossing down the jacket, thinking she would fold it and put it away later.

It didn't take long to search that well-ordered room or the closet with clothes hung so precisely for a wearer who would not return.

Finally, Max shook his head. "It's not here. The diary's not in the damned house."

He was right. Someone had beaten them to it. Once again, a quick, clever, determined figure moved ahead of them, blocking them. Someone else had known Harriet kept a diary—and been determined no one should read it.

They were at the head of the stairs when Max stopped and looked up.

"That's funny. Why should that trapdoor be open—if that's what it is."

"It must lead up to Harriet's widow's walk."

Careful, house-proud Harriet would never have gone off leaving the roof door open. The sunshine pouring in would quickly mark and fade the expensive oriental runner that lay below.

At least, she wouldn't leave it open unless she were in a great hurry.

Annie and Max were neck and neck as they reached the ladder, but Max paused to let Annie swarm up the rungs first.

The widow's walk commanded a magnificent panorama of the marsh, the mudflats, the open sound, and the maritime forest.

Annie's first reaction was surprise at the extent of the view. Her second, a sense of shock.

"Max, she could see both the front and back approaches to Elliot's tree house."

He tugged his crumpled map of the island from his back pocket and traced the curve of the salt marsh. As a crow flew, Harriet's house was on a direct line with Elliot's. Crows and Harriet standing in her widow's walk would not have their vision obscured by the sea pines and live oaks.

"I thought no one was around. Why, Harriet could see everything. She must have seen me come—and climb in that window."

Max reached down and picked up the pearl-inlaid binoculars and held them out to her.

Raising them to her eyes, she focused on the tree house. The kitchen window leapt to her eyes, every detail distinct.

"And look at this."

Annie whirled around.

Max held a Minolta camera.

Binoculars. Camera.

They both spoke at once.

"Max, do you suppose . . ."

"Annie, I'll bet . . ."

They turned and looked toward Elliot's tree house.

Annie felt like the Porsche had a big red *X* painted on it. She wasn't cut out for a life of crime—or even one of concealing evidence. She was uncomfortably aware of her purse, which held Harriet's film. Any way you cut it, that film was material evidence.

"Look, Max, we *have* to take that camera to Saulter."

"Perhaps you'd like me to present him your head on a platter, too? That camera's staying in the trunk until we can get to the mainland and get those photographs developed. We'll take the ferry over as soon as we finish talking to the suspects." On that point, he was immovable.

On one thing they did agree. Harriet didn't have the Minolta in the widow's walk as decorative art. She was prepared to take pictures. Presumably, she had seen Annie's arrival and photographed it.

"But the killer came, too."

"We don't know when," Max explained patiently. "She dropped the camera, scrambled downstairs so fast she just threw her jacket on the bed. She left the binoculars and camera in the widow's walk, and the trapdoor open. She was in a hurry, Annie. She was ready to confront you and haul you off to Saulter. Did she get the killer's picture, too? We've got to be sure before we let Saulter have that film."

The evening ferry didn't cross until six. Plenty of time to do their other interviews.

She finally tracked Fritz Hemphill to the tenth hole of the Island Hills Golf Course. She waited in the shade of a yellow pine just short of the green until he sank a thirteen-foot putt. He was playing alone.

It was a gorgeous day for golf, and Fritz looked perfectly at home on the exquisitely manicured course. In his pale yellow slacks, white ribbed pullover, and white golf shoes, he looked every inch the country club golfer, except for his short, crisp crew cut.

As he bent to retrieve his ball, Annie called out, "May I walk to the next tee with you?"

He pocketed the ball and waved her to the cart.

"No walking permitted, but I'd be glad to have you along for the ride." Despite the pleasantness of his voice, there was no mistaking the wariness in his eyes.

"Fritz, I might as well come right to the point."

The cart whirred onto the golf path.

"Elliot sent me a copy of what he intended to say Sunday night."

"So?"

"You know what he was going to say about you."

Fritz pulled a cigarette from his pocket, put it in his mouth, lit it, then blew out a stream of smoke.

"No. What was he going to say?"

It was like taking a step in the dark and missing a tread.

Annie spun through the brief number of facts she knew about Fritz. The very brief number.

Number one. He was an ex-cop.

That gave him his credibility and was a good part of the reason for his success. A cop telling it the way it is for cops. His hero cop, Dan Lundy, always fought against urban corruption and won. Fritz chiseled his prose with the gritty reality of a Joseph Wambaugh.

"If what you did came out, you might end up in jail."

The cart jolted to a stop. Fritz ignored her as he slid out and reached back to pick up his bag. As he slung the bag over his shoulder, he looked directly at her.

With a feeling of surprise, she realized she'd never looked into his eyes before. They were almost black and flat, like the eyes of a squid.

"Nobody ever proved a thing." His thin mouth stretched in an empty smile. "Funny thing is, Annie, dead men don't talk."

"He did it." Annie was adamant.

Max held up both hands. "No favorites yet," he protested. "We still haven't talked to Capt. Mac or Kelly. Besides, my money's on Emma Clyde. That is one tough broad."

"Max, you don't know how sinister it was. He snarled out of the side of his mouth, just like Al Capone." She paused portentously. "Besides, he was the only one who wasn't upset. And he said he didn't *know* what Elliot was going to say. He just waited for me to tell him—and the murderer is the only one who knows I didn't have a chance to look at those files."

"Right. But then again Hemphill may have learned a long time ago that the less you ante, the less you can lose."

"Maybe," Annie murmured doubtfully. "But we need to check into it. We've got to see if we can link Fritz to some dead men."

Max pounded the steering wheel once, hard. "By God, maybe it's just that simple. He was a cop. Maybe it was some kind of shootout, and maybe there are some cops or somebody who suspect Fritz didn't have to shoot. Something of that kind."

"Because why else would he stop being a cop? Fritz isn't old enough to retire like Capt. Mac. I wonder if he's really made all of his money from books?"

"Write all of that down," Max urged. "When we finish talking to everybody, we'll get onto these things. Like who might have seen Emma Clyde give the big push."

"We're getting some place, Max. We really are." She glanced down at her purse. "We need to get that film developed. Why don't we hire a boat?"

"Saulter'd be sure you were escaping and he'd haul you off to jail. Just be patient, Annie. Six o'clock."

She glanced at her watch. Two. Four hours to go.

The Porsche curved around Hook Point and turned onto the main road.

As they eased forward to a stop sign, their argument began again. Who should they see first, Capt. Mac or Kelly Rizzoli?

Fourteen

CAPT. MAC BEAMED. "Annie, this is an unexpected pleasure."

He was the first person that day to evidence any pleasure whatsoever in her arrival. She hated to replace his smile with a glower, but she wanted to do it before she got inside. Annie Laurance's progress in the winning of enemies and antagonists. How did Peter McKimsey do it? Subtly, Annie my girl, and with charm.

"I wanted to talk to you before I went to see Chief Saulter."

"Sure. Be glad to help." He looked over her head as he stepped out onto the front porch. "Isn't that your young man's car out there?"

"He isn't my young man."

"Oh, so there's hope for us old dogs yet. Hey there, Darling. Come on up."

They found themselves shepherded briskly around the side of the house to the patio and offered mint juleps. Capt. Mac's patio was the ultimate in comfort, the white plastic webbed furniture scattered around the figure-eight pool, the shiny black, obviously new outdoor barbecue without any stains of weather or salt corrosion, the woven hammock which swung invitingly in the dappled shade of the spreading live oak. Not a single weed marred the perfection of the flowerbeds of late-blooming marigolds and zinnias. No effort or expense had been spared.

Capt. Mac returned with the juleps in frosted glasses. Sprigs of fresh mint poked over the rims. He was an eager host, providing bowls of cashews and peanuts.

"Now, what can I do for you?"

Annie was enjoying the julep, and she hated to ruin the pleasant moment. Max's eyes prodded her, but he cowardly dropped a handful of peanuts into his mouth and remained silent.

"You know that Chief Saulter thinks I killed Elliot."

"I keep telling Frank that's damn nonsense."

With every word, Annie grew more uncomfortable. Here he was trying to use his influence for her benefit, and she was steeling her courage to accuse him of some kind of buried wrongdoing, including, of course, four homicides.

"Annie and I are trying to clear it up ourselves," Max said firmly, to remind Annie why they were there.

Capt. Mac managed not to look too astounded, but his obvious surprise discouraged Annie, too. How could she and Max hope to solve the crime by themselves?

"I wish you'd help us," she blurted. She very carefully did not look toward Max. After all, Miss Marple sought the support of Sir Henry Clithering. Max should understand, if he weren't such a jealous pig.

"Sweetheart, I'll give you all the help I can."

If Max had been a toad, he would have swelled. Such is jealousy.

"We think Elliot was killed because of the Sunday night session. After all, we all knew he was getting ready to tell nasty secrets about everyone there."

Capt. Mac swirled the ice in his glass meditatively. "I wouldn't take all that too seriously. Elliot loved to be the center of attention. It wouldn't have amounted to anything."

"But it did. You see, he sent me a copy of what he was going to say, and he was right—people had plenty to hide."

Capt. Mac put down his julep on a side table and reached for a cashew. "Oh, he did?"

She plunged into her narrative. "Emma Clyde pushed her second husband overboard. Hal buried his wife. Jeff Farley is a wife-beater. Fritz Hemphill . . ." Annie paused, then created,

". . . was a crooked cop. And Kelly Rizzoli attacked a woman once."

Capt. Mac ate another cashew. "Maybe those things are true. Maybe not. Even if they are, could they be proved? Obviously most of them can't be proved in a court of law, or some of those people would be in jail right now. That's something a policeman learns early on. It takes a hell of a lot in evidence to bring a charge and to make it stick. Most of what Elliot had was stuff that could embarrass somebody, make it a little awkward at the Club if the word got around, but he didn't seriously threaten anyone. It's like what he had on me." Capt. Mac lifted the pitcher to replenish their glasses. "I imagine you don't think as well of me since you read that. And I wouldn't like to have it talked about." He shot Annie an uneasy glance, then averted his eyes from her. "Damned embarrassing. Of course, what can I say?" He shrugged his powerful shoulders. "Nobody likes to be hit with a paternity suit. It ruined my marriage. I'm still paying for it—and I'll be damned if I think the boy is mine."

The three of them sipped their drinks, and no one said anything for a long moment.

For the first time, Capt. Mac looked angry, his face flushed and his mouth compressed. "I suppose it would have given him some kind of thrill to spill it in front of everybody." He ducked his head awkwardly toward Annie. "He knew I wanted you to think well of me. But I'll tell you for sure, I wouldn't have snuffed him to keep it quiet. I wouldn't have minded wiping that grin off his face with my fists. But I didn't get a chance to do that."

His flush faded, and he frowned. "I'll tell you, I don't see Elliot's big exposé as the crux of anything. So he insinuates that Emma gave her husband a push. So what? Who can prove it? And that's what you have to remember, accusations without proof are bullshit." He nodded toward Annie. "Pardon me, my dear. But that's how I feel about it. Elliot was a pain, all right, but that's as far as it went. Now maybe he could have queered things for the Farleys. I know they're up for the National Book Award. But for the rest of them, I don't take it too seriously. The only thing

Elliot's performance proves is that he was a heel. When you think about that, it occurs to me that maybe you should take a look at his ex-wife."

Max and Annie stared at him blankly.

"But somebody at Death On Demand killed Elliot," Annie said.

"Did they?" Capt. Mac shrugged. "Maybe. Maybe not. The back door was open." He paused. "His ex-wife is my next-door neighbor, Carmen Morgan. And is she a pistol."

They stood beside the Porsche.

"Look, Max, it's right next door. And Capt. Mac's pretty perceptive. He was a cop for a long time, and his instincts are good."

"He probably tried to put the make on her, and she turned him down."

"Max!"

"No kidding. We've got a platterful of solid suspects, and now he comes up with somebody who wasn't even there."

"He's smart enough to pay attention about the back door. I kept telling Saulter."

Max's voice rose in disgust. "How could this ex-wife know enough about your Sunday evening sessions to plant the dart and fix the lights?"

Annie didn't like being patronized. Who did Max think he was? Colonel Primrose?

"If she was mad enough to murder him, she'd find out. It would be a stroke of genius, wouldn't it, to kill somebody in front of a bunch of people with hot motives?"

Turning on her heel, she stalked toward the house next door.

The lawn was well kept, the house recently painted and guttered. That would be the work of the Halcyon maintenance company. The house had no touches of individuality, no hanging plants or flower beds.

Annie had just touched the bell when the door opened.

Capt. Mac was right. Carmen Morgan did look like a pistol. Silver-white, shoulder-length hair, a cerise tank top cut to the navel that emphasized a Dolly Parton cleavage and a Southern belle waist, and fingernails that must make thumb and finger precision difficult. Mike Hammer would have loved her—before he blew her away. A smell of camphorwood incense eddied from the dim living room.

She fastened shrewd, baby-blue eyes on Annie.

"I know who you are. Elliot got knocked off in your place." She smiled thinly. "Wish I'd been there."

"Were you?" Annie shot back, pleased at her own audacity.

"No such luck. Somebody say I was?" The baby-blue eyes narrowed. "You've been talking to that fat ex-cop next door. That jerk can't keep his nose out of other people's business."

"We thought you might have some idea who did kill Elliot," Max interjected smoothly, coming up silently behind Annie.

Carmen's face reformed as she looked at Max. Her pale eyes with their dramatic underscoring of lavender mascara widened in appreciation. This is the kind of reaction Magnum gets.

Annie felt her own face stiffen like plaster of paris.

The appraising eyes swept up and down Max's tall frame. "Why should you care, big boy?"

Big boy.

Gag.

"The cops have some dumb ideas. We're trying to set the record straight."

"You mean they want to pitch it on gumdrop here."

It took a minute to realize that she was said gumdrop. Annie opened her mouth to explode, but clever Max got there first.

"I'll bet they haven't even asked you for your help." He leaned revoltingly close to Carmen, oozing camaraderie.

"They didn't even bother to come tell me he was dead." Her porcelain pretty face turned brittle, and abruptly she looked a decade older. "I mean, I was married to the jerk for four years, three months and eighteen days, and nobody even tells me he's dead."

"That's awful," Max commiserated. "How'd you find out?"

"I got a friend at the police station."

Annie suddenly remembered the brawny motorcycle cop. A friend, indeed.

Carmen Morgan swivelled her platinum head to look again at Annie, a searching and not especially comradely look. "That's how I knew *she* was in a pickle. Bud, my friend, says they're going to arrest her tomorrow." She snorted. "Hell, you didn't kill Elliot. I can tell that by looking at you. You don't have the stuff."

While Annie was trying to decide whether to be complimented or offended, Carmen focused on Max.

"You come on in. I'll tell you what I can about my ex. The louse."

Annie moved in tandem with Max. She intended to stick to him like Nora to Nick, whether Carmen liked it or not.

The small hall was dingy with scuffed black-and-white checkerboard tile. A heavy smell of camphorwood combined with the two mint juleps to make her head feel dangerously unsteady.

"A beer, you guys?"

Annie started to decline, but Max grinned and said, "Sure. Let me help you," and he trailed Carmen into the kitchen.

Right on his heels, Annie followed. Max was not only a jealous pig and a sore-sport toad, he was now revealing himself to be a lecher of the first order.

Carmen opened three bottles of Dos XX's, and waved them to seats at the tan Formica-topped kitchen table. No light beer here. And apparently equally little cooking. The kitchen looked like a display in the home section at Sears, and just about as used.

Her body arched seductively toward Max, Carmen said, "What do you want to know?"

"Tell us about yourself." Max drew his chair closer to Carmen's. He would soon be on the same side of the table with her.

Annie gripped her bottle forcefully. Otherwise, she might have tossed it in his ingenuous face.

Carmen used both hands to fluff her long, silver hair. "True confessions?" she asked huskily.

Annie was delighted to note that Max looked a tad uncomfortable. He lifted his beer and drank.

"How about where you're from and how you met Elliot," Annie suggested tartly, smirking at Max's discomfort.

"I'm a dancer. I was working at a club down in the Keys, and Elliot came in. He was one big spender. Anyway, he was writing a book." She squinted reminiscently. "He told me I was like Sadie somebody, and I was wonderful material." She sipped at her beer and peered coyly and fuzzily at Max. The old bat was too vain to wear glasses.

Annie translated this: Carmen was a stripper in a joint, and Elliot was playing another role, macho novelist à la Hemingway.

"And you got married?" She cringed at the naked astonishment in her voice.

"Yeah. We went on a big party, and it seemed like a good idea."

Wonder what kind of idea it seemed to Elliot when he sobered up?

Carmen's mouth tightened. Annie added another five years to her age.

"Have you been divorced long?" Where had Max suddenly acquired his vast reserves of sympathy?

"Six months."

"Why are you staying here? Why don't you go back to Florida?"

Carmen swung on Annie furiously. "Why should I? I've got as much right to live here as anybody."

Max finished his beer, smacking his lips in pleasure, then broke the uncomfortable silence. "Did you know about the writers' meetings on Sunday nights at Death On Demand?"

"Yeah. Sure." Her eyes flicked over Annie's face. "You people give me the creeps. Death On Demand. Why don't you have a nice little shop that sells pretty things? You know, painted sea shells and birds in glasses. That kind of thing?"

"My uncle died and left me the bookstore," Annie replied in a strangled voice.

Carmen shrugged. "You gotta go with what you got. That's what I've always done." Consciously or unconsciously, she raised her arms and stretched her body sensuously.

Max leaned forward. "Did you know Elliot was going to say a lot of bad things about the other writers the night he was killed?"

"Oh, hell yes. He told me all about it."

"He did?" Annie shot Max a triumphant glare. "When did you see him?"

"He dropped by Friday afternoon. About five. To bring my alimony check. He was trying to chisel like always, two hundred bucks short. Said he'd lost a bundle on the commodities market, but he'd get the rest to me next week." She tugged at the cerise tank top, redistributing the wealth. "Hey, how do you suppose I can collect my money?"

While Max enthusiastically explained the law of probate, Annie thought furiously.

"Carmen, what did he tell you about the other writers?"

Elliot's ex-wife took a dainty sip of beer. "This and that. He loved to snoop around. I mean, he really liked to get the dirt on people."

"Did he tell you what he was going to say Sunday night?"

"Oh, sort of. I didn't pay a lot of attention. I wanted to talk about the money he owed me. I mean, try living here without a lot of bucks—"

Max leaned across the table and turned on a two-hundred-watt smile. "Try to remember. It could mean a lot."

"To you?" Carmen inquired huskily.

"To everybody," Annie interjected in an arctic tone. It would be hard for Carmen to remember. Her attention span was obviously limited solely to matters of importance to her.

But, with Max cheering her on, the woman dredged up some interesting information.

Some of it they knew—about Emma, the Farleys, and Hal. Some of it they didn't.

"Elliot said Fritz Hemphill was an idiot not to pay his wife alimony. I told him I sure agreed with that. Guys who don't pay their alimony are real geeks." For the first time, Annie noted the diamond-studded hoop earring hidden beneath the platinum hair.

"Is that all he had on Fritz?"

Carmen snorted. "Naw. That was why he had stuff on Fritz. Seems like his ex-wife is no chum, and she unloaded a bellyful to Elliot."

"What?" Max asked.

Carmen smeared the moisture from her beer bottle with a deadly fingernail. "Something about watching your backside with Fritz, not letting him come up behind you with a gun. Something like that."

A gun. That sounded more like it. Annie remembered Fritz's squidlike eyes.

"As for that jerk next door," and Carmen tilted her platinum head delicately toward Capt. Mac's house, "Elliot said he was a cool bastard all right, one who'd learned to keep his mouth shut."

It figured that Capt. Mac wouldn't broadcast information about a paternity suit.

"How about Kelly Rizzoli?" Max prodded.

"Nutty as a fruitcake, he said," Carmen replied, twirling an index finger by her temple significantly.

"Nutty how?" Annie asked, then thought, *Now I'm beginning to sound like her.* As if he could read her mind, Max grinned teasingly. She ignored him.

"Something about some tricks she'd played. Nasty ones, like killing somebody's cat."

Annie's skin crawled. *Psycho. Hallowe'en II.* Highsmith. Rendell. There were people who did things like that. But could they include Kelly, who had such a sensitive face and such an air of vulnerability?

Annie's recoil didn't escape Carmen's notice. "Yeah, you were sure having a swell party Sunday night. Lots of fun people there." Her pale eyes glinted maliciously. "Then there's the scoop on you. Elliot found out all about Santa Fe." Carmen's lip curled. "You think I'm just a cheap bitch, but I'd never do anything like that." She glanced over to Max. "You ought to ask her about Santa Fe sometime."

Santa Fe. What would Max think about Santa Fe? It had spelled the end for her and Richard. Thank God.

Annie looked directly at Carmen. "Yes, I can tell Max about Santa Fe."

There was a short, sharp pause, then Max interjected smoothly, "Carmen, did Elliot play the commodities market very often?"

Annie could have hugged him.

The widow grimaced. "Like clockwork. The sap."

"So maybe he really needed money."

"He *always* needed money," Carmen said seriously. This was obviously a subject close to her heart.

Annie turned to Max. "See, I thought there might be blackmail involved. I don't care what you say, he was extorting money from Emma Clyde . . ."

"Wait a minute," the blonde interrupted. "What makes you think so?"

"As soon as I made it clear I knew what Elliot was going to say, Emma asked me how much money I wanted. That must mean she was already being blackmailed."

"Not by Elliot." Carmen lost interest in Annie's theory. "No way."

"Why not? If he needed money, and you said he did, why wouldn't he take money to keep quiet about something like that?"

"Not Elliot. He was a chiseler, yeah, but he wasn't a crook. He told me once he thought blackmailers were slime, real slime. No way. You got to understand"—she got up and wriggled to the refrigerator—"he was a rat, but he really hated killers and bad cops and nasty, underhanded people. You know his favorite detective, Josh Hibbert, well, all that stuff was really him. The trouble is, he wanted to shove people's noses in their little messes. He liked to push people. That's why I dumped him. Cat and mouse, always a little push here, a shove there. I wouldn't take it. I told him to stick it." She squinted into the refrigerator thoughtfully. There were no more Dos XX's. "I guess he pushed somebody too hard."

"I think she's kinda cute," Max said, gunning the Porsche.

"You and every male in South Carolina."

"That is a sexist remark."

"You bet it is." Annie gently massaged her temples. "Wow, beer on top of two mint juleps. But it's a good thing we talked to her. She did know Elliot was going to speak Sunday night, and she knew why. She could easily have hidden the dart and tampered with the lights."

"Oh, Annie. Admit it. You just don't like the girl."

Girl. That was a laugh.

"She's about as girlish as a female anaconda."

"But to the right male anaconda . . ."

"I wonder how Elliot left his money?"

Max slowed the Porsche to swing back onto the main road. Massive yellow pines crowded the road, and through the open sunroof came the scent of sunbaked pitch. The scaly orange trunks rose ruler-straight.

"According to Carmen, he'd commoditied out of money."

"Sure, that would be her story. But wouldn't you think twice about that sweet girl if it turned out she inherited?"

Reluctantly, Max nodded. "That's an oversight, all right. We need to find out who gets his money—if there is any to get. That could make a difference."

"You know the motives for murder. Hate, revenge, fear, and greed."

"Or a combination thereof. Where do you suppose Kelly Rizzoli fits in?"

On the surface, their interchange was just as usual—light, flippant, and fun. Annie sensed an undertone, though, whether or not Max did.

She reached out and touched his arm. "Before we see Kelly, I want to tell you about Santa Fe."

Fifteen

"I'VE NEVER BEEN into true confession," he said drily. "What counts is now. Today." His dark blue eyes met hers directly.

Dear Max.

"I want to tell you. I know I don't have to." She couldn't quite resist reaching out to touch his cheek. "Let's go over to Indigo Beach."

She directed him to a rutted sandy lane.

Low hanging vines scraped the top of the Porsche as Max eased it around a fallen palmetto. He cringed for the paint job. "They could use a little machete work down this way."

Resurrection ferns laced the branches of a spreading live oak, and cinnamon ferns flourished beside a pond to the left. The undergrowth suddenly erupted with a flurry of movement, and a dusky gray white-tail deer plunged fleetingly across the narrow track to disappear into a thicket of bayberry.

A fallen southern red cedar blocked the track twenty yards short of the beach. They left the car and walked over the hummocky, sandy ground to a narrow boardwalk, half-covered by drifting sand.

Head-high sea oats, October brown, rippled in the onshore breeze. Nutgrass and sandspur rustled knee-high. As they stood at the top of the dune and looked over the littoral at the gentle surf, a ragged line of cormorants passed overhead. They walked down the dune to the flat-packed gray sand along the water's edge.

Annie reached down and touched an eddy of warm water.

"You don't have to tell me anything," Max insisted. "I know everything I need to know about you."

"I want to tell you." She frowned, picking her words. "Elliot must have talked to Richard."

Max was silent.

"I've never told you about Richard. It was right after I got out of school. I was living in Dallas and working as a model." She turned and began to walk up the beach, and Max paced with her. "Richard is a banker." She laughed. "That's not fair, really. I know there are all kinds of bankers, but Richard is like all of their worst qualities rolled into one. He is extremely cautious, extremely careful. He believes there are rules for every situation. We were engaged." She shook her head in self-surprise. "Actually, I can't believe now that I ever considered marrying him. Richard is extremely nice, extremely handsome, extremely . . . dull."

"Dull," Max repeated. "At least, you've never called me dull."

"Never. Anyway, Richard and I were engaged. Then a very old friend called me. She was in real trouble. She asked me to come to Santa Fe with her and not to tell anyone. So I told Richard that I had to leave town immediately, and that I would be back in a week.

"He wanted to know why. I told him I couldn't say." Annie winced at the recollection of the acrimonious dispute that followed. "Richard wasn't pleased. But I lost my temper, told him off, and went. A week later, when I got back, I wouldn't tell him why I'd gone, or what I'd done.

"Three days after that, he showed up at my apartment, and he was livid. He had a report from a private detective. It said that Anne McKinley Laurance entered a private nursing home on Sunday evening, gave birth to a son that night, and was discharged the following Wednesday."

"Your friend used your name."

"Do you know, that never occurred to Richard? He demanded to know how I'd hidden my pregnancy, since he knew damn well he hadn't gotten me pregnant, and who the hell was I sneaking around with?"

Max raised one blond eyebrow. "Is his bank on the FDIC worry list?"

"No, Richard is very bright about numbers."

"But, thank God, not very bright about people."

"That's what Elliot found out. The baby was immediately given up for adoption."

"Why did it have to be so secret?" he asked.

"You are perceptive, aren't you?" She bit her lip.

"You don't have to tell me any more."

"No, I want to tell you because I know what I did was illegal. You see, Emily was married. That wasn't the problem at all. She had hidden the fact she was pregnant from her husband. You have to understand, her husband was the oldest son of one of Texas's most powerful families—and a kind of crazy mean family, too. She didn't know it until she married Quentin, but his father controlled all of them, and I mean that literally. Everyone in the family kowtowed to that horrible, domineering old monster. It was just like Mrs. Boynton in *Appointment With Death*. Quentin and his sister both used cocaine. Their mother was an alcoholic. It was just an awful way to live—and all Emily could think about was getting her baby—the only grandchild—into a safe, *normal* family. So we went to Santa Fe, and she went into a clinic using my name, and three days later I signed the adoption papers to a wonderful couple who had wanted and prayed for a baby for years."

She half-turned and looked out over the surging green water. "I've always been so glad I did it. Emily and Quentin were killed in a plane crash a year later, and that little baby would have been swallowed alive by Quentin's father."

"Good for you," Max said warmly. At her look of surprise, he said almost roughly, "Richard may have been a damn fool, but I'm not, Annie."

"You don't care that I was a party to—I don't know what to call it. Fraud? Conspiracy?"

"I think you're wonderful. I've always thought so. I'll always think so." He couldn't quite resist adding, "Even if I don't have a serious job—like a banker."

They stopped at Death On Demand en route to Kelly Rizzoli's. Max insisted there was plenty of time before the ferry left to organize what they'd learned and then interview Kelly. He reached out to pat the glossy black head of the stuffed raven in the entryway.

"What's his name?"

"Edgar, of course."

Ingrid greeted them wearily. "Everything's okay. I think the rush is over. But I sold $689 worth. And you're out of Christianna Brands." She patted the stack of receipts proudly. Her eyes darted solicitously from Max to Annie before she added reluctantly, "Chief Saulter's been by twice, looking for you, and Mrs. Brawley phoned three times."

Bad news and good news. Annie stepped close to give Ingrid a hug. "Let's close up for now. And don't worry, Ingrid, Max and I are working on it."

Ingrid's face brightened. "Like Pam and Jerry North."

Not quite, but Annie wouldn't have minded a martini. Although that might be the final blow, after the mint juleps and beer.

Ingrid put up the Closed sign and locked the front door as she left. "I'll open up in the morning."

Did she think Annie would be in jail?

Max made himself comfortable in the largest wicker chair with the softest pillows.

"It's time to organize what we have." He propped a yellow legal pad on his knee.

Annie wandered restlessly around the store: the coffee area, the exhibit of watercolors, the central corridor with the soft gum bookcases angling away, the cash desk, Edgar with his glossy feathers and sightless eyes.

Sanctuary. That's what Death On Demand had been for her in the days following Uncle Ambrose's death. She'd always been so happy here, felt so safe. Had Saulter come by to arrest her? Carmen Morgan had thought the arrest would come tomorrow. How much time did she have left? The clock in the tall Queen Anne walnut case next to Edgar read 3:07. Time, time, she was running out of time.

She whirled around and started down the central corridor, then paused abruptly, her eyes on a level with the top shelf of the True Crime section, which held all the works of Uncle Ambrose's favorite author, Clark Howard. Howard, a 1980 Edgar winner for his short story "Horn Man," wrote everything well—short stories, novels, television and movie scripts, and nonfiction crime books.

Annie stared at the books until the titles scrambled in her mind.

They were losing sight of the most important fact.

"Max!" she yelped. She veered to her right, tangled with a fern, and slid to a stop beside his chair.

Agatha erupted from the base of the fern next to Max, stared reproachfully at Annie, and shot toward the dimness of the coffee bar.

Annie flapped her hands at Max's sheaf of paper. "What did you do with the stuff you put together on everybody when I was being bopped at Elliot's?"

Max riffled through his stack and pulled out several typewritten sheets. Annie grabbed them.

"We've got to fine-tooth-comb this stuff and see who's connected to a killing that Uncle Ambrose was investigating. Don't you see? It all goes back to Uncle Ambrose. That's important, not this penny-ante stuff like Capt. Mac and his paternity suit."

"First, we have to organize our material." Max looked extremely judicious, a non-eggshaped Hercule Poirot.

Annie didn't dignify this with an answer. Instead, she grabbed the dossiers. Quickly, she scratched out a list of people and places.

ANNIE'S GEOGRAPHIC CHART

Emma Clyde	Hal Douglas	The Farleys	Fritz Hemphill	Capt. Mac	Kelly Rizzoli
Billings	Wiesbaden	Columbia	Long Beach	Ft. Walton	Ft. Smith
Cincinnati	St. Louis	Kansas City	Saigon	Jacksonville	Ozark
N. Africa	Hollywood	Broward's	Loma Linda	Camp	Fayetteville
Memphis	Lake Tahoe	Rock	Los Angeles	Lejeune	Broward's
New York	Broward's		Broward's	Korea	Rock
Boca Raton	Rock		Rock	Miami	
Broward's				Silver City	
Rock				Broward's	
				Rock	

As she studied her chart, she felt her first qualm. On the surface, not a single one of these people had any connection with Uncle Ambrose's famous cases. But she didn't know enough about the three cases Uncle Ambrose had been investigating.

Fifteen minutes later, her hand cramped from note taking, she put down the phone.

Max came up behind her and reached down to massage her tight shoulders. "What did you plug into? Today's devotional?"

"The crime reporter at the Atlanta *Constitution*. His name's Sam, and he asked me out for a drink the next time I get to Atlanta." She swivelled around to look at the clock face. Oh, God, 3:22. Here they sat, Max scribbling another damn list and she trying to forge some link between Uncle Ambrose's missing manuscript and the suspects. And, darn it, nothing was working out.

Max bent over to look at her work.

"Nothing," she said bitterly. "Oh, obviously he was on the right track, but there isn't anything to link those crimes to anybody here." She ticked them off on her fingers: "Alden Armbruster stepped into his Lincoln Continental to drive to work. He turned on the motor and kerboom. There had been labor trouble at the plant (they made plating for artillery shells). They suspected Alden Armbruster Jr., who had made a recent trip to Miami, where he could easily have purchased the plastic explosive used to blow up the car. No fingerprints. No proof. Case never closed. Alden Armbruster Jr. lives and presumably thrives in New York City. No other suspects, and nobody here could be Alden Armbruster. The Vinson suicide: Amalie Vinson, the tire heiress, was found one June morning in her Waikiki penthouse, dead of a cocaine overdose. Could be accident. Could be suicide. There was a note. A scrap, actually. The classic—*I can't go on.* As any fool knows, find a written regret to an invitation, tear it artfully, and you have a picture-perfect suicide note. Worked beautifully in *The Moving Finger.* Chief suspect—her third husband, Bobby Kaiser, who doesn't live on Broward's Rock. Finally, the Winningham case. Cale Winningham, heir to a tobacco fortune, was known as a brutal, spoiled womanizer. Somehow, he'd married a nice girl, Sheila Hammonds. In the middle of a November night, Winningham killed her with a shotgun. His story was that they'd had trouble recently with prowlers. A month before, they'd been robbed. He heard a noise, got up, crept out into the hall, shouted, 'Stop or I'll shoot!' There was no answer, so he blasted. When he turned on the light, there was Sheila. He was devastated. He married another woman two months later. But Winningham didn't live long to enjoy his new wife. They were killed when his private plane crashed on takeoff a few months later. The FAA found sugar in the gas line. So Cale Winningham can't be on Broward's Rock. Unless he's a ghost."

Annie shoved her hands frenziedly through her hair. "Dammit, there's no link to Broward's Rock."

Max held up his legal pad. "Here's what really matters."

Max's list:

1. Emma Clyde gave Ricky a shove. Who saw the dirty deed? Check the Coast Guard.

2. Hal Douglas's wife ran around on him. According to Hal, she also ran out on him. Where is Lenora Harris Douglas?

3. Jeff Farley beats his wife. Would he or Janis kill to keep Jeff's brutality a secret?

4. Fritz Hemphill is apparently trigger-happy, with a past he was determined to keep buried. What did his ex-wife know?

5. Capt. Mac keeps his mouth shut. Did he hide anything more dangerous than a paternity suit?

6. Carmen Morgan knew about the Sunday evening session. She knew that everyone there would have a motive for shutting Elliot up. Does Carmen inherit? Where was she Sunday night?

7. Kelly Rizzoli. Elliot said she played some nasty tricks. What were they?

Max reached for the telephone.

3:33. She tugged Max's sleeve and pointed at the clock.

He covered the receiver. "Plenty of time," he soothed, as he dialed.

Agatha moved like a black shadow, jumping up to the top of the counter. She looked at Annie with her deep yellow eyes.

"What do you think, Agatha?"

The cat made a soft, throaty sound.

"If you could talk, you could tell us who came in here Sunday morning."

Agatha began to clean her face, licking her right paw daintily, then scrubbing furiously at her cheek.

Annie reached out, petted the silky fur, and tilted her head a little to listen to Max.

"Lieutenant Ferrill, did you investigate the drowning of Enrique Morales a couple of years ago?"

"Yes."

"This is Max Darling, attorney-at-law. I'm involved in a wrongful death suit, and I need to get a copy of the report on Morales's death. Could you send it to me by Federal Express?"

"Yes, I suppose so." A puzzled pause followed. "Wrongful death? That death was ruled an accidental drowning."

"There's some question of liability on the part of the yacht manufacturer, Lieutenant. Too low a railing on the afterdeck."

"That'd be hard to prove," Ferrill said drily. "The railing was four feet high."

Max swept ahead. "Did you interview the steward and the cook of *Marigold's Pleasure?*"

"Of course. Neither was aboard that evening."

"So Mrs. Morales and her husband were alone?"

The lieutenant paused. "Mrs. Clyde, that's what she calls herself. She and her second husband were alone."

But someone somewhere saw something, if Annie's blackmail theory were correct. "Wasn't there anybody else around?"

"We talked to the owner of another boat anchored close by. He corroborated the information we received from Mrs. Clyde. I think you're barking up the wrong tree. There wasn't anything wrong with the railing on that boat."

"Possibly not," Max agreed placidly. "But please send me the report."

After giving Ferrill Annie's address, Max hung up, marking a series of fat, black question marks by Emma's name. Annie was right. There was something there—or Emma wouldn't have immediately suspected her of a blackmail attempt. Maybe there would be something in the report, at the least a few more names to call.

He tracked down Jeff and Janis Farley's editor, just returning from lunch at The Four Seasons.

"This is Max Darling. I'm writing an article for a library journal, and I'm trying to get some information on personal factors that can affect book sales. You were recommended to me as an extremely knowledgeable observer of children's publishing. Anything you may tell me will be confidential. I'm not using anybody's name in this story."

"What do you want to know?" Her voice was clipped, level, and noncommittal.

"What would be the effect upon sales for a children's writer who was convicted of drunk driving?"

"Mr. Darling, that is a very peculiar question."

"There's been some concern among librarians that there is an inverse censorship at work affecting the children's market that isn't at work in adult writing. In other words, does the behavior of children's writers make a difference in their likelihood of sale? So, I'm asking you whether a D.W.I. conviction or wife-beating charge or anything of that nature could make a difference."

"I won't be quoted?"

"Never."

"Then, off the record and between you and me and the wall, it makes a hell of a difference. If children's writers have nasty personal lives, they'd damned well better keep them under wraps."

"Do you think it's possible for a writer to win a national book prize if something like this became public?"

"Forget it."

Annie was madly deciphering his cryptic notes as he finished the call.

"My turn," and she took the receiver out of his hand and dialed information for the alumni office at Washington University at St. Louis. It took patience to get the name of Lenora Harris Douglas's sister, Mrs. Bennett Berry.

"Mrs. Berry, I'm calling about your sister, Lenora Harris Douglas . . ."

There was an excited cry. "My God, do you know where she is? Where is she? My God, who is this?"

Annie felt a constriction in her chest. Martha Berry's cry told her almost everything she needed to know.

"Mrs. Berry, I'm sorry, you've misunderstood me. I'm calling to see if you have your sister's address."

"Oh. Oh, for a minute I thought . . ." Martha Berry took a deep breath. "No, no, I don't know where Lenora is."

"When did you last hear from her?"

"A postcard. Two years ago. From the casino at Lake Tahoe." Her voice quickened. "Do you know Lenora? Do you know somebody who knows her?"

"No, I'm sorry. I was calling about a reunion of our college class. That last address we have is a rural box number in California. We didn't get any answer."

"No answer. That's all I ever got. I went out, looked for her, but that cabin's empty, and I've never found a trace of the guy she married."

"Do you know anything about him?"

"His name is Harold Douglas. That's all we know. He took Lenora out to Hollywood with him, and that's the last we ever heard. She told me, the last time we talked, that he was crazy jealous. I asked her to come home, but she laughed and said it would be all right." Martha Berry paused. "Listen, if you do find Lenora, please tell her to call us. Tell her we've been worried sick because . . . well, she's a good girl but . . . All Lenora ever wanted to do was have a good time. We don't know why she hasn't called or written."

Annie hung up and drew a gallows with a noose. Girls just want to have fun.

There was no answer at the home of the former Mrs. Fritz Hemphill. Her office said she was out of town on a business trip and could be contacted that evening at the Vanderbilt Plaza in Nashville, Tennessee. Annie glanced at the clock. 3:50. They couldn't wait until evening. It was a wonder Saulter hadn't been by again—this time with a warrant. And they still needed to talk to Kelly and get Harriet's film to the mainland to be developed.

She watched the clock hands move as she waited on hold, but she was finally connected to the LAPD chief of detectives. He wasn't very forthcoming.

"Yeah. Hemphill was with us. For about ten—maybe a dozen—years."

"Why did he quit?"

"Ask him. By the way, who did you say you were?"

"I'm writing a feature on mystery novelists," Annie invented. "I understand he quit because he got in a little trouble."

"He quit because he inherited some money." The voice was flat. "If you want to know more about it, you might call a Mrs. Cynthia Harmon."

Cynthia Harmon ran a beauty shop in Long Beach.

"Who told you to call me?"

"Horace King."

"Horace— So you want to know about Fritz Hemphill." Her voice harshened. "Yeah, you called the right number. I'll tell you about Fritz. Horace can't say anything. He has to watch out, or they'll hit him with a slander suit. Me, I don't give a damn. Yeah, I can tell you about Fritz. He's a murderer."

"Who did he kill?"

"His best friend. Isn't that something? His best friend, Mike Gonzalez. He shot him in the back and then stood there and watched him bleed to death."

She was crying now.

"I'm sorry," Annie said feebly.

"We all ought to be sorry. A good man like Mike. I never liked Fritz, never, but I didn't say anything to Mike because a man doesn't like for a woman to knock his friends. But I always thought Fritz had cold eyes, like a snake. And that's what he was, a snake in the grass. See, Mike saved Fritz's life one time when they faced down some creeps in an alley, and one of them pulled a gun and was going to shoot Fritz. Mike got him first, saved Fritz's life. They were good pals then. Fritz was divorced, and Mike's first wife died of cancer and they didn't have any kids, so Mike made up a will and left everything he had to Fritz. He should have known . . . Anyway, Mike had this beach house he inherited from this spinster aunt, a beach house in Carmel, and you know what kind of money that is. Mike never even liked the place, said the people were too ritzy for him, but he made up a will, left it all to Fritz. Then he met me, and it was great, it was wonderful. I finally met a nice man, a man I could really care about, and Mike liked my kids, everything. We were going to get married in two months, and he went hunting with Fritz, and he died with the back of his head blown away."

"An accident—" she began.

"Accident! Lady, cops don't have accidents with guns."

Annie hung up, started to report to Max, then saw the time. "I'll tell you on the way. We'd better hurry. It's almost four."

"Don't you think I have time to do some phoning on Capt. Mac?"

The front door rattled. Chief Saulter stood on the verandah, peering into Death On Demand.

Without a word, Annie and Max dropped to the floor.

Sixteen

SHE'D NEVER REALIZED how hard heart pine floors were when crossed on hands and knees. Had Saulter caught a glimpse of them? But the door was mullioned and that would make it difficult for him to see.

She didn't draw an easy breath until they'd tiptoed out the storeroom door, darted up the back alley, and skulked on the far side of the hibiscus to Max's Porsche. As they roared off, she looked over her shoulder. No one followed. Of course, Saulter could find her, if he looked hard enough. But every second gave them another chance to find out more. And they had to catch the six o'clock ferry and develop that film.

Magpie Plantation was hidden deep from the main road; enormous, thick-leaved live oak trees and their dangling swaths of Spanish moss shrouded the tangled undergrowth, enclosed the narrow, dusty gray road. It was like driving in a terrarium, moist, green, dim, and somber.

"All we need is a crow on a fence post," Max muttered.

The Porsche curved around the crumbling remains of old Fort Hendrix, an earthwork fortification built in 1862 by the occupying Union forces to overlook Abelard Creek. They rattled over a narrow wooden bridge, and Annie said in a hushed voice, "There's the house."

Magpie Plantation was old, a lovingly restored antebellum survivor of sea cotton days. The railings of the broad double verandahs and the slender Doric columns glistened with fresh white paint.

With the motor off, a funereal silence enfolded them.

Max raised an eyebrow. "I'll bet they laugh a lot here. My God, the place looks like a cross between a southern Wuthering Heights and the summer home of the Addams family."

The silvery Spanish moss hung motionless. The onshore breeze didn't penetrate the thick stand of live oaks. The sound of their footsteps on the oyster-shell path was distinct in the brooding stillness.

Annie remembered Magpie Plantation from summer hikes with Uncle Ambrose. It had been a derelict then, untenanted, dank weeds choking the drive, the second-story verandah sagging. She'd known, of course, that Kelly had bought and restored the old house. But why wasn't it included in the spring tour of plantation homes? Most owners of the antebellum mansions gloried in showing off their prizes.

They were starting up the rose-bordered front walk when a scream, high and rising higher, pealed through the heavy air.

"My God, what's that?"

Max was squinting at the house's beautiful facade. "There," he shouted, and pointed to the second-floor verandah, where two figures struggled near the railing, one trying desperately to squirm free, the other, smaller one holding on tenaciously.

Max leapt up the steps and yanked on the heavy front door. It didn't budge. He sprinted down the verandah to the end and an ivy-laden lattice. He started up, Annie close behind.

"It won't hold both of us," he shouted in warning as the framework quivered.

Annie dropped back down and craned to see.

The larger woman broke free to clamber awkwardly up onto the railing. The smaller figure, Kelly, grabbed and clung. The two teetered precariously. Then Max was up and over the railing, and the three figures disappeared in a melee of arms and legs.

The scream sounded again, piercing and shrill, then abruptly broke off, followed by brokenhearted sobs.

"Max," Annie yelled, then she climbed up on the railing to start up the lattice.

He peered down from the second story. "Hold on, Annie. We'll be down in a minute."

By the time the front door swung open, Annie was standing beside it and breathing almost normally.

Kelly stepped back and motioned her inside. Her dark red hair was disheveled, her face pale. Max had an angry scratch on his right arm, and his shirt pocket was torn.

"We'll go in the living room." Kelly's voice was as soft and unhurried as usual. They might have been joining her for afternoon tea.

The living room was lovely. Delicate, white molded cornices decorated fourteen-foot-tall ceilings. A magnificent three-tiered crystal chandelier hung from a center medallion. Pale gray walls set off the draped turquoise hangings over the huge arched windows. The room was shadowy, but Kelly didn't turn on a light. Annie thought of the approach to the house. It was all of a piece, quiet, spooky, sinister.

Their hostess waved them to an American Chippendale sofa, then sat in a small but very fine Queen Anne wing chair, upholstered in rose and white.

Annie felt a curl of uneasiness. This was *Knight's Gambit* territory. Antebellum perfection below and a madwoman above.

Kelly turned politely toward Max. "I do owe you a very great thanks."

"No problem." Max took up two-thirds of the sofa, overwhelmingly masculine in a feminine room. "I became quite skilled in ascending and descending lattices in my younger days."

Annie filed that one away for further reference and possible inquiry.

Kelly didn't smile. She nodded soberly and continued to gaze at Max with haunted green eyes. "It's great luck you happened by. We are rather isolated here. What can I do for you?"

It was a courteous way of asking what the hell they wanted, and a clear indication the verandah episode was closed.

Kelly wasn't Carmen or any of the others they'd talked to. If anyone were capable of out-thinking the world, it was Kelly Rizzoli.

"It's Elliot," Annie began, beating Max to the punch.

"Elliot?" Kelly echoed coolly.

"He sent me a copy of what he was going to say Sunday night."

"Oh, he did? Would you suppose he had a presentiment?"

Annie shrugged. "I doubt it. Maybe more on the order of insurance."

"It lapsed, didn't it?"

Annie could swear there was a sick glimmer of amusement in Kelly's gorgeous eyes, but she plunged resolutely on. "I don't really want to tell Saulter what he was going to say about you."

"So you came to see me instead?" Kelly wore a shamrock-green turtleneck and boxy white slacks. She looked very slight in the delicate wingback chair. Slight but somehow imposing.

Annie nodded.

"If I can persuade you that what he had on me wasn't sufficient motive for murder, you will protect my good name. Is that right?"

"Right." Certainly Kelly didn't seem discomfited by her threat to go to Saulter.

Kelly looked away, her gaze seeming to fasten somewhere near the delicate Adam mantel. She spoke dreamily. "It's funny what can serve as motivation. That was part of Elliot's thesis, you know, that a writer's reality serves as the basis for invention. I find motivation quite fascinating." She shifted a little in her chair, looked at Annie. "In my latest collection of short stories, there's one I like particularly, 'Gideon's Morning.'" Her voice had a singsong, musical quality like the faraway fall of water. "It is his last morning, you see. His mother splits his skull with an axe as he sits at the breakfast table."

Max and Annie sat quietly, scarcely breathing.

She tilted her head like a bird observing a worm. "It's really quite understandable. She'd told him and told him and told him not to track mud across her clean kitchen floor when she'd just mopped it."

The vision of a blood-drenched country kitchen hung in the shadows of the room.

"Motivation. Yes, Elliot was right. We use everything we've ever known or seen or felt when we write. Sometimes, we pick up pieces of people's lives, like a crow attracted to the shine of a broken brooch. We take it all and put together something new and different, but it does spring from our past, our collective past."

"And your past," Annie said softly.

Kelly nodded. She looked childlike, sitting in that straight-backed old chair, her hands folded primly in her lap, her shoulders narrow beneath the green turtleneck.

"My past—and Elliot. That's what you came to talk about. My past and my present. You know, Elliot was right and wrong about me."

"Can you tell us?" Max urged, his voice low and careful.

Pensively, Kelly nodded. "It's interesting. Motivation again. Elliot didn't understand that it didn't matter to me if he told everyone—right or wrong. He got the story from one of my classmates, I suppose. It happened at the College of the Ozarks." She turned to Max. "Have you ever been to southern Arkansas? You might understand better if you've been there. Did you know you can go back in the Arkansas swamp country and go to a lake that's hooded by trees—and there will be snakes hanging from the branches?"

Again that slow, dreamy smile.

"Think about that, picture it. The darkness among the cypress and the still, emerald water and the thick-bodied water moccasins dangling from the branches.

"Arkansas—it can be very still and dark and ingrown. Very ingrown. Many families have kept to themselves for a long time. My family, too. But my sister, Pamela, and I went together to college. I knew Pamela wasn't quite right, but we thought she could go if I were there." Kelly's dreamy eyes looked beyond them, to a past and place they couldn't see. "We rented a tiny room in a boardinghouse two blocks from the campus. Pamela took art classes." Her voice was suddenly animated. "She can really draw quite well. When she's happy, she paints smiling children. When she's unhappy . . . They found the dog first, the dog next door. His throat was cut. Then a parakeet was strangled. Our landlady had a pet cat, a beautiful cat who had her own silk cushion and special foods." Kelly moved her hand, as if stroking a cat.

Annie didn't ask what had happened to the cat. She didn't want to know.

"Pamela?"

Kelly's eyes slowly focused on Max. "I told them I did it. I said it was an experiment in the psychology of stress, and I promised to make restitution. Do you understand why?"

"To protect your sister?"

"They would have put her away, and she wouldn't be able to bear it. I never make her stay locked up. I let her go out when she wants, but I watch her very carefully. Upsets like today don't happen often, but I think she sensed I was disturbed about something. That affects her. She'll be all right, now that she's had a sedative. She'll sleep until tomorrow, then get up and be cheerful, and we'll walk along the beach and search for a perfect sand dollar."

"Why not get her to a doctor? She's sick, Kelly. You should know that. You majored in psychology."

Kelly's green eyes didn't look the least dreamy when she turned them toward Annie. "You do know a lot about me, don't you?"

"Why don't you get her into a hospital?"

Kelly's skin was almost translucent, the veins blue-black near the surface. "Never. You don't know what it would be like. Have you ever been in a mental hospital? Tan walls and cement floors, people with empty, staring eyes, figures in green coveralls, and doctors who ineptly try to treat illnesses that no one understands." She paused, then spoke so low Annie found herself leaning forward to hear. "She would be so frightened, so terribly alone."

"It must all be in your college records," Max said briskly.

"About the animals. And that's what Elliot had. You said you didn't care if he told it?"

"Why should I?"

"Because someone might discover the truth about Pamela and insist she be put away."

"I won't let that happen." Kelly lifted her head regally.

She was cold and obdurate and a dangerous adversary. And very, very clever. She was also supremely confident of her cleverness.

Those shrewd, beautiful eyes watched Annie warily.

"Look, Kelly, I'll tell you the truth. Chief Saulter is going to arrest me tomorrow. He believes I murdered Elliot because he was threatening to raise my rent and drive me out of business. He even thinks I pushed my uncle into the harbor last summer, just to inherit the bookstore."

For the first time, Kelly looked surprised. Annie wondered immediately if it were consummate acting or if it had never occurred to her that Ambrose Bailey's death had not been accidental.

"That's absurd. You wouldn't have done that."

"Well, thanks. I'm glad you don't agree."

Kelly wasn't listening. Instead, she studied the diamond pattern in the turquoise rug.

"Ambrose murdered." Her gaze swung back to Annie. "Why?"

Annie briefly described the true-crime book and the missing manuscript.

"Oh hey, Annie." Max was impatient, irritated at this diversion. "You and Saulter both are way off base. Your uncle fell. I'd bet on that."

"So what happened to the manuscript?"

"You probably lost a box when you moved the stuff from his house."

"Lost a box? Do you think I'm a nitwit?"

"Do you lose things sometimes?"

What a low blow. "Just because I mislaid that script."

At least he had the grace not to bring up the fact that it had almost cost him a producer.

"Where did we find it?"

"Okay, okay. I left it on a park bench. But a silly damn script is not the size of a box with a manuscript." Annie was tired of this battle. She turned to Kelly. "Anyway, my neck's on the block, and Saulter won't even listen, so Max and I have decided to find out everything we can to solve the crime. Will you help us?"

"How can I help you?" Kelly was still cautious, but interested. And perhaps tempted?

"Sure you can help. You know these people; you are extraordinarily perceptive. Maybe you'll see something we've missed." Max was busy exercising his charm. Max was world class when it came to wheedling. He could wheedle a seat five minutes before takeoff on a sold-out People's Express. He could wheedle a box-seat at game-time at the Super Bowl. He was *magic,* and Annie watched with reluctant admiration as Kelly received a concentrated dose.

"I might at that. Tell me what you have." A faint flush stained those marble-pale cheeks. Max was a marvel, and Annie was controlling a sharp impulse to give him an elbow in the ribs.

They started with number one, Emma Clyde.

When Max finished summing up, Kelly moved her hands, and Annie was reminded of seaweed swaying in water.

"Oh, yes. I can see it happening. Emma is quite capable of a carefully conceived, excellently executed plan. If she decided her second husband was a mistake—and she couldn't see any way of divorcing him without losing a great deal of money—I don't believe she'd hesitate for a moment to murder him. I find it quite revealing that she told you she had wanted to see him early the next morning about some investments. She was clearly thinking about him in terms of money. And it's very suggestive that she immediately assumed Annie's intention in bringing up the matter was blackmail. I consider that significant, too. I would almost feel certain she was already the victim of blackmail."

"If she can plan so well and won't stop at murder, why wouldn't she get rid of the blackmailer?" Max asked.

"But she did," Annie jumped in. "That's why she killed Elliot.

He was blackmailing her, so she set it all up, stole the poison, killed Jill because she interrupted that, then hid the dart in my store and fixed the lights. It sounds reasonable to me."

"No, no," Kelly objected calmly. "You are misreading Elliot's persona entirely. My dear, he sought power, that was his overriding desire—to manipulate and coerce, to inflict punishment." A tiny smile rippled over her pond-smooth face. "He was not a very attractive person, dear Elliot."

"What's blackmail but a clear exercise of power?" Annie demanded.

"In a limited sense. Do you think, in Elliot's mind, that the receipt of money could compare in any way with the power and pleasure he would take from standing up in front of the Regulars and publicly stripping each person there emotionally naked?"

"By God, you're right," Max declared.

Where had Max acquired his perverted weakness for blond anacondas and redheaded vipers?

"So you think he meant every word of his threat to reveal all Sunday night?"

"Of course. I have no doubt that, had he lived, we would all have learned some fascinating particulars about each person there." Was there a touch of regret in her voice? Viper, indeed.

"So you agree that the motive for his murder must lie in his actions that night?"

"I have no doubt about it."

"How about his ex-wife? How about Ambrose Bailey?"

Neither of them even glanced Annie's way. Max was crinkling his eyes at Kelly, and she was responding on cue. Annie knew she would do well to remember his expertise in the future.

"You've certainly thought this through very thoroughly. Who are the other candidates?"

Max was spilling all to their new confederate. "The next person we talked to was Hal Douglas." Then his face abruptly went blank, and Annie knew he'd remembered her own comment that she suspected a romance between Hal and Kelly.

Kelly waited.

With Max struck dumb, Annie explained about Hal's emotional outburst.

Kelly was unruffled. "His wife could have run off with someone."

"Did you know he had a wife?"

"I knew there was an emotional block."

Annie stopped short of announcing her belief that Lenora was in an unmarked grave near that Lake Tahoe cabin. Instead, she skirted. "What do you think about Hal? Could he kill someone?"

"Hal is passionate. I can see problems if he loved someone deeply and discovered infidelity, but I have trouble imagining him cold-bloodedly killing Jill—or Harriet."

"Jill's death may not have been intentional," Annie suggested. "The autopsy revealed she had a very thin skull—and she was only hit once. Perhaps the killer simply intended to knock her unconscious." Annie reached up and touched the sore spot, still a little swollen, behind her ear. "As for Harriet, nobody really knows what happened. Maybe she saw someone go into Elliot's house and followed them. She may have accused that person of being the murderer and something happened to convince her she was right. The killer had no choice."

"That seems possible." Max nodded.

Kelly was skeptical. She stood and walked slowly to the mantel and lightly touched a piece of painted tinware. "Hal would do things in a rush. He might knock Elliot down or shoot him, but I can't imagine he would plan and carry out this complicated murder."

An attack on Hal made her uneasy. What might she do to protect Hal? Were she and Max naive? Did Kelly know all about Lenora, and was she determined to protect Hal at all costs? She'd already revealed that she would go to great lengths if she cared for someone. Witness her determination to shield her sister.

"Hal writes pretty complicated books."

Kelly merely smiled patronizingly and shook her head.

"How about the Farleys? Solo or together."

Kelly leaned back against the mantel, very much at ease now

that Hal wasn't the subject. "They're possible, quite possible." Her dark red hair swung as she nodded. "There is repression there, and violence."

She wasn't at all surprised to learn of Jeff's attacks or Janis's protective response. But again, she thought outright aggression would be more likely for Jeff than the carefully premeditated death by dart.

"I wouldn't rule them out, though, psychologically speaking."

"What about Fritz Hemphill?" Did Max have to look as if he awaited a guru's pronouncement?

Kelly reached out and traced her fingers over the raised pattern in the upholstery of the small Queen Anne wingback. "Fritz is a dangerous man. What did Elliot have on him?"

"Apparently he blew away his best friend so he could inherit a valuable beachfront cottage at Carmel."

"Fritz is a planner, the kind of person who takes what he wants."

"Then there's Capt. Mac." Max's voice was as curdled as sour milk. "A paternity suit."

"At least he didn't kill somebody," Annie exclaimed protectively.

Kelly's green eyes darted from Annie to Max, brightly, perceptively.

Annie was getting pretty damn sick of perception.

"So Capt. Mac's libido caused him some difficulty. Not surprising. But he's capable and intelligent. A cool customer. Of course, that's what you would expect from someone who's headed a police force. Tough. Ruthless. Very savvy."

"Capt. Wonderful," Max said sarcastically.

Kelly slipped gracefully into the wingback chair and looked at him, amused. "You asked for my opinion. I didn't say I liked the man—either."

Max scooted away from that one. "Well, off the top of your head, who's the most likely suspect?"

Kelly gave them an enigmatic smile. "I'd rather know what each of you thinks. Your choice will be so revealing."

Seventeen

THE BREEZE through the open sunroof ruffled Annie's hair, which hadn't been combed in some time. As the Porsche rattled over the wooden bridge, and they left the ruins of Fort Hendrix behind, she blew out a whoosh of relief. "My God, that woman's enough to give you the creepy crawlies for life. I don't think Hal can be the good old boy everybody takes him for."

"I'm not taking him for a good old boy," Max said drily.

Her lips quivered in a smile. "I guess I have a perverse streak. I was pretty well set on Emma, until Kelly said she could be the villain. Now I keep thinking of Emma's good points."

"Such as?"

Annie laughed. "She's a nice guest. She brought extra chips and clam dip Sunday night."

"And a poisoned dart?" He gunned the motor, then turned right onto the blacktop.

"Hey, wait. Where are you going? Let's go back to the shop. I've got some ideas, and we have to hurry before the ferry leaves."

"I'm thirsty."

"Who do you think you are? Phil Marlowe? We can't spend the afternoon slaking your insatiable thirst. We've got work to do."

But he was already past the checkpoint and turning into Parotti's tavern parking lot when a siren sounded behind them. The Porsche smoothed to a stop, and Max turned an indignant face toward the big motorcycle cop. "I was going twenty-eight miles per hour. A motorized wheelchair could have passed me."

Annie recognized the young giant as the second of the Broward's Rock force, the one who'd dusted for fingerprints in Death On Demand after Elliot was killed. Now he placed ham-sized hands on the doorsill and ignored Max to fix her with a gimletlike stare out of his beady eyes. She started to bristle even before he spoke.

"Just a word to the wise, Miss Laurance." He radiated a thick scent of spicy cologne.

Was there ever a phrase better designed to incite rebellion?

"You'd better stay put. The chief told me to keep an eye on you."

Before Max could pull on his barrister's wig, Annie attacked. "Do they pay you extra to be officious?" she demanded, gray eyes glittering dangerously.

Max held up a hand, clearly a warning to cease and desist.

"Sure, I'm official," the cop retorted.

"Officious," she repeated loudly. "As in rude, overbearing, and gratuitously self-important. Just like Inspector Slack."

The young giant's face turned a dull plum color. "You can talk just as fancy as you like, lady. But you better watch your step, or you're going to jail." With that, he swung on his heel, remounted his motorcycle, and roared off in the direction of the village.

Annie slammed the front door to Death On Demand so hard the front window quivered and a display copy of *Break In* tumbled down. "I'm *mad*."

"Cool down, Tiger." Max moved down the central aisle, carrying the sack from their side excursion to Parotti's tavern.

Flicking on the lights, she followed, too infuriated to take time to pet Agatha, who registered her contempt with a resentful yellow glare.

Max put two six-packs of Bud Light on the coffee bar, then opened the refrigerator.

"Want a beer?"

"I'd rather have that cop's head on a platter."

"Annie, Annie," he said mournfully. "What are we going to do with your temper?" He lifted the beers from their cardboard cartons and put all but two away. "I'm doing my best to keep you out of jail, and that famous Laurance temper's going to get you tossed in the can before nightfall. Honey, didn't you ever learn it's easier to sweet-talk your way out of trouble?"

She banged a stack of *Sugartowns* into a neat pile. Some of the flush began to die out of her cheeks, and she could almost smile. "Okay. So I've got a short fuse."

"That's not all bad—depending upon what you're triggering." His dark blue eyes glinted meaningfully.

She reached up and ruffled his hair. "Stow it, lecher."

"Seriously, sweetie, you're going to have to button your lip. The chief isn't like that director you reamed out when they were casting 'Sailors Ashore.' "

"That sorry clown took his feebleminded script too seriously." She put her hands on her hips, ready to do battle. "At least Saulter hasn't made a pass at me." Her brows drew together. "I wonder why the hell not?"

Max laughed uproariously. "My God, you can't have it both ways."

"Well, just let him try," she said in a steely voice.

He opened two beers and handed one to her. "Come on, chum, cool off. You waste too much energy being mad."

She tilted up the brown bottle, then set it down without tasting its contents. "You know something, we are incompatible."

"Just because I believe in avoiding trouble?"

"That's one reason. But it typifies . . ."

He grinned and reached across the coffee bar to touch a finger lightly to her lips. "Typify's the kind of word Kelly Rizzoli likes. She could undoubtedly draw up a list of incontrovertible reasons why you and I should avoid interpersonal relationships." His hand traced the line of her cheek. "But she'd be wrong."

She should firmly push his hand away, but another kind of short fuse was ticking.

"Everyone says it's foolish to pursue relationships that will deadend—" She didn't finish. Max's lips got in the way. The coffee bar was an obstacle, but neither paid any attention to it. Who moved first? Who cared? Their lips met, and Annie stopped analyzing, analogizing, and pontificating.

The phone rang.

Annie didn't quite have her breathing under control when she answered.

Max looked savagely at the phone.

"Yes, Chief?" she said icily.

"Understand you and that pet lawyer of yours are out bothering people."

"It's a free country. Or so I thought."

"You have no call to go around interviewing people. Mrs. Morgan resents it."

"The ex-Mrs. Morgan knew all about the Sunday night session —and she was pretty annoyed that Elliot wasn't forking over her alimony on schedule," Annie said furiously.

A voice broke in. "Hey, you people better leave Carmen alone." She pictured a meaty face with beady brown eyes.

"Butt out, Bud."

So that was Inspector Slack's name.

"Ms. Laurance, I'm calling to give you another chance. You keep your face out of my investigation. I've got enough trouble on this island without you and your boyfriend playing detective. Bud was just giving you some friendly advice."

"I have some friendly advice for Bud," she retorted. "His pal, Carmen, is a real pistol, and she wanted money—"

"Hey, lady, you watch your mouth about Carmen. What d'you mean, she's a pistol?"

"And, furthermore, Chief, have you found out who inherits Elliot's money?"

"Of course."

"Who?"

"That's no business of yours."

"If you're going to slap me in chains tomorrow, you can bet my lawyer will *make* it his business."

Finally, Saulter spoke, and there was just a hint of consideration in his voice. "He hadn't changed his will."

"So Carmen inherits?"

"Yes."

Bud was still fuming. "Hey, wait a minute. Nobody's going to hang a rap on Carmen. Me and her were on the beach Sunday night."

Not Inspector Slack, Annie decided. Mike Hammer on a vacation.

"Bud, get off the line." After an instant, there was a click. "Okay, Ms. Laurance, you and your boyfriend have your fun—but I'll be over to talk to you in the morning. And you better have some good answers." He hung up.

She replaced the receiver. "The tumbril's going to roll first thing in the morning." Her voice was light, but she glanced up at the clock. "Oh Lord, we've got to get cracking. It's ten after five. Come on, Max, let's split up the work. You summarize what we learned from everybody, and I'll call around and see if I can find out where everybody was when Harriet was killed."

Max spread out his notes from the day on the table nearest the coffee bar. He draped himself comfortably in a chair, took off his brown cordovan loafers, wiggled his toes, and drank some more beer.

She called Emma first.

"Yes?" The mistress of mysteries was not cordial.

"Emma, where were you between five and six P.M. Monday?"

There was a chilly pause. "I understand Harriet died about then," she said finally. "Is that what prompts this call?" She laughed softly. "You are indefatigable, aren't you? I was here, my dear. In my office. Working."

"I thought you wrote in the mornings."

"That's right. And in the evenings, too, when I'm close to the finish."

"How about 9:45 Sunday morning?"

"Now that's something new." Her tone was assured and amused. "Is there a corpse no one's told me about?"

"No. That's when the murderer hid the dart in Death On Demand."

"Oh my, you and Mr. Darling do seem to be clever at discovering things. I'm sorry I can't be more helpful. I was working. The next time I get involved in a murder, I'll be sure to order my time better."

Emma sounded quite good-humored now. She certainly didn't feel threatened by their investigation so far.

Annie took a flyer. "How about ten-thirty P.M. Wednesday, July seventeenth?"

"Is there any semblance of reason behind that question?"

"Somebody pushed Uncle Ambrose off his boat."

"Interesting that you know the exact time."

Annie would have given a hot reply, but Emma swept on.

"Sorry, dear, I don't keep a diary—and I wasn't skulking around the harbor that night." The line went dead.

It didn't take long to ring up her list.

Hal Douglas didn't seem affronted by her question. "Yeah, I was jogging about the time Harriet was killed, but I took a path through the bird refuge. I didn't see a soul," he said cheerfully. "As for Sunday morning, I was asleep. And I don't have any idea about last July." His voice dropped. "Do you really think somebody murdered your uncle?"

Annie was relieved when Janis Farley answered rather than Jeff. She replied to the questions in a low, uneasy voice. She and Jeff, she insisted, were at breakfast together Sunday morning and were playing Scrabble Monday evening. Annie could imagine her looking over her shoulder as she spoke.

Fritz Hemphill listened, then said distinctly, "Go to hell."

Before he could hang up, she threw out, "Do you still have the rifle you used to shoot Mike Gonzalez?"

"Funny thing, Annie. Dead men don't talk." His voice continued, cold and uninflected. "Neither do dead women. Sure, I got that gun. I still hunt with it."

Capt. Mac was encouraging. "Have you found out anything?"

"A lot. Some of it, you wouldn't believe."

"I'd believe it. I was a cop for a long time."

It wasn't hard to ask him. "Where were you when Harriet died?"

"In and out. No alibi, unfortunately. I'm transplanting some crape myrtle, so I was around the patio most of the time. You know, the privacy on Broward's Rock is great, but sometimes I wish I had a nosy neighbor."

"There's Carmen Morgan," she offered.

He chuckled. "The lady doesn't spend a lot of time in her garden."

The bedroom was her more likely habitat, but neither of them said it.

"Have you talked to Saulter about Harriet?" she asked.

"Yeah, but there isn't much to report. Place was wiped clean of fingerprints. Saulter thought that was interesting. I did, too. It might indicate the killer was caught by surprise. Otherwise, you'd think he would be wearing gloves."

Capt. Mac said he was probably in the shower Sunday morning. He remembered that he'd spent the evening working on his car the night Ambrose drowned.

Annie rang Carmen Morgan.

"Monday afternoon? Geez, I don't know. I don't keep track of my time like a shop girl."

"That was just yesterday," Annie reminded her in a long-suffering tone which caused Max to look up and grin.

"Sure. Yeah. Well, probably I was watching a game show. That's what I was doing."

Sure.

"What're you going to do with the money Elliot left you?"

"Money? What money?"

"You know. He never changed his will. You'll inherit. Just like a widow."

"Gee, I didn't know that! Gee, that's great." Her effort to sound surprised was as fake as her spiky eyelashes. Annie was glad she didn't have to act for a living. She claimed to be asleep Sunday morning and probably was playing bingo on a Wednesday night in July.

Kelly Rizzoli sounded dreamy. "Around six? I don't know, really. I sometimes walk down by the rock garden. It's peaceful as dusk comes."

Just Kelly and the earthworms, Annie thought.

Max was exhibiting, for him, great industry, shuffling papers and occasionally writing in spurts, so Annie, despite her meager results, stubbornly drew up a chart.

She carried her work to his table and plopped the chart on top of his papers. "Can you believe this?"

He studied it.

ANNIE'S ALIBI CHART

	9:45 Sunday	*6 p.m. Monday*	*10:30 pm Wednesday July 17*
Emma Clyde	working	working	?
Capt. Mac	showering	transplanting crape myrtle	car repair
Farleys	breakfast	playing Scrabble	don't remember
Fritz Hemphill	—	—	—
Kelly Rizzoli	?	walking in the garden	?
Hal Douglas	asleep	jogging	don't remember
Carmen Morgan	asleep	game show	bingo?

She ran her hands distractedly through her snarled hair. "These jerks would never make it in a Freeman Wills Croft book." She thumped the table in disgust. "Look at that. Not a single one has an alibi. How can that many people be invisible every time a murder takes place?"

"Everybody says writers are loners. Maybe it's so."

"Not only loners, weirdos," she muttered. "Every time I talk to Kelly Rizzoli, I feel like I'm in a deserted cemetery at midnight, consorting with a vampire."

"You can't expect charts to solve anything," Max continued with irritating placidity. "Life doesn't imitate art. Old mysteries can't help us solve this."

"Sure they can. Why, I'll bet I figure it out before you do. I know a lot more about murders than you ever thought about."

He gave her a smile that could only qualify as patronizing in the extreme, pushed her chart aside to pick up his top paper, and waggled his paper, filled with his dark, sloping scrawl. "Here's what we have to find out."

She ignored the proffered sheet. He quirked an eyebrow, still looking superior and amused, then swung his feet to the floor and stood.

He held his papers high as he moved up the central aisle. "When I get the answers to these questions, we'll know everything that matters." He picked up the phone at the cash desk.

Annie paced back and forth in the coffee area, pausing occasionally to look up at the watercolors. Of course she knew more about murders than Max! He had the usual male conceit, so certain he knew more than she did. By golly, she would show him. The little gray cells, that was the ticket. In all of this mishmash of information, there had to be a key to the villain. No alibi. That indicated a great deal of confidence on the murderer's part, didn't it? Confidence— Okay, she had confidence, too.

But she did prick up her ears to hear his half of the conversation. Fair was fair. After all, she'd let him see her alibi chart.

He was as slick as the hide of a greased pig.

". . . calling from Beaufort County, South Carolina. We have a homicide here, actually a triple homicide, and we need some information on a Miss Kelly Rizzoli. You've got her down for a couple of misdemeanors, around '78, '79. If you can pull it up on your computer, we'd appreciate the help. Sure, I'd be glad to hold."

"So if you get some stuff on Kelly, then we'll know about everybody," Annie kibitzed.

He covered the receiver. "Except for Harriet. And that's moot."

"I know that one. Elliot accused her of lifting a plot from somebody."

Max gave a small shrug. "We know she wasn't the killer. But that would hardly be reason enough."

She remembered Harriet's contorted face that day at Death On Demand. Max was wrong. That day, Harriet was mad enough to kill.

Annie spread her hands out. "How can we guess what's reason enough? Remember what happened to Gideon in Kelly's short story?"

Max waggled his hand for her to be quiet. "That's right," he said into the receiver. "That's the one. What've you got—well, I'll be damned. Sure. Listen, we appreciate your help. If we can ever give you a hand—"

He hung up, then turned to Annie, his blue eyes gleaming with excitement. "He remembers, all right, and he thinks Kelly is just as nutty as her sister. In fact, he believes Kelly did every bit of it herself." He scrunched his face in distaste. "She forgot to mention the chicken house. Apparently, she—or Pamela—set fire to the chicken house behind the place where they boarded."

"Ugh."

"Yeah. So maybe Kelly had more to lose than some embarrassing talk about her crazy sister."

"Maybe Pamela's not crazy. Maybe she's a *prisoner*—a variation on *Flowers in the Attic*."

He didn't laugh. "Actually, nothing about Kelly would surprise me." He ran a hand through his thick blond hair. "Maybe Carmen summed up the party pretty well. Annie, did you have any idea what your Sunday Night Regulars were like?"

She tried to remember back before Sunday. Sunday seemed a thousand years ago.

"I always thought Emma Clyde was a lot smarter than she acted. You know, she looks like the average housewife shopping in the housewares section at Winn-Dixie."

"That's on a par with calling a cobra a house pet."

"I really liked Hal Douglas. He has such an all-American face."

"Just your average neighborhood wife-killer," Max sang.

"And Kelly seemed so vulnerable, like a coed at a bad hang-out."

"Very bad, but she's the den mother."

He lightly touched her elbow, and they started back down the central aisle.

"I never did like the Farleys. They give me the willies."

"Another all-American pair." Max walked behind the coffee bar, honing in on the refrigerator.

As he lifted out another beer, she mused, "Nobody much liked Fritz. He's such a cold fish."

Max carefully fitted the church key to the bottle cap. "Then there's Capt. Wonderful," and he shot a sly look at Annie.

She leaned against the coffee bar. "Why do you hate him so much? He's the only normal one of the bunch."

The cap snapped off, and foam rose over the lip of the bottle. "No cop is normal."

"That's not fair. Besides, he has a piddly motive."

Handing her the first bottle, he uncapped the second. "Keeping a paternity suit quiet doesn't seem worth a poison-tipped dart. But a man who'll cheat on his wife will cheat anybody. I intend to nose around him a little more."

Annie took a delicate sip of beer. She'd better ease up on her quaffing. She needed a clear head, especially if she were going to show Max up. He thought he was so smart. Of course, if the murderer's picture were on Harriet's film, neither—

She popped straight up. The beer jostled and overflowed as she gestured wildly at the wall clock.

"My God, Max, it's almost six!"

Eighteen

THE PORSCHE leapt forward. Annie clung to the red leather rim of the dash. The clock flashed 5:52.

"Don't worry, this girl can fly. We'll make it. Besides, Parotti probably doesn't leave on time."

"Yes, he does," she yelled back over the whip of the wind through the open sunroof. The live oaks passed in a blur. "He's a little martinet. You'd think that damned ferry was the *Queen Elizabeth* the way he acts about her schedule."

In answer, Max pressed harder on the accelerator.

Annie thumped back against her spine. They had to make it. They had to.

The Porsche zoomed around the last curve and roared toward the checkpoint. He braked hard, received a pass-through wave from a startled Jimmy Moon, then floorboarded it, and the sports car burst forward like a two-year-old headed for the winner's circle.

Success was theirs! The car screeched onto the dock just as Parotti gave the preliminary toots announcing imminent departure. The ferry horn mingled with the high, abrasive whine of a siren.

Annie twisted in her seat and saw the motorcycle turning off the blacktop.

"Hurry, drive onto the ferry!"

Max twisted to look, too. The Porsche didn't move. "A work farm is not my idea of a pleasant way to spend the rest of October."

As the motorcycle drew alongside, she glared at Max in bitter disappointment.

Once again, the massive young policeman loomed beside the car. A waft of spicy cologne tickled Annie's nose. "Eighty-six miles per hour. You people think this island is a goddamned racetrack?"

Annie jounced in the seat. They had to hurry! The ferry always left on time. The clock flashed 5:59. She could see Parotti peering at them from the ferry cabin.

"Officer, I apologize," Max began smoothly, "but we have important business on the mainland."

"You may have business there. But she don't," and he jerked a thumb at Annie.

"Wait a minute—" she began angrily.

Max spoke out of the side of his mouth. "Stop snarling. Let me handle this."

"She ain't leavin' the island."

"She isn't under arrest so—"

The squinty-eyed giant smiled. It was as charming as a barracuda doing ballet. "I got a warrant right here." He thumped his brown khaki chest. "You get on that ferry, I arrest her."

Parotti yanked the whistle. Final call.

Annie glared at Bud, then leaned forward as if to kiss Max goodbye. At the same time, she pulled open her purse, fished out the roll of film, and jammed it in his hand.

"Go ahead," she whispered in his ear, then slid across the seat, opened the door, and jumped out.

Max looked from her to Bud and back again.

"Max, go!"

The Porsche jolted forward and rolled onto the ferry. The horn tooted, and the ferry chugged out into the sound.

Annie, arms folded, faced Bud.

His meaty face furrowed. "Hey, what was the big hurry?"

"Wouldn't you just like to know?"

□   □   □   □

Annie rented a battered chartreuse bicycle at Henry's Bikes By the Day or Week, picked up tacos-to-go at Maria's Cantina, and pedaled furiously back to her tree house, taking the shortcut across the Forest Preserve, cool and dim now as dusk settled over the sea pines. She pumped vigorously, treating the bike path like a Le Mans speedway, to help ease some of her frustration. What a lousy deal. She *deserved* to be in at the kill. Or, if not actually the kill, the moment of truth when the murderer's identity was revealed.

Parking the bike beneath the outside stairway, she ran lightly up the wooden steps, unlocked the front door, and carried the take-out sack to the kitchen. She wiped her face, flushed from exertion. She felt like a piece of saltwater taffy that had been dropped in the sand. It was easy somehow to picture Max lounging comfortably in the Porsche, enjoying the cool sweep of water off the sound—and carrying in his pocket the solution to their mystery.

She plumped two beef tacos in the microwave to warm, ducked into the bathroom to wash her hands and face, retrieved the tacos, liberally doused them with hot sauce, and poured orange Gatorade into a yellow plastic cup. Carrying her meal into the living room, she settled comfortably in the wicker divan with a soft red cushion behind her. As she ate, she imagined Max's reaction to this feast (utter horror) and studied her ceiling-high shelves filled with her own very favorite mysteries, many of them quite valuable and difficult to find. She had most of the Constance and Gwenyth Little books. All but one contained the word *black* in the title. Her favorite? Probably *The Black Shrouds*. There were the Leslie Ford, Mary Roberts Rinehart, Mary Collins, Eric Ambler, and Patricia Wentworth titles. Plus Phoebe Atwood Taylor, Rex Stout, and all the Christies, of course.

She finished the first taco, drank some Gatorade, and was reaching for the second taco, when her hand paused. Almost every one of these books, except the Ambler titles, contained magnificent denouements where the detective faced the circle of suspects and, *voilà,* through brilliant ratiocination, triumphantly revealed the identity of the murderer.

Hercule Poirot in *Towards Zero.* Asey Mayo in *Out of Order.* Nero Wolfe in *The Zero Clue.*

Why not Annie Laurance at Death On Demand?

A trap. All she had to do was set a trap for the murderer—

The second taco forgotten, she jumped up and hurried to the telephone. It rang the instant before she reached it.

Bother. She licked hot sauce from her fingers, picked it up, and barked an impatient hello.

"Has the Revolution begun?"

"Huh?"

"You sound beleaguered. Uptight. Stressed." Max dropped his bantering tone. "Is that cop bothering you?"

"Oh, no. No, no. Listen, I've got a great idea!"

"Whatever it is, wait until I get back. I'll—"

"There isn't time. I've got to trap the killer before Saulter comes after me in the morning. And you can't get back until tomorrow."

"I'll be back at nine tonight."

"Did you take your water wings? The ferry doesn't run again until ten tomorrow."

"Mr. Parotti and I are drinking beer at a tavern down the block from a one-hour photo shop in Savannah. We are in hearty agreement that the rich get richer, the poor get poorer, and the working man gets screwed every time." George Jones sang "He Stopped Loving Her Today" in the background. "So cool it till I get back."

She ignored that. "Max, this is *genius.* I'm going to phone everybody and tell them I've just found a diary of Uncle Ambrose's at the shop, and now I know the truth. I'll act all upset and frantic, then I'll break the connection."

George Jones's wail carried clearly over Max's thundering silence.

She practically danced with eagerness. "It's perfect. The murderer will have to come after me. I'll call Saulter and have him watching."

"You think somebody as smart as our killer is going to fall for the oldest trick in the book and come running with a marlin spike?"

"Sure. Yes. Hell, yes. It *always* works for Nero Wolfe."

"Annie, it's all well and good to read those books, but you can't take them so seriously." You'd have to be deaf to miss the patronizing tone of his voice. "Flee, all is discovered. Lordy." He chuckled. "Okay, you have fun, and I'll be back about nine with the goods. I've got to go buy Parotti another beer."

She replaced the receiver very gently. She was in control. Otherwise, she would have thrown the entire instrument into the marsh. She glowered at the phone and wondered how Grace Latham had resisted bloodshed through her years of association with John Primrose.

She'd show him. Nine o'clock. She reached for the receiver, then paused. Maybe he did have a point about the flee-all-is-discovered ploy. She nibbled thoughtfully on her thumb. Oh. She turned an idea over in her mind and smiled. Sure. That would work. She would entice everybody back to the Scene of the Crime, then, just like Miss Marple who drew on her experiences in St. Mary Mead, she would cull from the recesses of her mind the appropriate parallel to a fictional murder, and the answer would be clear. Annie reached for the phone.

Saulter's lip curled as he picked up the mug of hot milk. Dammit, his stomach felt like somebody'd dropped in a handful of live coals. This case was becoming a coast-to-coast sensation. Three murders since Saturday night, and what did he have to show for it? One autopsy report that sounded like something out of John Dickson Carr. God, now he was beginning to think like those bloody writers. But who'd ever heard of killing anybody with succinyl-choline? And why'd medicines have names like Hungarian dancers? Damn crazy thing. Well, he wasn't going to be fooled. This was a setup, from first to last, trying to make it look like a nutty writer'd done it. Murder, when you got down to it, was always simple.

This time it was murder for money. That little sun-streaked blonde didn't want to lose the shop she'd murdered to get. She didn't have a penny until Ambrose drowned, and she inherited from him. She'd plowed every cent of his estate into the store, and she wasn't about to lose it.

Saulter gulped some milk and winced.

He'd made it pretty clear he was going to arrest her tomorrow, and now all he had to do was sit back and wait for her to do something foolish. Too bad Bud stopped her from taking the ferry. If she'd made a run for it, he'd have had all the proof he needed.

The problem was, he didn't have any evidence.

Just give him one tangible piece of evidence to tie her to the crime scene. Of course, her fingerprints were all over the circuit breaker box at the store, but her smartassed lawyer would make mincemeat of that. And so far there wasn't anything at the vet's or the Edelman murder.

Evidence. Something to put the nail in Annie Laurance's coffin. Or anything else that would tie her to Morgan. He glared at the last two boxes of papers from Morgan's house. He was sick and tired of reading this guy's stuff. But a careful cop keeps looking.

The phone rang, his hand jerked, and hot milk sloshed over his fingers. God, if it was another of those reporters . . . He lifted the receiver.

"Saulter here."

"Chief, you've got to get over to Death On Demand. I've called a meeting of all the suspects there in half an hour. We'll catch the murderer tonight!"

The pain in his stomach flared. He'd get this wise-guy little murderess if it was the last thing he did on Broward's Rock. "Ms. Laurance, if I come over there, I'll have a warrant for your arrest in my pocket," and he slammed down the phone.

That little dingo. As if he didn't have enough troubles without her horning in on his investigation.

Annie took a two-and-a-half-minute shower, dried off quicker than pelican diving for mullet, and dressed in a flurry—white linen slacks, a yellow cotton pullover, and yellow flats. She glanced at the clock as she raced out the front door. Everyone was due at Death On Demand in fifteen minutes. She needed to make coffee and organize her thoughts. It took a minute to start the Volvo. She had hardly driven it since Max arrived. Her golf clubs rattled in the back seat as she drove up the rutted road toward the blacktop. Not even a sliver of moonlight pierced the thick canopy of the swamp. When she reached the main road, she picked up speed until she turned into the oyster-shell lot behind the harbor-front shops.

Her footsteps crunched loudly across the broken shells. It was a soft Carolina night, the air as silky as Agatha's fur. She unlocked the front door of Death On Demand, flicked on the lights, and hurried toward the back. Agatha peered inquisitively after her, then jumped lightly to the floor and padded toward the coffee bar. Annie poured a twelve-cup measure of Kona beans into the grinder, then turned it on. Good hostess prepares to receive murderous guests. She grinned and took a deep breath, delighting in the heady mixture of freshly ground coffee and old, musty books.

She glanced around the coffee area. Oh, good grief. She must clear out Max's papers. No point in letting the suspects know just how much they had on them. She gathered up the sheets and paused to read Max's list of questions.

1. Whose goose would have been charbroiled if Elliot had finished his talk Sunday night?

2. Why did the murderer show up Johnny-on-the-spot when Annie was in Elliot's tree house?

3. Was Elliot blackmailing Emma? Annie says yes; Carmen, no. Carmen should know. *(Thanks, Max.)*

4. Were Carmen and the dumb cop really on the beach when Morgan was killed? Pretty convenient timing.

5. Did Harriet score twice with her camera? What if she didn't?

The coffee finished dripping into the pot. Annie found her favorite mug, *The Yellow Room* (Rinehart, not Leroux), poured a cup, and leaned against the coffee bar to think.

Her guests began arriving promptly at eight.

Annie greeted them cheerfully, but her perspective had indeed changed since Sunday evening.

Emma Clyde's cornflower blue eyes scanned the coffee area with the same shrewd intensity. Her dress, a swirling mixture of orange and magenta, contrasted as sharply with her stiff bronze curls. But Annie would never again see her as a clever housewife. She didn't carry chips and dip tonight.

"So you've called a meeting of the island residents who are most knowledgeable about crime," Emma observed. "I feel so flattered to have been included." Her tone was tart.

Kelly Rizzoli and Hal Douglas came in together, spookily reminiscent of their arrival Sunday. Then she had seen them as incipient lovebirds. Now it was difficult not to see Grace Poole and Bluebeard.

Capt. Mac came down the central aisle, his tanned face grim. He looked at Annie questioningly. The Farleys stood at the edge of the coffee area. Janis tried to keep her bruised face in the shadows, but Annie saw Emma's eyes widen.

Fritz Hemphill arrived last. He gave no greeting to anyone, and his dark eyes sparkled angrily in a set face.

"Grab a cup of coffee," she offered. "Then if you'll take your places—where you sat Sunday night—we'll get started."

They moved around the coffee bar, but there was no repartee as they took their cups to the tables.

"Now that we're all here—"

"Not quite." Hemphill's voice rasped like a rusty gate. "Where's the boyfriend? And your twittery clerk, Ingrid?"

"Nobody could possibly think Max and Ingrid had anything to do with Elliot's murder. Max never met him until that night, and Ingrid wasn't on Elliot's list."

Hemphill wasn't deflected. "So Ingrid's not in the party. Okay, I buy it. But where's the boyfriend? Searching our places while we sit here?"

"Of course not," she objected hotly. "He's not even on the island."

"That's true. I saw him take the ferry at six," Hal agreed. "But what happened on the dock with you and the cop, Annie?"

Annie stood with her back to the coffee bar and felt control slipping away.

"No big deal," she responded quickly. "Max had some errands to run in Savannah, and I didn't go with him."

"So how come you got left at the dock?" Hal pressed.

"Because that charming cop was going to arrest me if I left the island." Her voice wasn't so good-humored now.

Emma attacked. "So you want us to figure out the crime and save your skin."

"Everybody will breathe easier if we solve the crime. I see no reason why anyone should oppose that—except the murderer."

No one said a word. Seven pairs of eyes watched Annie stonily.

It was time. *En garde.* Annie pointed at the nearest table. Color blazed in Jeff Farley's pale cheeks above his sleek blond beard. His thick horn-rimmed glasses glittered in the overhead light. His chest moved beneath his caramel-colored sweater as his breathing quickened. Janis, her shoulders hunched, pressed her knuckles against her mouth. Her thick, pancake brown makeup was designed to hide the ugly bruise on her cheek. Instead, it emphasized the alabaster fairness of her neck.

"Jeff Farley couldn't afford to let Elliot Morgan live," Annie began.

Emma Clyde leaned forward, her eyes intent on Jeff's face. The others sat as quietly as mice when a cat nears.

"Jeff is sick." Her voice shook a little, because this wasn't nice. It wasn't fun to peel away the protective layers to a wounded core. "He hurts Janis. Elliot knew this, and, if he put it in a book, it would be the end of everything for Jeff as a writer."

Farley stumbled to his feet, the chair clattering to the floor behind him.

"Jeff, no. No!" Janis's voice rose in a desperate cry.

Capt. Mac was across the brief space in two strides, pinning Jeff's arms to his side. Without a struggle, Farley sagged against the stronger man.

"Sit down, and don't move again." Capt. Mac gently pressed the younger man back into his seat, then turned toward Annie, his face rock hard. "Don't you think this is a little much? Let's leave the investigating to the cops."

"Only the murderer should object," she said steadily.

"People don't like having their dirty laundry spread out in public."

"This isn't public. We were all here Sunday night." She looked from face to face. "We are all under suspicion until we find the murderer."

"That's quite true," Kelly said mildly.

"Go for it," Hal joined in.

Capt. Mac, his face tight with disapproval, shrugged and returned to his table.

Annie knew she didn't have a friend in the house.

"Emma."

The square-faced, sharp-eyed woman nodded curtly. "Here." She took a deliberate sip of coffee. "Good brew. As we used to say, the atmosphere is stimulating. I wouldn't have missed it for the world."

"You don't miss much, do you?" Annie demanded. "You know, if you aren't the murderer, I'll bet you know who did it."

Those keen blue eyes regarded Annie without a quiver. But Annie knew she'd hit the truth. "What do you know, Emma? Why don't you tell us?"

Again, Emma sipped her coffee, taking her time. She smiled, but it was as artificial as a potted plastic plant at a gas station. "I know one thing."

They all turned toward Emma and waited expectantly: Jeff Farley, his hands balled in fists, his face still flushed; Janis Farley, her eyes enormous, her arms crossed tightly over her chest; Kelly Rizzoli, her dark red hair falling softly around her face, her green eyes not the least bit dreamy; Hal Douglas, his pudgy face closed and empty; Capt. Mac, his dark eyes watchful, alert.

"I know a fishing expedition when I see one," Emma said caustically. "You don't know a damned thing, Annie."

Annie eyed her adversary. "But you know a lot of tricks, Emma. You're the smartest one in the room. You know the best defense is a good offense—and you know damned well you pushed your husband over the side of your yacht."

Something moved in those calculating, observant eyes. "I know I can afford a slander suit. One more crack out of you, and I'll call my lawyer."

Annie ignored her and leaned her elbows back against the coffee bar.

"Murder will out, whether it's ever proved or not. Nobody can prove it, but there are some people in L.A. who know Fritz Hemphill blew away his best friend in a so-called hunting accident so he could inherit some property in Carmel."

As usual, Fritz looked the part of a Broward's Rock islander: pale pink cotton broadcloth shirt, a blue ribbed pullover, gray slacks. So civilized. Except for those dark, hot eyes.

Annie met that gaze boldly. "How many cops have you ever known to have an accident with a gun, Fritz?"

When he made no answer, she nodded slowly. "Elliot knew. He knew about Jeff and Janis, Emma, and Fritz. And he knew about Kelly and Hal."

That ideal couple watched her unblinkingly.

"Kelly keeps her sister a prisoner. She claims the girl is mentally ill. I wonder what the truth is? Maybe somebody should talk to her sister. As for Hal, nobody's ever seen his wife since she disappeared from their cabin at Lake Tahoe. He didn't like the way she ran around with other men."

Hal looked like he'd been jabbed in the throat. His head swung toward Kelly. Her face was as placid as a tidal pond, and she reached out to touch his hand.

Capt. Mac slammed his palm hard against the table where he sat alone. Harriet had been his companion Sunday evening. Coffee slopped out of his mug and ran in a slow trickle across the table. He ignored it. "Goddammit, you've gone too far. And I'm not going to sit here like a schoolboy waiting to be scolded." His face, dark with anger, turned toward the others: "I'm next. What did Elliot have on me? A paternity suit, if any of you give a damn." He rose and faced Annie. "I've tried to be helpful to you. I don't think you killed Elliot or Harriet. Or Jill Kearney. But I do think you've let your so-called mystery expertise go to your head, young woman, and I've had enough of it."

He snatched up his soft cap and started down the central aisle. Other chairs scraped. Everyone was leaving.

Her denouement was collapsing like an overcooked soufflé. Now was the time—if she were Hercule Poirot or Nero Wolfe or Asey Mayo or Miss Marple or Miss Silver—when she would raise her hand and point at the guilty party, and the curtain would ring down.

There was one small problem.

She didn't know who in the *hell* the murderer was.

Her suspects were moving with stiff alacrity up the central aisle, and nobody was saying what a good time they'd had.

Emma Clyde paused at the head of the pack, looked back, and taunted, "I assure you, Annie, Marigold Rembrandt would have done it better."

That was the last straw.

Dammit, one of them was a three-time—no—four-time murderer, counting Uncle Ambrose.

"All right," she called out angrily. "You can all laugh now. But I'll have the last laugh tomorrow when I give Chief Saulter a photograph of the murderer."

The exodus stopped.

"Where in the hell did you get a picture of the murderer?" Emma demanded.

"The murderer's not so damned smart. Did it ever occur to any of you that Harriet had a clear view of Elliot's house? And she was up in her widow's walk Monday afternoon—with her camera."

Nineteen

MAX TAPPED a Scott Joplin intro with his fingers on the glass counter and watched the clock. In another five minutes, he'd know what Harriet had captured in her film. Would it be Annie? And someone else?

That reminded him of his list of questions. Elliot had collected information about the Sunday Night Regulars, and he had intended to blab everything he knew. When Annie pretended she knew about Elliot's information, Emma immediately suspected her of blackmail. That suggested she'd been blackmailed before. But Carmen insisted her ex-husband wasn't a blackmailer—Max stood up straight. Blackmail. Why did people blackmail? He thought about it with growing excitement, and he thought about everyone who'd been at Death On Demand Sunday night and the traditional reason for blackmail.

"Your pictures, mister." The clerk shoved the package across the counter with exquisite boredom.

Max grabbed them. There was Annie, climbing in the kitchen window of Elliot Morgan's house. And there—by God. It was the face he expected.

"Can I use your phone?" he yelled at the startled clerk.

He made a long distance call, using his Sprint number, but the line at Death On Demand rang busy.

It was very quiet in Death On Demand. So quiet Annie could hear the click of Agatha's claws as she glided up the central aisle to see why her mistress stood by the front door.

"Agatha, I may have blown it."

Curious bright yellow eyes stared at her unblinkingly.

"Emma made me mad." She spoke conversationally. Max had always warned that her temper was going to land her in deep trouble someday. Just because Emma had taunted her with that crack about Marigold Rembrandt was no excuse to have let slip about the film.

Her face furrowed in concentration. But no matter how hard she thought, it didn't change the truth of the matter. She'd told them about Harriet's camera—and she'd said she'd turn the film over to the chief tomorrow.

The bookstore was quieter than a graveyard at midnight. She swallowed, lunged across the few feet of space, and shoved home the deadbolt.

She gulped some air, then jumped to one side, her heart racketing in her chest as she stared wildly down to see what had touched her leg.

Agatha lifted a dainty paw and swiped again at her shin, thoroughly enjoying this new and active game.

God. A murderer somewhere outside and a cat with lousy timing inside.

Annie moved precipitously again, dashing to the cash desk and pulling open the drawer. Agatha flowed up to the counter and crouched, purring deeply. Annie scrabbled through the drawer. A letter opener. Wonderful to slice butter. Rubber bands. Band-Aids. Aspirin. Paper clips. A new package of golf balls. She ripped open the package and stuffed the three hard balls into the pocket of her slacks. It wasn't much, but they hadn't called her Dead-Eye on the softball team for nothing. She would at the very least go down firing.

Okay. She had some ammunition in case the killer broke in this minute, and now she'd call the chief. He *had* to listen this time.

She reached for the phone and realized her hand was shaking. She'd always felt absolute disdain for the wumpety conduct that landed gothic heroines in a pickle up to the top of their lace nighties. She had always been confident that she would never be guilty of repairing to the second tombstone at midnight in the company of a man with a mustache. Not she.

And here she was, trying to breathe silently so she could listen for the telltale noises that would signal the murderer's approach.

Her hand rested on the receiver. A faint frown touched her face.

Why wasn't the killer poking a rifle through a window and blowing her away? Or unleashing another poisoned dart? Or wielding a handy cosh?

Indeed, why was it as quiet as the proverbial graveyard?

Nobody was trying to break in.

Was someone lying in wait for her outside?

She lifted her hand from the telephone and rubbed her knuckles thoughtfully against her cheek.

Let him—or her—lie. She wouldn't stir a step until Max came, and nobody could handle the two of them.

She breathed more easily, and checked her watch. Max and Parotti might be boarding the ferry this minute. It wouldn't be long, and when he got back, they'd take the pictures straight to Saulter.

But if nobody were reacting to her startling revelation about Harriet's camera—it meant nobody but Annie was pictured in those films. That's why the doors remained closed. No one knocked. No one called.

"Dammit."

Agatha stopped purring.

"Not you, sweetheart." Annie stroked the silky fur, but Agatha twisted away and dropped to the floor.

If she alone were pictured in the films, she and Max were back to Square One.

The whole evening was a fiasco. Perhaps the only solution was to look at everything with a fresh eye. Start at the beginning— with the murder of Uncle Ambrose. She paced down the central aisle, her eyes scanning the bright jackets to her right and left with disappointment. Her books had let her down. She *should* have been able to turn and dramatically unveil the villain, but her denouement had fizzled like day-old champagne. She passed the espionage/thrillers section and noted an Ambler title, *The Light of Day.* She felt just about as competent as Arthur Abdel Simpson.

She tucked her hand in her pocket and gripped the first golf ball. Maybe she should retire as a mystery bookseller and concentrate on her golf.

Reaching the coffee area, she stared up at the five watercolors, without experiencing the usual spurt of pleasure in them.

The old lady with faded blue eyes stared at approaching death without surprise as the heavy car hurtled closer in watercolor number one. The ancient servant strained to see in the second painting. The third pictured an active man's closet full of trophies and sports equipment. The young man exhibited disgust as he handed the letter to his sister in the fourth picture, and guests watched as their host raised a glass in a toast in the fifth.

What good did it do to know all about murder and murderers and be caught wanting when it mattered?

She knew these stories backward and forward. The sporting man who opened his library window on a snowy evening to someone he trusted—

Someone he trusted.

Annie stood very still and stared up at the third painting.

Trust.

Uncle Ambrose's murder.

Uncle Ambrose himself.

She stared at the painting and could see her uncle, his thoughtful, intelligent face. He had been smart, savvy, tough, perhaps a little cynical from his years as a prosecuting attorney in Fort Worth. He knew just how bad people could be. He knew that murderers were dangerous predators.

He was researching *murders.* He would never have turned his back on someone he suspected of being a killer.

Uncle Ambrose was nobody's fool.

So he had been killed by someone he trusted, just as was the man whose closet was pictured.

It was exactly as Hercule Poirot always insisted: the character

of the victim revealed the identity of the murderer. Staring up at
that painting of a jumbled closet, remembering her uncle, knowing the Sunday Night Regulars, she knew who had committed the
four murders on Broward's Rock.

Swinging around, she ran up the central aisle, and grabbed up
the telephone receiver. Agatha flashed into the darkness, seeking
sanctuary beneath her favorite fern. Annie held the receiver to her
ear, then stiffened.

The line was dead.

Max leaned sleepily back against the car seat and enjoyed the
breeze lifting off the water as the ferry chugged peacefully across
the sound. He felt a great sense of satisfaction. He'd tell Annie
how he'd figured it out even before he got the pictures. All it
required was an orderly mind, the ability to shuck away the extraneous and focus on the important. Poor Annie and her flee-all-is-
discovered ploy. He shook his head and smiled, then smothered a
yawn. Almost there. Well, he'd be tactful with her.

The lights went out in Death On Demand. Annie moved away
from the switches and ran swiftly down the central corridor, a golf
ball clutched in her right hand. She slid like a wraith into the
storeroom and felt her way across the floor to the back door.

This was the tricky part.

The murderer must be waiting for her outside. That dead phone
line was no accident. It was intended to prevent her from calling
the chief, which meant, in turn, that the films did contain the
murderer's picture. She had no intention of remaining in Death
On Demand like one of the Ten Little Indians.

She edged open the back door and peered out into the alley. It
was darker than the dirt heaped beside an open grave. As quietly
as a water moccasin slipping through a marsh pond, she eased out
of the screen door and crept up the alley, every nerve end alert for
a betraying rustle. Reaching the end of the alley, she surveyed the
broad expanse of lawn, dotted with sea pines, that lay between the
shops and the parking area. Her blue Volvo sat in solitary splen-

dor near a clump of wisteria. God, what she would have given at that moment for a little urban clutter and excitement. The shops and their parking lot, closed at night, were separated from the houses by the golf course. The nearest habitations were the marina condos, several hundred yards to her left. Lights shone cheerfully from several of the condos.

Could she scream loudly enough to get help?

Not in time. The Broward's Rock murderer liked to bash his victims. It behooved her to avoid all contact. If she could just reach her car—

Darting from palmetto palm to azalea thicket to palmetto palm, Annie plunged into the shadows nearest her Volvo and fell headlong over a body.

She didn't have to see to know it was a body. She could *feel* it. Her first, panicked, instinctive fear was for Max. But he couldn't be back yet. Frantically, she felt the still form, found the slowly beating pulse in the throat. A man's throat. A familiar smell. Cologne. My God, it must be *Bud*. Maybe Saulter had listened and sent Bud to keep an eye on her, but obviously the murderer had spotted him. She patted his pockets. Keys. A lighter. Shielding it with her hand, she flicked it on. Yes, it was Bud, with a smear of blood at the side of his head.

And no gun in his holster.

Annie crouched by the unconscious policeman, then hurtled toward her car, yanked open the door, jumped in, slammed and locked the door. She poked the key in the ignition, turned it, and nothing happened.

The phone dead. Bud knocked out. Her car disabled.

She was one sitting duck.

The murderer could get her now. The slam of the car door was unmistakable. He had to know where she was.

Minutes ticked by. Nothing happened.

She gripped the steering wheel. Okay, the murderer was after the film—

"Oh, God!"

Annie unlocked the car door, jumped out, started for the shop, stopped, flapped her hands frantically.

How could she have been so dumb?

She wasn't the target. The killer was after Max! Max's trip to the mainland had received full play at her abortive denouement—and this murderer thought fast and moved faster. The ferry would be back any minute, and the murderer would be there, waiting, ready to attack.

Car dead. Bud out. Phone off.

She had to get word to Saulter.

By the time she could knock at a condo, persuade someone to let her in, call the station, get Saulter, and convince him, it would be too late for Max.

Forever too late.

Her watch gleamed in the dark.

Five minutes to nine. The ferry was due back at nine.

Annie set off in a jog toward the condos. She'd find a bike. Steal one. Nobody locked up their bikes on Broward's Rock. Then she saw a gleam of metal in the bushes near where Bud lay. She tore at the branches of wisteria. It took only a moment to get the keys out of Bud's pocket. As she kicked the motorcycle to life, she remembered those long-ago summer outings on dirt bikes with Uncle Ambrose and gunned the motor.

Had anyone seen her race across the island, it would have been the stuff of legends: "Listen, my child, you shall hear of the night Annie Laurance flew by here." But instead she took the bike trail across the Forest Preserve, which, understandably, was not heavily populated at nine o'clock on an October night, and erupted into public notice at the checkpoint.

Throttling down, she squealed the cycle to a pause and shouted at a startled Jimmy Moon, "Call Chief Saulter. Tell him the murderer's after Max at the ferry landing and to come quick!"

The motorcycle jolted forward. Annie careened through the village streets and curved around the last corner to see the ferry bumping into the dock. She killed the motor and let the machine roll to a stop, then jumped down and began to run. She dared not call out. The killer had Bud's gun. The murderer much preferred a quiet knockout, but the gun would be used if necessary. She had no doubt of that.

She ran up the blacktop, her flats slapping against the pavement. The Porsche bumped slowly off the ferry.

A dark figure stepped out into the road and hailed Max.

The Porsche stopped.

Annie was close enough to see a figure bend near the window. She gripped a golf ball, raised her arm and let fly.

Twenty

HER GOLF BALL struck Capt. Mac square on the temple just as Max slammed open the car door and creamed him across the chest.

The police car, red light whirling and siren snarling, slid to a stop on the dock. The lights from the police car showed Capt. Mac struggling to get to his feet and reaching beneath his black turtleneck sweater.

"He's got Bud's gun!" Annie shouted as Max turned to dive toward McElroy and Chief Saulter reached for his own gun.

Her second golf ball bulleted into Capt. Mac's hand just as he drew out the pistol. Then Max's flying tackle dumped the older man on his back.

Chief Saulter trained his gun on the two of them, retrieved Bud's gun, then gestured for Max and his quarry to stand with their backs against the patrol car.

Parotti stumped off the ferry, his head jutting forward pugnaciously. "What the hell's going on here? Can't a man drink a beer in peace and quiet after a hard day?" Then he squinted at Max. "You still here? Got car trouble?"

Max jerked his head toward Capt. Mac, then rubbed his neck. "Ouch. Capt. Mac's the murderer. He tried to jump me. Didn't you see it?"

Parotti grumbled, "I was down below, but you people are making enough noise to raise the dead."

Capt. Mac kept trying. "Saulter, I was going to make a citizen's arrest. Darling's the man you want. He's—"

"Give it up," Max advised. "I've got the pictures, McElroy, showing you on Elliot's steps. Harriet had a talent for photography."

Capt. Mac slumped back against the police car, his face stolid.

Max yanked on his pullover sweater which had twisted around his chest in the struggle. The whirling red light on the police car revealed an ugly scratch on the side of his face.

Annie was preparing to move forward, offer a handkerchief, and make sympathetic coos when Saulter, snapping handcuffs on Capt. Mac's wrists, said, "So you solved it, Darling."

She stopped in midstride. "Oh, no," she objected energetically. "I solved it. I figured it out and came to save Max's life."

"Save my life! Hell, I knew it was Capt. Mac. Why do you think I rammed the door against him? I probably dented the hell out of it—"

"You just stopped in the middle of the road, and he was getting ready to cosh you. If it hadn't been for me—"

"For God's sake, I *had* to stop. He called out that he had you at his place, and if I ever wanted to see you again, I'd better cooperate."

"You just looked at Harriet's pictures," she said derisively. "I *deduced* it."

"Oh yeah! How?"

She described the third watercolor at Death On Demand. "And, of course, once I *thought* about it, it was easy. It had to be Capt. Mac." She leaned forward to explain. "You see, it was just as Hercule Poirot always says. The character of the victim is all-important."

"Look, Annie, admit it," Max urged, "you made a lucky guess."

"Guess, my monocle. It was an exercise in *reason*. One: Uncle Ambrose was smart. He was writing a book about murderers. He knew how dangerous killers are. He spent his life putting them behind bars. Would he turn his back on somebody he thought was a murderer? Hell, no. So that meant he wasn't afraid of the person who killed him. Two: What was Uncle Ambrose going to do the very next week? He was going to make a trip to do some research on his book. His first stop was to have been in Florida. Silver City." Annie turned to look toward the heavyset man in handcuffs. "You told us you didn't have anything to do with the Winningham investigation. You know something, Capt. Mac, I'll bet that's not true."

McElroy's face looked like a slab of rough-cut stone in the whirling red flash from the police car. He stared back at Annie with an ugly glint in his eyes.

"He trusted you. And you killed him."

"You don't have any evidence," Saulter objected.

"When you investigate, you'll find out," Annie insisted. "Once you know where to look, it will all come apart."

"A lucky guess," Max repeated disdainfully. "I'm the one who figured it from information we received. Emma Clyde was the key. Obviously, she was being blackmailed. That's the first thing she expected when Annie pretended to know what Morgan was going to spill Sunday night. And Carmen insisted Elliot wasn't a blackmailer. So where did that leave us? There was a blackmailer on Broward's Rock. And who was the only person in that bookstore Sunday night who lived in a two-hundred-thousand-dollar house and didn't have fat royalties to pay for it?" He pointed at the sullen figure of the ex-cop. "There he is. Living in a rich man's house—but retired from a police force. Where did he get the money to buy a place here and live like a man of leisure? I wonder how much Winningham paid him? Somehow he knew something that would convict Emma of murder. He lived like a king by keeping things quiet for money. That's what Morgan figured out. If an investigation into McElroy's finances ever began, he would be finished."

"Yeah." Saulter nodded. "I finished up going through Morgan's papers tonight. He'd gotten a copy of the Coast Guard report on the investigation into the drowning of Emma's husband.

"It didn't mean anything by itself. But it fits into your theories real nice. Guess who was in the boat anchored next to *Marigold's*

Pleasure? Guess who told the Coast Guard there were no cries for help that night?"

"So," Max declared grandly, "I figured it out."

"Oh no." Annie shook her blond head. "I did it."

Heads lowered, hands on hips, Max and Annie glared furiously at each other.

Twenty-one

CHIEF SAULTER stood just inside the bookshop door. He peered at Edgar.

"Pretty nice place here."

Annie forbore to remind him that the last time he came in, he thought she was a murderess.

"Nice cat." Saulter reached out to pet Agatha. Instead of streaking away as any perceptive feline would, Agatha rolled over on her back and kneaded her paws.

Annie leaned on the cash desk and pondered feline intelligence. Then she looked up and down the empty aisles of Death On Demand. Where were all those customers who'd thronged the place when they thought Annie was killer-of-the-week? Ingrid had opened the store that morning and left when Annie arrived because it was crystal clear the rush was over. There wasn't a single person present to see Saulter eat crow.

Saulter opened his mouth, closed it. Apparently crow wasn't delicious.

She was too kindhearted to let him suffer. "How's Bud?"

Saulter's saturnine face twisted in a genuine smile. "Can't be too uncomfortable," he said drily. "Carmen Morgan's got him in bed." He paused and added stolidly, "Resting up from his head wound."

She and the chief looked at each other with mutual understanding.

Saulter shifted his weight from one big foot to the other.

"Thought I'd let you know everything's falling into place against Capt. Mac. It's just like you and that young man thought."

She started to bristle. How could Max try to take credit?

"You figured it right. Capt. Mac couldn't afford to let Ambrose go to Silver City. I've been on the phone this morning. You know how he told you he didn't have anything to do with the Winningham investigation?" Saulter snorted in disgust. "Not much. He just ran the whole thing. Seems the chief then, Al Canady, why, he was a drunk. The city manager told me Capt. Mac was a great guy the way he ran the department and never seemed to mind that he was just the assistant chief." Irritation roughened his voice. "Who knows how many times he got paid off? Course, he really hit it big with the Winningham case. Then he anchored next to Emma when she pushed her husband over. We'll never prove that, 'cause Mac's not saying a word. But it's pretty clear she was paying off somebody, and we can bet it was Mac. That's why Mac murdered Elliot. And he had to kill Dr. Kearney when she caught him at the clinic, stealing the—" He paused; it was still too hard to say. "—stuff. And Harriet was watching Elliot's place and saw you and Mac arrive." The chief shook his head disapprovingly. "Breaking and Entry. You shouldn't of done that, Ms. Laurance."

"I know," she said humbly. "But you seemed so suspicious of me, I felt I had to look out for myself."

"Guess you were pretty upset about the investigation," he said uncomfortably.

She toyed with the spike holding phone messages (four from Mrs. Brawley).

He peered intently at the floor. "I really liked old Ambrose. Kind of lost my cool when I figured somebody pushed him overboard. Should have known it wasn't you. I always did wonder why nobody heard a splash in the harbor. Think I've figured that out, too. Ambrose must've gone over to McElroy's house that night for a drink. Bet Mac hit him from behind, then dumped him into his saltwater pool to drown. When he was—when he was finished— he hauled the body out and took it to the harbor." He rubbed the back of his hand against his nose. "Anyway, should've known you didn't do it."

Annie surprised herself. She reached out and patted his arm. "I can understand. Uncle Ambrose was a wonderful person."

The chief finally looked at her directly. "So anyway, no hard feelings?" He stuck out a callused hand.

She shook it. "Chief, what about the others?"

"We're scratching around. I've got the Tahoe people looking for a grave by that cabin, but I don't expect anything to come of it. Too much territory. Fritz Hemphill—he got away with murder, I don't doubt it. It'll never be proved. As for Mrs. Clyde—Capt. Mac won't say a word, so she's still out of our reach. I sent the district nurse to talk to the Farleys and Miss Rizzoli. The Farleys have agreed to some counseling. That Miss Rizzoli—she's a nut case, isn't she? Some little group of friends you had there."

He squinted at her. "You intend to have any more of those Sunday night meetings?"

"God. I hadn't thought about it."

She ticked the survivors off in her mind: Emma, the Farleys, Fritz, Kelly, and Hal.

Saulter grinned. "There'll be more writers coming to Broward's Rock. I'll bet you can start them up again in a few months."

She knew that was the most generous gesture he could have made.

"And that boyfriend of yours can help keep everybody in line. Especially if he sets up down the boardwalk from you."

"Sets up?"

"Yeah. He's measuring the empty shop right now."

"What for?"

"His detective agency."

As Saulter left, Max came in, grinning smugly and carrying a tape measure and notepad. The two men exchanged chummy greetings in the doorway. Saulter promised to take Max fishing.

Annie opened her mouth to attack, but Max spoke first.

"I'm only doing what you asked me to."

He was odiously pleased with himself. He draped the tape measure around Edgar and tied it in a bow, then grinned at her.

"I *asked* you—Max, I never asked you to be a private detective. That's ridiculous. You can't be serious. How could a private detective agency have any business on a little island like this?"

"Why not? When word gets around how ingeniously I solved these murders when the authorities were stymied, people will flock to my agency."

He solved the murders! She'd get to that absurd proposition in a minute. "Dammit, Max. You are impossible. When we talked about you doing something, I meant something *real*. This is just the same old thing. Max, can't you be serious?"

He reached out and took her hand and drew her near.

She came reluctantly.

Then a little closer.

"Max," and her indignant voice was muffled against his shoulder. "Why can't you—"

"Annie—"

The bell above the door jangled. They leapt apart guiltily as Mrs. Brawley poked her head inside. Her foxlike nose twitched and her bright eyes glinted, but there were more important matters than love. She darted to Annie, took her firmly by the sleeve, and started down the central aisle toward the coffee bar.

Annie was irresistibly swept along, and Max followed.

". . . called and called. I know I'm the first one. Now, here're the answers."

Mrs. Brawley pointed to the first watercolor.

"That's from *Easy to Kill*. And the next one's *Funerals Are Fatal*. Then *Murder at Hazelmoor; The Moving Finger*, and *Remembered Death*. All Agatha Christies. My dear," she chided, "is that quite fair?"

Carolyn G. Hart is the author of eight "Death on Demand" mysteries featuring Annie Laurance Darling, including *Something Wicked,* for which she won an Agatha and Anthony, *Honeymoon with Murder,* which won an Anthony, and *A Little Class on Murder,* which won a Macavity. She lives in Oklahoma City with her husband, Phil. She is currently at work on her first "Henrie O" mystery, *Dead Man's Island.*